Published 2001

Cover Design: dawn m. drew, INk. graphic design services corp.

Canadian Cataloguing in Publication
Dancing with the Dead
ISBN 1-894372-12-3

Vernon Oickle -1961-
Canadian Literature
Canadian Fiction - N.S.
Edited by Yvonne Wilson

ALL RIGHTS RESERVED. No part of this book may be reproduced in any form without the written permission of the publisher except brief quotations embodied in critical articles or reviews.

Copyright ©·2001 by
DreamCatcher Publishing
Suite 306, Dockside, 1 Market Square
Saint John, New Brunswick
Canada E2L 4Z6
e-mail dcpub@fundy.net
www.dreamcatcher.nb.ca
Telephone: Toll Free 1-800-693-4188

Printed and bound in Canada

The Canada Council | Le Conseil des Arts
for the Arts | du Canada

ACKNOWLEDGEMENT : This book has been published with the assistance of the Canada Council for the Arts.

Dancing with the Dead

by

Vernon Oickle

Other books by Vernon Oickle

1993   -Life and Dealth After Billy
-Friends & Neighbours: A collection of stories from The Liverpool Advance

1997   -Busted: Nova Scotia's War on Drugs

1999   -Queens County (photo book)

2001   -Ghost Stories of the Maritimes

For Nancy

Acknowledgements

How do you thank those who have helped make your life-long dream become a reality? It's really impossible to put into words how I feel about the process that has led up to the realization of this book. All my life, I have wanted to write. It has been a long, and sometimes frustrating road to reach this destination, but finally here it is.

Dancing with the Dead began many years ago with an idea I had for a story. Since putting the first words to paper, the story has evolved and taken many different twists and turns, but this book is the culmination of many hours of hard work. It also represents my determination not to give up. But I didn't do this alone. Over the years I've had a great deal of input and many long discussions with people who shared in my vision. Along the way I've received support from my colleagues Marg Hennigar, Theresa Hawkesworth and Lisa Brown. I've received encouraging words in times of despair from my good friend Marci Lin Melvin. All of these people have shared this ride with me and I thank them from the bottom of my heart. I also must thank another colleague, Jodie Turner, for taking my photograph that appears on the book's back cover.

Writing a book takes a great deal of teamwork on the homefront and without the support and encouragement of my wife Nancy this dream would never have become a reality. Through many years of writing and rewriting, Nancy has been my crutch, helping with the children and holding down the fort. While my name is on this book, Nancy deserves at least half the credit, for I could never have done it without her.

Lastly this book would never have happened if not for the team at DreamCatcher Publishing and particularly, Yvonne Wilson who has tirelessly given me guidance and advice. I am grateful that Yvonne saw something in this story that was worth telling. Her expert editing skills guided me through many hours of writing, rewriting, cutting and rearranging. They say a good book editor is as important as the author. I now know that's the truth.

Vernon Oickle
Liverpool, Nova Scotia
June 19, 2001

Chapter 1

Thank God Nanny Vera wasn't the type of woman to give up easily or I would have been buried out behind the old barn with the rest of the dead babies.

I was born on March 25 in 1922. My mother always said people born on that date were blessed. According to Mama's theory, on March 25 Christians remember the coming of the Angel Gabriel to the Blessed Virgin Mary. That was the day of the conception of Jesus by the Holy Ghost. By Mama's reasoning, that made March 25 a special day. She believed people like me had angels watching over us ... maybe even Gabriel himself.

"You are a lucky child," Mama said. But over the years, I've grown pretty sceptical of that theory. I've never seen an angel. That is, near as I can remember. Not that I'd know what an angel would look like. Then again, I'm not sure why God would send an angel to look over someone like me, especially after some of the things I've done.

It didn't matter what I believed in. Mama's faith was strong and unwavering. She had good reason. When I was a child, she told me to be mindful of how I spoke to God. "After all," she explained, "it is only by His grace that you are walking this earth. You are only here because He has allowed it."

I was born in Nanny's rambling old homestead, just down the hill from the small, unpainted house where I grew up. There weren't many doctors around when I was born. Babies arriving in Liverpool back then were brought into this world by midwives. These were women who themselves had a batch of kids. Even Doc Halliday, the town's only resident doctor for many years, hadn't arrived yet. So midwives did the work. They had no special training but knew from their own experience how to deliver babies, and they knew when things were wrong.

The midwife who helped deliver me was Flossy Garret, a haggard old woman with thirteen children of her own. She lived on the other side of Liverpool with most of the other poor people, but you can't dispute her success as a midwife. Even the rich women of Liverpool got Flossy's help. That's saying something about how good Flossy was at delivering babies. Most of the time, the rich snobs in this town would have nothing to do with that crusty little woman who seemed to walk as if she had a permanent bend in her spine. But in her time, Flossy helped to bring over one hundred babies into the world, and of that number only nine died. That's quite an impressive record considering she didn't have the modern luxuries and equipment that doctors and hospitals have nowadays, or any medical training.

Some folks said Flossy was a witch. They claimed she had special powers and that she could see into the future. Strange things happened when Flossy was around, but I never believed in such things. I dismissed them as mere coincidence even though she did look like a wicked white-haired witch.

When I was ready to be born, Mama sent the Old Man to fetch Flossy as fast as he could. As my luck would have it, Liverpool was hit by a major spring snowstorm that day and travelling was difficult, especially since people mostly went by foot. From the moment Mama's water broke to the time the Old Man brought Flossy back to Nanny's house, more than three hours had passed. That was a rough period for my mother. She was in a great deal of pain and passing lots of blood. When Flossy arrived, the delivery had already started. I don't know why I was in such a rush to come into this hateful world, but I was well on my way ... and I wasn't coming without a fuss. Even in my birth, I had to make things complicated. It's a pattern I would follow throughout most of my life.

As soon as Flossy took one look at Mama and the amount of blood she was losing, she knew there was trouble. "Somethin's really wrong. He's comin' feet first," she said, getting right to work. Since I was already engaged in the birth canal, Flossy didn't have much choice but to try to make the delivery as easy as possible. I was coming and there was no stopping me.

"It don't look good to me. I'm afraid I can't give the little fella much of a chance," she told my parents as she tried to work a miracle. "He's wedged in there pretty tight. ... I don't think he wants to come out, but if I don't get him out, he's either gonna be dead or retarded 'cause he can't get any air ... he can't breathe. He's gonna smother."

In Flossy's many years of experience she had delivered several breached babies. "Most times," she pointed out to my exhausted and distraught mother, "when I see a baby comin' feet first, I try to turn him. But this little guy's already started to come down. I got no choice but to bring him out this way. I gotta tell 'ya this looks bad. When babies come feet first, most times they don't make it."

Naturally the news devastated my parents. They had wanted a child very badly and now they were facing their worst fears. Flossy held nothing back. She was blunt and I suppose that was a good thing. But it seemed she didn't have much compassion for my parents. "I'll try my best, but you better be ready for the worst," she said. It may have seemed heartless, but I don't believe Flossy wanted them to build up any false hopes.

Flossy worked hard and finally, after putting Mama through what must have been pure hell, she announced my arrival. Only there wasn't much to celebrate. "I was afraid of this. He ain't breathin'," the old woman said. "He's pretty blue. That tells me he didn't get any oxygen. If he lives, you better accept that he'll probably be mental. Maybe we should just let him go. That might be easier for everyone."

My parents were horrified at the suggestion. "No, I don't think so. We can't do that," Mama cried. "He's our son. No matter what God's givin' us, we're gonna love him and make him part of our family. You must do whatever you can for him."

With my parents' insistence, Flossy went to work on the lifeless body that was me. She tried for five or ten minutes to make me cry, but couldn't get me to breathe. In one desperate last-ditch effort to bring me to life, she gave me a couple of good cracks on the butt. There was nothing. There was no life. "He's gone," she said as Mama and the Old Man cried over their misfortune. Why had God done this to them, they wondered.

"It's not God's fault," Flossy insisted. "It's just the way things were meant to be. Maybe there's a reason this little guy wasn't s'pposed to live. Things happen for a reason. They are as they are and it's no good to question them. You just got to accept that and move on. You can have other babies."

As far as the old woman was concerned, I was dead and should be buried out behind the dilapidated barn as quickly as possible. "There's nothin' more we can do, 'cept bury him." Her blunt statement was almost as heartless as it was cold. She wasted no emotions. Wrapping me in a blanket, she then tossed me onto the bed, next to Mama. "Take a look before they bury him. The longer he lays 'round here, the harder it'll be on you," she told Mama. Then she instructed my Old Man to get one of the wooden feed boxes from the barn. "We'll bury him in that."

In those days it was common to bury babies on your property. It happened all the time. I don't know how many babies were actually disposed of there behind my nanny's barn, but I know there were a few. Nanny Vera had once showed me some of their graves and it's only by the desperation of one old woman that I didn't end up there with the others behind the barn in that makeshift burial ground. Although I don't know how hard she would have tried if she had known how I'd eventually turn out.

"Just hold it a minute," Nanny Vera interrupted. "I've seen this happen before. I'm not ready to give up on this baby just yet."

Chapter 2

I loved Nanny Vera very deeply. We seemed to have a special bond. She was small but feisty with blue hair. She stood only five feet tall but was full of energy and always ready to embrace life. She could spout the Bible with the best of them, but she could also stand her ground when the going got tough. I remember Nanny pretty well, although she died when I was young. It makes me sad today that I didn't have more time with her. I think I missed the chance to know a wonderful woman. She died of a stroke when I was only five, but we spent a lot of wonderful time together. We did many fun things. She seemed so busy all the time, but always allowed me to help with her chores. We dug worms out in her garden and went to the river to fish for eels. She liked fresh eels out of the water and into the frying pan. To Nanny, these were a treat, but I didn't much care for them. They tasted distinctly oily and salty to me, but Nanny liked to fry them up good and brown. She said they tasted kind of like a cross between chicken and haddock, but I don't know about that. I didn't even like the looks of them, slimy and black and curled up in the frying pan. I guess you've got to have a certain kind of taste to enjoy something like that. I didn't have it.

I liked it when we used to go back in the woods behind Nanny's house in the summer and pick berries. She made jams and jellies from blueberries, raspberries, brier berries and chokecherries. I loved them all, especially in the winter when it was cold and bitter outside. There wasn't anyone around these parts that could make preserves like my Nanny Vera. Those were good days. I'm thankful I got to spend such quality time with her before she died, even if it was only a few short years. What's more important is that I owe her my life.

Old Flossy had told my parents to accept their loss without question. But Nanny wasn't about to give up on her grandson so quickly. "Don't listen to that ol' witch," Nanny snapped as my parents mourned for their baby. "She doesn't know everything."

While the others all but had me dead and buried in the cold ground, Nanny went to work. Mama always said it was a miracle. I was dead, there was do doubt about that. But unwrapping my limp, lifeless body, Nanny gingerly rubbed and massaged the bluish skin of my chest and stomach with her weather-worn, but gentle, hands. Slowly she moved out over my little legs and arms and then, ever so carefully, over my head as if trying to coax the blood into circulation. She wouldn't give up, Mama said. After a few minutes, I started to breathe and then, "just like that," Mama said, "you let out a blat that shook the wall plaster loose."

If it hadn't been for Nanny, everything else would have turned out differently. Reassured that I was going to keep breathing, Nanny wrapped me in cotton batting. Then she placed my tiny body in a small cardboard box and sat it on the open oven door where the stove would provide warmth like an incubator.

All those who had assembled for my birth gave thanks for the miracle they witnessed, except Flossy. Mama said it seemed as if the old woman was angry or disappointed that she had been wrong about me. I think the cranky old witch resented Nanny's interference. Anyway, after that Flossy said there was no way I should have survived my birth. She was adamant right up to the day she died, at eighty-three, ten years after I was born, that I should have never taken a breath of air. I'm not too sure if she looked at my miraculous life as a work of God or something from the bowels of Hell, but she scared me. The way she looked at me sometimes caused my blood to freeze ... her cold, icy stare would send shivers up my spine, making my flesh crawl. I think she believed I was the Devil incarnate because she always kept her distance from me. Maybe she saw something no one else could see. Perhaps she knew something about me that others couldn't know. It's possible, I suppose, she knew how I would turn out. After all, everyone in town said old Flossy had special powers.

Nanny saw things differently. She said I was a gift from God and that I was blessed. "On the day you were born," she told me with much faith in her words, "He reached down with His own hands and touched your heart, making it beat. That makes you special." Of course she would always caution that my life's journey was still my own to chart and that I controlled my own destiny. "But God will always be on your side if you welcome Him into your mind and heart." Her words were reassuring and comforting for a child who often lost his way. If she were alive today, I'm sure Nanny Vera would be disappointed at how I turned out. I couldn't blame her. I'm disappointed in myself.

I can't say I was particularly religious, but my mother, just like Nanny, lived by the Bible. She was raised in a family of Reform Baptists and her parents were terribly strict with her. Perhaps that explains why she had such deep faith in the scriptures. She believed my life was nothing less than a miracle.

Kids my mother's age had a difficult upbringing under their religion, particularly when it came to discipline. The girls weren't allowed to have their hair curled, wear earrings or any jewellery for that matter, attend dances, or do anything that might make them attractive to the boys. They believed such frivolous things were evil, the work of Satan himself, designed to lure the young girls to a life of sin and promiscuity. As for marriage, the girls weren't allowed to have a husband until they turned twenty-one. Any girl wanting to marry before that age, had to have the written permission of her father. That's what had happened in Mama's case. She was only four months shy of her twenty-first birthday when she got married and Nanny Vera, acting on her dead husband's behalf, had to sign her away or the pastor wouldn't have performed the ceremony. And if couples weren't married in church, then their union was blasphemy.

My parents married five years before I was born and I think for the most part it was a happy union. If they had any major troubles, they kept them to themselves. My parents never believed in airing their dirty laundry in public or in front of me. I respected them for their integrity.

I found the religious trappings amusing, but my mother didn't appreciate my sense of humour when it came to her faith. I meant no harm and I think she knew that. I used to joke with Mama all the time that if my grandparents had been so strict with her, how did she and my Old Man get together? And why, I would probe, could they not have waited the other four months instead of having to go through all the trouble of securing written permission to get married sooner? It didn't matter how many times I asked, she'd never give me an answer. She'd only acknowledge my questions with a sly, almost sheepish, smirk. I have no idea what they may have been, but my parents obviously had their secrets.

Chapter 3

Liverpool's the only place I've ever called home and it's here on the South Shore where I want to be buried when I die, which shouldn't be that much longer ... if God is willing.

My life had gotten off to a rocky start, but it didn't stop there. I was a sickly child. It seemed whatever ailment was going around, I'd get it. Some people are like that. We have a weak constitution. Flossy used to tell Mama that I got sick so often because, while I was lucky that I had escaped Death's clutches the first time, she believed the Grim Reaper was still after me. What a wicked woman to say something so terrible in front of a small child. No wonder I didn't trust her. Nanny Vera, on the other hand, would soothe my aching body with her tender words. She would comfort me when I was sick, explaining that when I was ill, God was testing my faith to see what kind of person I would become. He was making me strong through such adversities, she would say, while giving me a reassuring smile and gently squeezing my hand to let me know I could believe her. "Into everyone's life a little suffering must come," she'd say, adding that God was paying extra attention to me because I was special. Every time I got sick and then recovered, she'd say in her best I-told-you-so voice, "There, God has seen you through and now He has made your body stronger to fight off the germs ... to fight off the evil."

But once it was a little too close for comfort. I wasn't sure if God was going to come through for me. When I was seven, I developed Rheumatic Fever. Nanny had died by this time and I missed her terribly. I was sure I was going to see her soon. The fever had confined me to bed for two weeks and Mama later told me that she had accepted I would die. She had been prepared to place my soul in God's care. I knew that my condition must have been grave for my mother to have given up. I was deathly ill with a high fever and was near delusional for several days, but I wasn't too sick to overhear Doc Halliday talking to my parents one evening. The diagnosis wasn't good.

"I'm afraid the boy's got the fever pretty bad," he said. "I've done everything I can and the prognosis is not good. The medicine doesn't seem to be working. All we can do now is wait and try to keep the fever in check ... and pray, if you think that will help. But you should be prepared for the worst."

My parents didn't say a word but continued to maintain their silent vigil at my bedside. It has to be tough for a doctor to look parents straight in the eyes and tell them their only child may not survive. If the fever got any worse, Doc Halliday feared it would attack my vital organs. Particularly, he said, I could develop rheumatic heart disease and if that happened, I would surely die. Nowadays they have developed antibiotics to fight the fever, but seventy years ago these medicines didn't exist so I was on my own ... or at least I was in God's hands.

I don't remember much from those days when I was in the fever-induced daze, but I recall seeing the concern and anguish on my parents' faces as they watched the life of their only child slowly drain away. They were helpless as the sickness worsened. Three days after I took sick, the fever reached one hundred and three degrees and I lapsed into a near coma. I recall how strange I felt in that state. It's like I was asleep but still awake. I was aware of things around me but couldn't speak or move. I lay there, helpless, like a rotting log, unable to reach out to my parents. But even though I was deathly ill, I never felt alone. And it wasn't that I knew my parents were in the room with me. It was as if someone else was there with them. I couldn't recognize him or even say if the person was real, but I'm sure there was a presence beside me, watching as I fought to hang on. I have never been able to figure out if there actually was someone else there or if that person was only in my imagination, an inducement of the high fever. Either way, whoever it was made me feel warm on the inside, and soothed my troubled thoughts, much in the same way Nanny Vera used to make me feel.

I didn't understand then, but I know now, that I came close to dying. Then on the evening of the third day of the high fever, it was old Flossy, of all people, who came to my parents with a possible remedy. Entering my small bedroom, Flossy handed them two fresh mackerel, explaining, "It's not a sure cure, but it might work." Her deep, husky voice was as clear to me as my own reflection in a mirror. I may have been nearly unconscious, but I knew it was her.

I was drifting in and out of consciousness, but I heard most of what she was saying. I wasn't sure why she would offer to help us since she didn't believe I should be alive anyway. But I wasn't in any position to argue. And besides, why would I want to discourage her if the old woman really could help?

"I remember seein' it used when I was a kid for the fever, but I ain't never tried it myself. The old people swore by it. They said it always worked, but there ain't no guarantees that it will. And if the fever's already gotten to his heart, it's gonna be too late," she told them without hesitation in her distinct, gravelly voice.

My parents were desperate to try anything, even if it sounded far-fetched. They did as Flossy instructed without question. They knew of the woman's reputation as a healer using the old ways, and hoped she might have a cure. Besides, nothing else had worked. All the acceptable medical treatments had failed so my parents kept an open mind, going with their hearts. As Mama put it, what did they have to lose?

First Flossy placed one of the mackerel next to the hot skin of my right foot. Then she took some clean, white cloth that she had instructed Mama to fetch and wrapped it around my foot and the mackerel. She used some rope to secure the cloth and the fish snugly in place. She then repeated the exercise for my left foot. "Make sure these bandages are kept good'n tight and in place for twelve hours. This won't work if the bandages are removed too soon," she warned before retreating from my bedroom.

I don't remember much after that. I seemed to slip deeper into my coma-like state. But by the next morning I awoke early and was feeling fine. Mama had remained in my room with me every night since I had become ill. We couldn't believe how quickly I seemed to recover.

"It's a miracle," Mama said, praising God for rescuing her son once again from the clutches of Death. "God must have something really important planned for you," she said, clutching her Bible against her breasts and kissing my forehead. "We must never forget what He has done for us."

I'm not sure God had much to do with my miraculous recovery. I was giving credit to old Flossy's prehistoric remedy. The fever had broken overnight. It had been over twelve hours since Flossy had come to my bedside with her old-country remedy when I awoke. Sceptics later dismissed any notion that the old woman had saved my life, but her method seemed to work when everything else had failed.

I can still hear the Old Man's reaction as my parents carefully removed the bandages. As the cloth slipped from my feet we were shocked to discover the mackerel had been cooked overnight as they drew the fever from my body. It was unbelievable. How could something so simple and primitive work? I now owed my life to Flossy, and I wasn't sure how I felt about that, considering how she viewed me. But I was thankful she had found her way to my sickbed that night. I surely would have died if she had not come.

I have never understood why the old woman came to my aid. "It's just somethin' I felt I had to do," she would later tell Mama. "Some things don't need explain'. You can't always find the answers you want so it's no good lookin'."

Had Flossy been able to see into the future like people believed she could, I know she wouldn't have come that night. If she had had a sense of my true nature and knew of the evil deed I would some day commit, I'm sure she would have allowed me to die. Or perhaps she knew my destiny and understood that nature dictates everyone must fulfil their fate, no matter which dark path they go down. Her reasons for coming to my rescue continue to haunt me even after all these years. She was a mysterious woman, and now I was in her debt. Even to this day, such a thought sends shivers up my spine.

Chapter 4

The ways of the old country were all around Liverpool. It was a different time and, in many ways, a different place but we had everything we needed. Most of the time, Liverpool was a wonderful place to live and raise a family. But things were rough in those days. We had to scrape to get by. Sometimes you didn't know where your next meal was going to come from. Work was scarce and the First World War had just ended. People didn't know how they were going to make ends meet. But somehow, "with the grace of God," Mama always said, we survived.

My folks and me didn't have much, just barely got by most of the time. But that didn't stop my mother from helping others. No matter how bad things got for us, even at times when we didn't know if we were going to have enough food for our own supper, Mama would always make a little extra for a neighbour who was sick or another friend who had lost his job in the dying economy. That was how my parents operated. They always put other people first, usually sacrificing themselves to help someone else. Whenever I would ask my mother why we would share our food when we barely had enough for ourselves, she always quoted a passage from the Bible. Recalling the words of John the Baptist, she would take me by the chin, look me squarely in the eyes and say, "Whoever has two shirts must give one to the man who has none, and whoever has food must share it."

Mama always made her points with such profound statements, but the Old Man was not to be outdone. Whenever we had these discussions around the supper table and the Old Man was home, he'd throw in his two cents worth, whether we asked him for it or not. He'd pipe up in that fake bravado voice he used when mocking well-educated men of means, adding his own piece of philosophy. "He who possesses a surplus, possesses the goods of others," he'd say.

Don't ask me from where he managed to pull such wisdom. He wasn't a well-educated man. Book learning was important for my generation, he stressed, but he didn't read. "I never had time for books. I went to work when I was nine years old," he'd lecture. "But you, Jack Webster. You got a chance to do something with your life. Get a good education and the world will be yours." That was his philosophy. Everything hinged on a good education and he tried to make me see that. I respected my Old Man because he learned through life's school of hard knocks. He was a proud man and feared no challenge, big or small, just as he always extended a helping hand to his neighbours in their time of need.

"There may come a day, God forbid, that we might need their help in return," he would point out in his most matter-of-fact voice. "Never turn your back on a neighbour in need."

I often wish I would have inherited my Old Man's common-sense as well as my mother's undying love of life. Many times over the years, I fear, I've failed to live up to their fine examples. I failed to live up to their expectations and to my own. They would both be disappointed in how their son turned out.

My parents struggled to make a comfortable home for me. I'm thankful for that. They did the best they could and they did it with the sweat of their brows and the strength of their backs. The will to beat the odds was their strongest ally, and sheer determination was their hallmark. We didn't have much money when I was a kid, but we were rich in a lot of ways. We had no luxuries. We didn't even have running water in our little shack that doubled as a house, but at least we had a roof over our heads to keep the weather out and I don't recall ever starving or freezing in the winter. "There's more to life than money," my Old Man would say, taking me by the shoulders and giving me a gentle shake. "Someday you'll learn to appreciate what we've got, but until that day comes, you'll just have to make do."

It's not that I didn't appreciate the obstacles that lay before my parents in their struggles to make us a comfortable lifestyle. It's just that as a child, I couldn't understand why some people in Liverpool seemed to be so well off, while others were barely getting by. I remember my Old Man would work for fifteen cents an hour when he first went to work down at Tupper's shipyard. An honest living in those days, but hardly enough to support a family. But he didn't complain. My Old Man did odd jobs at the shipyard and he didn't question any of the tasks that were assigned to him. He didn't have any special trade or training. He did whatever needed to be done to earn enough money to feed me and my mother. "You just gotta do what you gotta do," he'd say, dismissing any concern for his own well being. "Sometimes you may not like the task at hand, but it's gotta be done. When that happens, the best thing to do is get at it. The more you think about it or complain about it, the harder it gets."

Both my parents went through life with this work ethic. They knew no other way. They only had the one kid, just me, but I found out some years later there had been another baby boy about four years older than me. He had died when he was five or six months old. My parents never talked about that, so I don't know what happened to him or even what his name was for sure. I think it was James. People in town said my mother never got over it, that she carried the pain from the loss of her first-born to her grave. It seems the baby died in his crib one night for no apparent reason while the Old Man and my mother were sleeping. They had wanted a large family with many children, but after I was born, the Old Man said they couldn't afford more kids. "It's hard enough finding the money to put food in one kid's mouth," he'd say, dismissing any further thought of more children.

He really wasn't a bad father. He was dedicated to us and a hard worker who always put his family first. My mother and me, we didn't see him all that much. The Old Man worked long hours and when he came home early, I'd usually be getting ready for bed so we only ever had a few minutes together.

Most nights I'd be sound asleep when he came home and he'd already be off to work long before I ever got up in the morning. But on some of those nights when he came home late, I heard him sneaking into the house so as not to disturb me and Mama. We only had three rooms: two bedrooms and a kitchen, and there was a little outhouse out back for when we had to go. There wasn't much chance of keeping any secrets from each other. When the Old Man came home some nights, I'd hear my mother and him talking, maybe even occasionally arguing over the money situation or other problems that married couples have. Sometimes he wouldn't even come home. He'd work an extra shift for the additional money, staying at the shipyard overnight. He was a hard worker and a good provider. You could never take that away from him. He was proud, too, refusing handouts no matter how much in need we were. "I'll take care of my family my own way," he'd insist and that was all there was to it. Whenever he spoke in that manner, it was no good arguing with him. You couldn't win if you went toe to toe with that man. Even when he was wrong, he'd never give in, standing his ground until you saw it his way.

That's the way life was for us kids growing up in this small, backward town next to the ocean. I sometimes wondered why the Old Man didn't go to one of the other towns further up the coast to try and get on the fishing boats; the money was better there, but I never had the guts to ask him about it. I didn't want him to think he was failing me and Mama in any way. I figured he was doing the best he could the best way he knew how and he'd probably be insulted or hurt if I suggested such a thing to him. My father wasn't the kind of man you could easily talk to. He was extremely private. I never felt comfortable talking to him and I regret that now. Maybe it's because we never got the chance to spend much time together, or maybe it's just because men didn't open up in those days. I don't really know what it was that kept us from talking and I never had the chance to ask him when I got older. The Old Man died when I was fourteen.

That would have been 1936. They said it was a heart attack that took him out, but he was only forty-eight and he looked pretty healthy and strong to me. I don't remember him ever being sick or missing a day of work in his life. He was a heavy smoker, and with the way he worked it's possible everything finally caught up to him. His heart probably couldn't stand the strain any longer.

The Old Man was at work when he died, which seemed fitting considering how much time he spent there. I didn't see him the night before or that morning, but I remember people in town saying he was down in the holds of one of the boats docked at Tupper's when he keeled over. Just like that, they said. No warning. No nothing. They quickly called Doc Halliday down to work on him, but there wasn't much he could do. The Old Man was long gone before the doctor arrived. The men who were with the Old Man when he died said it was over in just a few seconds ... here one minute, gone the next.

I really wasn't surprised that morning when I heard the Old Man had died. If my mother was alive today, she could tell you we were both expecting something terrible to happen that day.

"A forerunner is a sign that someone in the family is about to die," Mama would explain in her most serious voice. "Not everyone can see them. Only people who are 'tuned in' can see forerunners. It is a gift," she said.

"Some gift," I'd answer.

"Don't mock those things you don't understand," she'd scold, her voice turning stern. "There are many things in this world that we don't understand or can't explain, but that doesn't mean they aren't real."

Usually a forerunner is a figure, mostly a large strange man, always dressed in black and he appears out of nowhere. That's exactly what happened that night before the Old Man died. It was shortly before midnight. I was in bed and just about asleep when this weird sensation washed over me, like the feeling you get when you think someone's looking at you. That's what it felt like and when I opened my eyes, there he was ... plain as day. A tall, strange man dressed in a long black overcoat and wearing a big-brimmed, black hat, standing at the foot of my bed staring down at me. I couldn't make out his face because the room was dark and the hat created a heavy shadow, but I knew it was a man and it scared the shit out of me.

I let one God-awful scream out of me when I opened my eyes and saw him there ... just like you're standing here beside the bed right now. It only took my mother a few seconds to get from her bedroom to mine, but by the time she got to my bed, the man was gone and I was shaking like the last leaf clinging desperately to a naked branch on a brisk fall day.

"You've just seen a forerunner," she said, sitting on the end of my bed in an effort to comfort me. "This isn't good. Something bad's gonna happen to someone in the family."

"What, Mama?" I asked. "What's gonna happen? To who?"

"I don't know," she answered. "But I just know it's a sign."

Little did we know that the messenger of Death had been warning us about the Old Man. But neither my mother nor me were terribly surprised when the knock came at the door at 6:15 that cold autumn morning. I remember the time exactly because the messenger arrived at our house just as the first train of the day arrived in Liverpool. The 6:15 from up the west'rd way came to town every morning and made two stops. It first pulled in to Tupper's and then went up to the sawmill before heading off down the coast and eventually into Halifax. You could set your watch to that morning train. It was always on time.

I had just gotten up and was getting ready for school when the man from the shipyard arrived. "Mrs. Webster," he blurted out, "you must come to the wharf right away. There has been some trouble."

The man was anxious, insisting that she come right that instant. "You must come now. There really is no time for delay."

"Jack," I remember her turning to me and saying in a dull, monotone whisper that did not betray her emotions, "you will have to fix your own breakfast this morning. I've got to go to your father." She remained calm, but I could barely hear her speak. Bracing herself against the plywood kitchen counter, she paused for a few seconds as if catching her breath and calling upon some inner being to deliver to her the strength she would need to get through the events of this dreadful day. Somehow she knew he was gone. "I fear something terrible has happened and I'm needed at Tupper's. I don't know how long I'll be. Get ready for school and be gone. I'll see you later."

I could tell the messenger had delivered bad news to Mama, but I remained hopeful that if anything was wrong with the Old Man, he'd recover and everything would be all right again before we knew it. But it wasn't meant to be.

Needless to say, I didn't bother with breakfast. Food was the furthest thing from my mind. After Mama left with the man from the shipyard, I hurried into my coat and boots and quickly followed after her, not fully prepared for what I was about to witness. My heart broke to pieces when I arrived at Tupper's wharf. At first they wouldn't allow me too close to the boat, but I pushed forward through the crowd of dock workers just in time to watch three men pass his limp body up from the boat's hold to two others waiting on the deck. They then placed his lifeless form onto the wagon that removed his remains to Cushings Funeral Home. Cushings has been a part of the Liverpool landscape for more than a hundred years. In the beginning it was owned by a family named Cushing. First the father, then the two sons. They were kind people and ran a quality business. They no longer own it. Some huge company out of the city bought it about ten years ago, but it still seems like a good operation. I think the funeral business is something everyone should consider when you're looking for a career. It doesn't matter how tight money gets, people are going to die so you know you're always going to have customers. If I were to ever start my own business, that's what I'd look at.

Watching Doc Halliday explain to Mama that the Old Man had died, and seeing her arms wrapped tightly around her frail, slender frame hugging herself for warmth from the crisp Atlantic wind blowing in from the ocean, I knew right then and there that our lives would be forever changed.

"If it's any comfort," the doctor told her, "he didn't suffer."

"No. It isn't," she responded as she left the wharf. "That's no comfort at all."

I felt bad that the Old Man had died, but I didn't cry. I couldn't. "Grown men don't cry," he had told me from as far back as I can remember. Since he was gone, I now had to be grown up. I figured he wouldn't have liked it if I beat myself up over something I couldn't control. I kept everything to myself. I know

now that when someone dies it's okay to cry. It's all right to be sad. I was sad about the Old Man's death, I just dealt with it on my own.

The funeral was nothing special. It couldn't be. Mama couldn't afford anything fancy and now with the Old Man gone, she had to watch every cent she had managed to squirrel away. But giving my father a proper burial was still important to Mama, even if it wasn't a slick one. She asked the men at Cushings to keep it modest, but still make it nice and, of course, the service would be held at the church. The undertakers did a fine job. He looked good dressed in his Sunday best, as he called them. For the Old Man, that meant a black suit, off-white shirt and navy tie. I think it's the only good set of clothes he ever owned because, as he would say, "What the hell do I need fancy clothes for down on the wharf?" He did have a point.

Now there he was dressed in them fine clothes one last time, laid out in that pine box that was covered in some kind of white satin-like material. I know it wasn't real satin. Mama could never have afforded anything that fancy. Not that her heart wasn't in the right place. Being a practical woman though, she understood the challenges she would face as a widow with a house to keep up and a child to take care of. After the Old Man's death, I remember Mama speaking to me about the cost of the funeral, and although she was disturbed that she couldn't do more for him as a final gesture of her love for him, she was also quite matter of fact about the whole situation.

Two nights after the Old Man died she said to me in that drawn out whispered voice that betrayed her heart-break, "Jack, I hope you're not disappointed that we can't do more for your father at the burial tomorrow, but we really have to watch the money. It's more important that we go there tomorrow and show him how much we loved him than it is to spend a lot of money on a fancy funeral just to impress everyone else in this town. Don't ever let anyone around here make you think any less of yourself because we can't afford a fancy funeral. It's not the money you spend on the dead that's important, it's how much you loved and cared for them while they were alive that matters. Your father knew we cared for him and that's what we must remember. If anyone wants to talk, let them. You just hold your head high and know that your father is smiling down upon you. He knows how brave you're being and he can feel your love way up there in Heaven. That's all you have to remember."

My mother was always practical, even at the worst of times. When most people might cave in to the pressures, Mama seemed to have some hidden reserve of strength to get her through. That was an asset she would have to call upon many times after the Old Man's death. It was also one of the things that I admired most about her.

I was fourteen and not prepared to look upon death's face, but Mama forced me to do just that on the morning of the Old Man's burial. Before my father died, I had never seen a dead body. Now I think people should try to get to funerals of people who are not so close to them - strangers even - before a loved one dies and you're obligated to go. Mama had spent a great deal of time by his side at the funeral home in the days after he died, but I had avoided the place. I didn't know what to say, what to do or where to put my hands. However, on that morning Mama insisted I had to go. "If you don't see him one last time before he's buried, you will always regret that," she gently explained, understanding I was struggling to come to terms with many emotions. "This will be your last chance to say goodbye to him. You had better make the most of it. Once he's gone, he's gone forever. You don't want to go through the rest of your life wishing you had taken the chance for one final goodbye. You owe this to yourself."

Somehow Mama convinced me to go but it wasn't easy walking into the funeral parlour. It was cold and still and quiet, like the inside of the outhouse on a cold January night. That's what I remember the most, how quiet it was. The only flowers in the room were a bunch of plastic red ones Mama had brought from home and placed near the head of the casket. While I had expected Mama to be emotional at this final meeting with the Old Man, she never shed a tear that morning. I'm sure she loved him, but she was too strong to break down in front of me. She didn't want me to see how worried she was ... but I knew.

We had the whole place to ourselves that morning and after Mama said her final goodbyes and kissed him on the cheek, she left me alone. "It will be good for you to have some time with him alone," she said as she turned and walked away, leaving me there to do my own thing ... whatever that was.

What do you say to a dead man? I stood there beside the casket and looked down upon him, remembering the last time I had seen him alive, two nights before he died. Now he looked peaceful, just lying there. His face was relaxed. The stress lines on his forehead and around his eyes were gone. I must have remained there beside the casket for at least ten minutes, not moving or making a sound. Then finally I said aloud, as if he could hear me, "Well, Old Man, I guess this is goodbye. You and me never had much chance to be together. It's hard to know the right thing to say now. But I want you to know that you were all right as a father. I knew you wanted to be around more, but with your work and all, I understood that you couldn't be. But it was okay. I know you were only doing what had to be done. I don't want you to worry about Mama. Now that you're gone, we'll pull together and make things work. We'll be fine."

With that I felt an uncontrollable urge to touch him. I don't know what came over me. I reached into the casket and touched his forehead. It was cold like a china plate in a refrigerator, but somehow I felt warm inside. The old people believed that if you touched a dead person it erased your grief and made it easier to say goodbye. I was glad Mama made me come.

About twenty minutes later, as we gathered in the church for the service, I remember whispering to Mama that the Old Man looked good and seemed relaxed; that he appeared to be resting peaceful. Maybe my youth made me naive, but I felt I should say something to reassure her. I don't know if it helped, but she whispered back, "I'm sure he is, Jack."

"Do you think he was afraid of dying?" I asked, as the six men from Tupper's brought in the pine box and began the long, slow procession to the front of the church.

"Not likely," Mama replied sharply, as if scolding me for entertaining such thoughts. "If you live life according to the Bible and do as God tells us, then you have no reason to fear death, Jack. Your father was a good man. He provided for us and never strayed from the path that God set for him. He is at peace now and we must not be sad for him." Then she shushed me in that stern but comforting motherly way. The minister was about to begin.

After the funeral we tried to get on with our lives ... but it wasn't easy.

In the months following the Old Man's death, things went from bad to worse for me and my mother. She had to find extra work to make up for the money that the Old Man would have been earning. He was gone, but she still had a house and a kid to look after. It was difficult for a woman on her own back then. There was no such thing as life insurance for our kind of people. They didn't throw money around like they do nowadays. There wasn't any welfare, and she wouldn't have taken it anyway. That would have gone against her grain; against everything she believed in. My mother rose to the challenge with pride and dignity. She fought against the odds and somehow we survived. She earned every black penny she got by scrubbing floors, doing other people's laundry and cooking for other folks. It was hard, but honest, work, cleaning up other people's dirt just for a few cents. But through it all she never complained and she remained strong and committed to her cause. She was proud that she could take care of things now that the Old Man was gone. She understood her lot in life and made the most of it. She never expected much and she never got much. She was a fine woman and a good mother. I was lucky to have her and there are times now I wish she was right here by my side.

My mother never had an easy life and, when she died, I think she was simply played out. Her old body just couldn't take it any more. She was sixty-six when she lost the fight, but she was working right up to the end. Doctors said it was leukaemia that finally killed her, but they never found it until she was dead. Probably they couldn't have done much for her anyway.

The years following my father's death were difficult, but we survived somehow, by sheer determination and depending upon each other for support. With my mother out of the house most of the time and my Old Man gone, I was pretty much left to fend for myself. I was fourteen and ready for independence. I liked being on my own with no one to watch over my shoulder all the time. I also started looking around for work. I figured if I could find a few odd jobs, I could earn my own money. That would relieve some of the pressure Mama was shouldering. I didn't have much luck at first. Then, after kicking around town for a few months, I finally got a break, landing some work at the newspaper office after school. That's when I first met Mrs. Jones. I'd usually work from three in the afternoon when school got out to about eight o'clock at night, or until the work was done, whichever came first.

Liverpool had its own newspaper back then, housed in the red brick building on Main Street where it's still located today. But "The Crier" in those days was a much better paper than it is now. At one time it was something people looked forward to every Wednesday morning for all the news from these parts and from around the world, especially during the war and depression years. Now it's run by a big chain with all the decisions made in a corporate head office somewhere that's out of touch with this community. It isn't much of a paper any more. There's nothing in it to read. All they're concerned about is the bottom line and to hell with the news.

When I was growing up, the paper was run by Mrs. Theresa Jones. She took over after her husband, Jake Jones, died from diabetes. He went into some kind of coma and never recovered. After a month and a half, he died. Jake Jones had suffered with diabetes all his life. He had been born with it, but folks said he always seemed to face the challenge head-on as if he was determined not to let the disease control his life. By the time Jake Jones died at the age of forty-two, he had lost most of his eyesight and had been forced to a wheelchair as poor circulation rendered both his legs nearly unusable. Prior to his death, the doctors were considering amputation. They were afraid gangrene might set in. That was a shame for such a vital young man to be knocked down in the prime of his life. After he died, people said, if you were in the newspaper office late at night and listened close, you could hear the creaking of his wheelchair as if he was still in there working.

I'm sure her husband's death was a sad thing for Mrs. Jones, but she didn't take it lying down. She was only a young woman, but she knew what had to be done. Since she wasn't one to shy away from a challenge she rolled up her sleeves and jumped in with both feet. She had spunk and die-hard determination. I admired her fortitude and courage. She wasn't from Liverpool, but that didn't matter. She was originally from some place up in Ontario, but she became part of the town's fabric as if she had been born and raised here. Jake had met her while he was going to law school, but she seemed to fit right in with all the locals. There was something about her that people liked, a natural honesty and disposition that attracted them to her much like a moth is pulled to an evening light. They appreciated her work ethic and respected her opinion. She was different than the other ladies around here. Mrs. Jones rocked the boat and earned the people's respect in the process. While the Liverpool women were either content to be housewives and pop out babies like gum balls from a candy machine, or were so caught up in climbing the social ladder that their life passed them by, Mrs. Jones was blazing a trail for today's younger generation of career women. With pen in hand, she broke new ground and wouldn't back down from the men who ran this town.

Mrs. Jones returned home with Jake when he came back to Liverpool to take over the newspaper from his father, Senator William "Willy" Jones. Since he was the only male child in the Jones family, the paper went to Jake when the Senator became too sick to run it. Everyone in Liverpool knew he'd end up with it someday. We all thought he should. He was a fine fellow who deserved better than what he got from life. Unlike some of us, he had no choice in his destiny. When Jake died, Mrs. Jones rose to the challenge. Fighting off a threat from Jake's three sisters, Mrs. Jones wrested the paper from the family. She took over the business, running the newspaper with a tight fist and an uncompromising editorial policy. She didn't mince words when it came to laying the truth on the line. She believed in telling it like it was and always shot straight from the hip. Of course, that didn't sit too well with everyone around here, especially some of the town council members who wanted things done their way. Those she confronted labelled her a cranky old bitch, but I liked her. I found her honesty and integrity refreshing. She was good to me and I never had a problem with her. I always believed that if you used people well, then they'd use you well in return ... so we got along. But I can tell you, she never backed down from no one or from any argument. She'd stand her ground and face the enemy head-on like some soldier going out on the battlefield, only words were her weapon and she used them wisely.

"If you want to make a point, the best way to do it is with as few words as possible," I remember her saying as she pecked away at her typewriter. "The wise person is the one who chooses his or her words with caution and forethought. Never rush head-first into an argument without being properly armed. Such stubbornness usually spells defeat." Mrs. Jones knew of what she spoke when she told me about stubbornness because if there was one person in Liverpool who best exemplified that quality, she was it. She claimed she had gotten her fighting spirit from her traditional Irish upbringing, and her blazing red hair was proof of that heritage. It was the hellfire and brimstone that turned her hair that colour, she joked. I simply labelled it good old fashioned spunk, because that's what she had.

When I started working at the paper I was mostly cleaning up and running errands, but eventually they got me doing many different jobs such as setting hot lead type, darkroom work, proof reading, and just about anything else that needed doing to get the paper out on time. On some days I even delivered the papers to the news stands. Fittingly they called people like me a Devil. That's because I was basically the printer's errand boy. Nowadays they got fancy computers and expensive camera equipment to put out newspapers. Back then it was done with elbow grease from start to finish. It was hard work, but rewarding too. I liked it very much. It taught me to pay attention to the world around me. Besides that, the people were great to work with, especially Mrs. Jones. The money wasn't the best, but it was fair for the times. I'm sure she paid me what she could afford. I was thankful that she found something for me to do. I couldn't be picky. Jobs were scarce and I was grateful for the chance to earn my own way. It gave me my own money so Mama wouldn't have to worry about giving me handouts. I gave her a little to help with the household expenses, and I kept the rest to spend. After I started working, I don't remember my mother having to give me money ever again. I'm proud of that. I earned my way in life. No one ever gave me a handout.

Chapter 5

There were five of us in our "company" as we called the group. Me and two of the guys lived in the same part of town up on the hill. People used to call it Hangman's Hill because in the 1700s they used to hang the criminals up there. According to local legend they had a hanging every week. Although I never saw or heard anything myself, my Old Man told me the old people swore the neighbourhood was haunted. They claimed that, if you listened on certain foggy nights, you could hear the trap door spring open with a loud thud or sometimes you might even see one of the ghosts that supposedly roamed the hill. They hung the last man up there in 1802. After that they tore down the gallows. But the ghosts of all the men who died there still walk the grounds where they drew their last breath ... or so they say.

As for me, I'm not so sure I believe in all those old tales and all that mumbo-jumbo. Then again you never know what's real or imagined. After all, I know for a fact that forerunners do exist.

Liverpool was a small town. The streets were nothing more than rough horse paths. The settlement grew up along the banks of the Mersey River near an old Indian village. There was a small group of buildings hugging the bank near the docks, that we called the business area. We had one gravel road running through the centre of Liverpool that linked us to the rest of the world. I remember the day in 1953 when they put down the first pavement. It was a big event. We even held a special celebration with a parade and town picnic to mark the occasion.

It was a different world then. Slower paced. Little things like pavement were a big deal. People struggled to survive. At that time, there were only two places in town to get a half-decent job: Tupper's shipyard and the sawmill. But it was hard to get employment at the sawmill. You had to know someone on the inside in order to get hired. Once you were in, though, the money was good. Naturally everyone wanted to work there. Tupper's had been in Liverpool for as long as anyone could remember. In fact, the shipyard grew as the town grew, becoming the cornerstone of this little seafaring community. For almost two hundred years, ships plying the North Atlantic have come to Tupper's wharf for repairs and to unload their goods like molasses and sugar from down south. In return, they'd take lumber from the forests around here. That's how the sawmill got started. During the height of exporting activity, before the turn of the last century, there were no fewer than a dozen sawmills up and down the river. It was a good time for the lumbering industry, but by the turn of the twentieth century it had all but died out and the mills slowly disappeared until only one remained.

The hill where we lived was considered the place for Liverpool's poor citizens. Three of us lived on the wrong side of the tracks. Everyone had their place and no one ever went anywhere they didn't belong ... except us kids. The other two boys in the company were from the main part of Liverpool, the ritzy area where people with money lived. The children from the two social classes weren't supposed to mingle, but that didn't stop us. Even though their standing was different than ours, that didn't prevent the five of us from becoming friends. We were too young to pay any attention to that bullshit. That's the kind of crap that adults get hung up on, particularly in those days when your social standing determined which circles you would move in or who your friends were. Kids are usually much wiser than adults when it comes to such foolishness. Kids can get beyond the superficial crap that often divides a community. We liked each other and that's all that mattered to us. We spent time with each other after school and on the weekends. We hung out at the local soda shop and we'd play some ball in the summer or go skating on the pond in the winter, building a fire on the shore so we could stay on the ice long after dark. We did the kind of things five young guys would do together. We weren't angels though. When we were young we did our share of bad things. We broke into a few houses looking for cigarettes or booze. Punk stuff. Things I'm shameful of now, but it paled in comparison to the trouble we would get into later on.

It was great having a group of friends that you could count on for anything. If one of us got into trouble, the others would be there for him. We'd help each other and things would work out somehow, no matter how large the problem. We were too young to really know what was going on in the world around us or to really even care. I'm sure there wasn't anything we wouldn't do for each other. We had a special bond that withstood many tests and lasted for years until, some time later, it finally reached its breaking point. That's the way it is with good friends.

As we got older, we started sneaking around drinking and smoking. And our behaviour sometimes got us into some serious trouble, but we were smart enough and our mouths were quick enough that we could talk our way out of just about anything. One of our favourite haunts was old Ralph Burchell's barn. We used to sneak there two, maybe three, nights a week. The barn was over on the south side of town where that new baseball field is now. We went there often and whenever Ralph would catch the five of us inside smoking, he'd freak out. He'd go crazy, cursing and swearing, ranting and raving like some kind of madman. "Get out. All of ya," he'd scream, spewing obscenities with his arms thrashing about. The old man would chase us out and threaten that he was going to tell our parents what we were doing in his barn ... but he never did.

I wish now he would have reported us. Our lives might have turned out differently if he had. Ralph Burchell seemed like a mean old bastard on the surface, but deep down inside I believe he had a special kind of heart. He understood we were doing what boys usually did. He was worried about his barn and for good reason. He kept all his winter's hay in there for his cattle and if he lost that, he'd be in deep trouble. Smoking around the hay was stupid and dangerous. Naturally, when he'd catch us, he'd be pissed. Who could blame him? But that didn't matter to us. He didn't want us in there, so that's where we wanted to be.

Old Ralph was tall and mean looking. All the kids around Liverpool were afraid of him because he looked so hateful all the time. And, just for good measure, the old man carried a shotgun loaded with buckshot wherever he went. Even though he never used it on us, I think he would have if we'd given him reason to.

One night, though, we gave him reason. Although it was an accident, we burned his barn down to the ground. It was early in the summer, I remember, because all the farmers had just put their critters out to pasture. I'd say we were about twelve or thirteen - it was about a year before my father died. We went out to old Ralph's to have a cigarette and one thing led to another. We were fooling around, wrestling in the hay when someone dropped a cigarette in the straw on the floor. By the time we noticed the smoke, it was too late. The fire moved quickly across the barn floor, like it had a life all its own. There was nothing we could do except get the hell out of there.

I felt bad for what we done. We all did. Old Ralph lost his whole barn that night. It was a good thing it was early spring and that year's haying hadn't started yet. But that was little consolation. Because of the fire, he had no place to put his new crop or the critters for the next winter and I didn't think there was any way he could afford to build a new barn if he had to do it from scratch. But, somehow, he eventually managed to build another one out of pieces of old lumber he found about town and some that people gave him. And luckily, a neighbour let Ralph use a part of his barn to store his hay until he built that new one. But we still felt guilty.

If anyone knew we were in the barn on the night of the fire, they didn't tell and we sure as hell didn't come forward on our own to confess. We were too scared to face the truth. Relieved that we had gotten away with the crime, we all promised never to tell anyone, but I know now that we should have told. It would have been the right thing to do. We suspected old Ralph Burchell knew we were responsible for his barn fire. He had caught us smoking in there many times, but he didn't tell on us. Maybe he figured that if we were real men we would have told the truth and taken our punishment. I expect he was disappointed in us for not taking responsibility for the trouble we had caused. If we would have come forward at that time, then things might have turned out differently later on. If we had been made to pay for our mistakes at a younger age, perhaps we would have avoided our future trouble.

Fate's a funny thing, but I think you can control your own destiny if you make the right decisions along the way. If you make the wrong ones, then God help you. You might think we should have learned our lesson after that night of the barn fire, but you never know how you're going to react when your back's against the wall. People react differently when they're under pressure. That's when you do things you wouldn't normally do if you'd been thinking straight. That's a lesson I learned the hard way.

Hank Thompson was my best friend. We were almost the same age and we grew up together on the hill. His home was practically next to mine on the rough dirt path that the locals called a road. There were seven homes along the narrow, rocky road that eventually came to a dead-end. Just like the lives of the people who lived there, the road went nowhere. As some of the town's original settlers, the Websters and the Thompsons had lived on the hill for several generations. Hank goes as far back as I can remember in my childhood. We were inseparable, practically bothers. He was almost one month older than me, having been born February 29 - a leap year - and I arrived March 25. Hank thought the fact that he was born on such an unusual date made him special because his birthday only came every four years. Physically, Hank was bigger than me. Tall and stocky with big, broad shoulders. He looked strong and tough, but he never came across that way once you got to know him. Boyhood competition was a big part of our relationship. It's funny that when you're a kid, those insignificant things like who's older or who's the tallest, or who is the strongest or fastest, or who has the biggest dick, really mean something to you. You get caught up in all those insignificant things while the rest of the world whizzes past. Right now, though, it doesn't matter who was the oldest or the biggest or the smartest or the richest. You learn too late in life that all these things mean very little in the long run. It's too bad you're not born with that knowledge. If you were, you'd be able to avoid a lot of problems further down the road. Instead, you stumble through life making mistakes as you go. Of course the real catch to surviving is to recognize those mistakes and then correct them. It's even worse when you know your mistakes but don't do anything about them.

Hank was a good guy, the best of the lot. I liked him very much. We played together when we were smaller and when we got older, we did many of those grown-up things as partners. We even got in trouble together long before the other guys came along. One time, when we were ten, we got caught breaking into one of our neighbours' houses to steal cigarettes. It wasn't anything serious. Nothing more that the kind of minor trouble kids often get into, especially boys. But that didn't matter. "A wrong is a wrong," my Old Man scolded as he tanned my ass. He didn't spank me often, but when he did he used an old strap he brought home from the shipyard. I could hardly sit down for three days after the cigarette incident. If you look close you might still see the red welts on my butt. I'm sure he must have left permanent marks. The Old Man was usually gentle. When he raised his hand to me, I knew he meant business. Stealing was something he wouldn't tolerate.

"No matter how bad things get or how much you want something, you never steal it from anyone else," he lectured. "Someone worked hard to get those things you want and to take it from them is like taking their security. Once you take that, you can't give it back."

It took several weeks before my Old Man forgave me for the theft, but he never let me forget what I'd done. "You must remember the pain you caused and you must learn from it," he told me.

Hank got into trouble too. Although he never would admit it to me or anyone else, I know his old man hit him ... many times. His old man had a reputation for being a mean son-of-a-bitch and I sometimes saw that hateful streak firsthand. Hank's father was a religious fanatic, a creep who gave me the shivers whenever we were in the same room. As I said before, I don't have anything against God or religion, but his old man took it to the extreme. In his house, Hank's old man was the master. He ruled the roost with an iron fist and believed in that old saying, spare the rod, spoil the child. I'm sure Hank's old man used the rod many times. I never saw anything too dramatic myself, but I know it happened ... I could see it in Hank's eyes every time his old man was around. I heard stories about him hitting the kids and their mother. The rumours were all over town. Hank was too proud to ever admit that anyone could ever discipline him. But I think his old man beat him and his young brother, Jimmy, a lot more than anyone ever really knew.

I remember seeing black and blue marks on Hank many times, especially on his arms and back and sometimes even on his legs, but he never told me how he got them. And I sure as hell never asked him any questions. That was his business and I respected his privacy. I figured I wouldn't have wanted anyone asking questions if it was me. I didn't pry. But the truth was, I didn't really know what Hank was going through. How could anyone know if they have never faced it themselves? My Old Man was strict, but he wasn't abusive. There is a very distinct difference. It's sad to think any parent could hurt their children, but I know they do.

Breaking into that house to steal cigarettes was stupid, but it was only one of the few times we got into any serious trouble. We weren't all bad, though. I've always figured we were pretty good kids. We liked spending time outdoors. We went fishing and swimming when the weather was nice and in the winter we'd go skating down on the old Mill Pond. The kids still use that pond today. It's a good place for skating. The ice gets pretty thick. We also did a little hunting in the fall. Mostly, though, we set rabbit snares. The hunting was good back then. Plenty of rabbits around these parts. But nowadays the coyotes got them all eaten up so it's pretty slim picking.

In the summer we'd go camping together, just the two of us out in the woods. It was great taking our blankets and getting away from everyone else. We'd go to this secret spot outside of town that we called Pine Grove. It was a wonderful place. Big, high pine trees with thick branches that formed a natural canopy as if shielding us from the rest of the world. No one would ever know you were in there because there weren't any roads running past it. It was a good hike from town so people hardly ever came up that way even though it was worth the effort. There was a small clearing next to a pool of water with all kinds of brier bushes growing around it. We called it Brier Lake. It was great for swimming. The water was so clear that you could see all the way to the bottom in some places. But it was deep out in the middle and the current was quite strong where it fed into the river. We built a raft that we pushed out to the middle of the lake to dive from. We spent many days out there at the lake, just the two of us and it was fantastic ... as if the world stood still for us. Sometimes

I wish we would never have left that place.

Pine Grove was a magical place where me and Hank could go and forget our troubles. Later, when we got older, the other guys would come out there with us and we'd have a great time swimming and sitting around bullshitting at night. We would build a fire in the little clearing, spread out our blankets on a bed of brush and spend the night under the stars talking about our hopes and dreams, and making plans for our future. I miss that place. I miss those days when everything seemed so simple. We still had our lives ahead of us and we had no knowledge of the mistakes we would soon make.

That magical place is gone now. It's called progress. They cut down all the big, beautiful trees and sold the logs to the sawmill. It's a pity what they've done. I can't tell you how many days and nights we spent out there, but I know it was a great part of our childhood and teenage years, when we'd go out to that little clearing to party. It's places like that where friendships can become something special. I wonder if Hank knew how much he meant to me.

We went through a great deal together, me and Hank. Some good and some bad. He was at my side when my Old Man died. He helped me through that difficult time in my life simply by being there and not asking any questions. He gave me space and that was good. That's exactly what I needed. I had to deal with his death in my own way, but I also knew I had a friend that I could count on. In return, I was there for him when his family's house burned down. We were sixteen. It was an awful night, but somehow everyone got out in one piece. Hank's old man fell asleep smoking in bed and the house went up in a matter of minutes. It was a hard time for Hank and his family. He stayed at my house for a few days until his mother arranged for them to stay at her sister's on the other side of town. They were there a few weeks until they found a house of their own to rent. It wasn't too far from the hill, so we could remain close. Damned shame though. When you have a fire like that, you lose everything. Personal belongings and keepsakes that you can't replace are gone forever. Hank had a tough time coming to terms with the fire. I stuck by him every day until he got back on his feet. It was the right thing to do. Friends do that for each other ... that, and a whole lot more.

Even though we were such good friends, Hank was still the kind of guy you sometimes love to hate. He often acted like he knew everything, but really didn't know his ass from a hole in the ground. You never argue with people like that because you can't win even when you know you're right and they're wrong. I never argued with Hank. I accepted him for what he was, a friend I could count on no matter how pigheaded he was. I could forgive him for that one small human flaw. There are worse things in life than a know-it-all.

Hank liked to give advice, especially when you didn't want it. I remember he was there when I went out on my first date with Patty Fergusson. She was a cute little thing with dimples and straight blond hair down to her shoulders. She was very attractive and popular in school. I really do think Hank believed he was being helpful when he tried to give me pointers on how to get into her pants that first night, but I never listened. As much as I loved him as a friend and brother, I knew he could sometimes be an asshole.

"I had my first woman when I was twelve," he'd brag to us with his chest stuck out in rooster fashion. But we didn't believe him. He claimed he had been with Susan Harris, a girl a few years ahead of us at school who had a reputation for being easy. I knew none of it really ever happened ... and believe me, I'd know. Even so, I let Hank blow steam whenever he was around the other guys. It made him feel like he was important and the centre of attention. I allowed him to have his fantasy.

Privately, though, I've come to think Hank used the bullshit to hide the truth about himself. Truth was, I don't remember Hank being too comfortable around girls. I say that now thinking back to this one particular hot summer day when we were thirteen. We had been heading out to the lake for a swim when it happened. On our way, we had to pass another smaller lake, called Beavertail Lake. It was used regularly by the townspeople because it was closer than Brier Lake and a lot easier to reach since, in order to get to Brier Lake, you had to walk at least an hour out of town and climb over Wild Cat Rock. It was a difficult hike, especially in the heat and humidity that we often get around here in the middle of summer.

Beavertail was used a great deal on hot days. That's why we were so surprised by what we discovered there this particular time. Me and Hank were going along minding our own business when we heard some rustling from a little patch of pine trees located next to Beavertail. At first, we thought maybe it was a deer or some other wild animal, but as we crept closer for a look we found Molly Burns and Jacob Dixon naked as jay-birds going at it right there on the ground for the whole world to see.

Molly was the daughter of bank manager, Hiram Burns. She was the second oldest of four girls. Her family was all snooty and the girls were raised to be prim and proper, with their big, floppy hats and frilly dresses decorated with fancy lace and ribbons. I can't help but chuckle when I think of what old Mr. Burns would have said if he had seen his precious Molly all sweaty and dirty, and huffing and puffing as she rolled around in the underbrush with Jacob on that hot day. He would have died right there on the spot, I'm sure.

Jacob was one of us second-class citizens of Liverpool from the other side of the tracks. His father and two brothers worked in the woods, cutting logs for the mill. It was an honourable way to make a living, but there's no way the Burns family would have condoned any kind of relationship between the two, that's why we were surprised to see them out in the open like they were that day. It's obvious they had been caught in the heat of passion, since they hadn't taken any precautions to hide themselves. Molly and Jacob were each about ten years older than us and we could tell by the way they were doing their business that this wasn't their first time.

"Come on, Hank, let's get a better look," I coaxed, inching ever closer to the thrashing bodies. Naturally, as an excitable young man, I wanted to stay and watch from our precarious hiding place under the bushes. We had a good view from this vantage point and I was enjoying the show, especially since I had never seen a naked girl in the flesh before. Although I would have never admitted that to the others. At our age it was important to let the others think we had experience with girls, so most of us lied about our sexual exploits. That's why I was so caught up in the heat of the moment that day. Molly Burns was a nice looking young woman and I was enjoying the sight of her shapely body thrashing about the underbrush as Jacob rode her like a stallion.

But Hank wasn't impressed. "Com'n Jack," he pleaded. "Let's get out of here before they see us. They'll be pissed if they catch us spyin' on them. That Jacob Dixon's pretty tough. I heard he took on three fellas one time. I don't feel like tanglin' with him today."

It was obvious Hank was uncomfortable and wanted to leave immediately. I made him stay a few minutes, but finally gave in to his insistent nagging, fearing that the two lusting lovers would catch us if we continued to argue.

Later, whenever I brought up the subject of what we had seen that day, Hank quickly changed it. "This ain't the time or place to talk about that," he'd say, quickly changing the subject.

Boys like to talk about such things. It's healthy and part of growing up. I often tried to engage my friend in such conversations. It never worked with Hank, though. If I ever tried to ask him what he thought of Molly's boobs bouncing around like they were, he wouldn't answer. I never thought much about it until years later, but I wonder now if maybe Hank didn't like guys better than girls. I never saw or heard anything specific to make me think such things about him. It's just a feeling I had and something I always kept to myself. Maybe that's because I can't convince myself that he was different. Regardless, Hank and me were good buddies and that's all that was important. If he liked boys better than girls, he certainly wasn't going to talk about it, especially to his friends. It just wasn't heard of. And in those days it never crossed my mind that Hank would be something like that. If it had, we probably wouldn't have been such good friends. There was no way you could associate with guys like that. That's just the way things were back then.

Besides my best friend Hank, there was Levi Taylor. He was strange, but likeable most of the time. There's no other way to describe him. Levi came from a good family who lived on the right side of the tracks. Mama always told me that I should avoid people like Levi Taylor because we would never fit in with each other. "You'll never get along," she'd say, pointing out our many differences. "You two come from different worlds. I don't know what you see in him." But I failed to see why we couldn't all be friends regardless of how much money they had or we didn't have.

Levi was tall, but not too skinny and pretty good looking too. He had the girls after him all the time and I often felt jealous because he was getting all the attention. I remember he had the thickest head of red hair I have ever seen and he was a good student. He had no choice in that. He was going to be somebody, or at least he was going to be if his old man had anything to do with it. Mr. Taylor was a piece of work. Levi's father would throw a fit every time he saw Levi with us. "You don't belong with those kind of boys," he'd say to Levi, snapping his high-society nose into the air. He didn't think we were good enough to be hanging around his precious little boy, but we didn't care. Truth was, we liked having Levi around because we knew it pissed off the old man. I'm sure they were thinking of him when they came up with the word asshole.

Actually we often wondered if Levi was good enough to be around us. After all, the whole town knew of his father's wandering ways. It was no secret that Mr. Taylor was having an affair with Doc Halliday's wife, Doris. We may not have come from families with much money, but at least our fathers weren't out screwing some doctor's wife while the doctor was out saving lives. What a hypocrite. How dare he think we weren't good enough for his little boy.

The Taylor family made its money from lumbering. They didn't work the woods themselves. They were too good for any type of menial physical work. Mr. Taylor owned some of the largest woodlots in the outlying areas surrounding Liverpool and paid dozens of men meagre wages to cut the logs for him which he'd turn around and sell to the mill for a hefty profit. Levi never talked about his family much and that was okay with us. A bunch of young shits like us got better things to do than listen to that crap. We had no room in our lives for such foolishness.

Sometimes though I pitied Levi. His parents gave him anything he could ever want and all he ever wanted was to be with his friends ... to be normal. That usually led to many arguments between Levi and his old man and some of those confrontations were wild affairs. Levi was a year older than me and Hank, and he backed down from no one, not even his father. He could hold his own against his old man and always rose to the challenge.

"I want you to stay away from that bunch off the hill," the senior Taylor would demand. "They're no good. They will never amount to anything. You're better than that. I want you to find some friends of your own kind."

"They're my friends," Levi would fire back, targeting his counter attack directly at his father. "I like them. You don't even know them, yet you've decided you don't like them. You don't even give them a chance. They're good people. It shouldn't matter if they got money or not. When I'm with them, I don't have to put up with any of this shit. They let me be me, which is more than I can say for you."

When the two Taylors took to screaming up there in that beige and yellow house with its fancy verandah nestled under the chestnut trees at the end of Birch Street, you could sometimes hear them way down at the other end. That's when you knew they were just like everyone else despite the show they put on around town. They still had their troubles and the money didn't matter. They didn't care who could hear them when they got into a fight. Levi's old man never apologized for his stern way of parenting or his smug, upper-class attitude. He figured it was nobody else's business how he raised his son. And honestly, I don't think anyone else really cared. Levi was an all right guy in our books, but we had other things to worry about than to listen to those two going at each other's throats.

Ben Weaver was another one of those regular guys you could always count on when you needed a helping hand. He lived near me and Hank, just a bit further up the hill along the path, which meant his family travelled in the same lower-class social circles as us working poor. Ben was built short and stocky like me, only he might have been a bit heavier. He reminded me of a tank, the way he was put together. I used to tell him he looked like a brick shithouse and he'd laugh like a fool. He had a good sense of humour when I first met him. That would change years later.

Ben always seemed to be around, even when you didn't want him to be. He was one of those people who seem to be there when you get up in the morning and who are still there when you go to bed at night. I sometimes wondered if he was sleeping on our front doorstep like a lost puppy.

Regardless of the frequency of his visits, Ben was a good guy and fun to be around. I liked him very much and appreciated his company most of the time. He was like me in many ways. Kind of shy, but not afraid to try new things. That kind of personality can get you into a heap of trouble and Ben always pushed it to the limits. Sometimes he could go too far. One time, he went over the edge.

Neither of us were exactly good students, but Ben was the worst. He was more interested in having a good time than learning. He loved to play practical jokes in school. We went to a small school that used to be located up there across from where they built the new fire hall. They tore it down a few years back to make room for a parking lot. It was a two-room brick building painted white. I remember we had to go up these freaking huge set of cement steps to get inside where the classrooms were. There was grades primary to three on one side and then grades four to eight on the other side. After that, you went to the old high school for grades nine to eleven. We didn't have grade twelve when I went to school. Hell, most of us were lucky if we could get to grade eleven.

I remember that building very well. We had those old desks where you sit two-by-two next to each other. Ben always arranged it so he was sitting next to one of the girls ... and it didn't matter who. He especially loved to sneak spiders into school and put them on the girls' backs so they'd drop onto the desk in front of them or crawl over their necks. Talk about scream. You've never heard anything like it. Almost bust your eardrums if you were unlucky enough to be sitting in the desk in front of them, or even worse, beside them. He could cause some shit, that guy, and he never quit. Yup, he was forever the jokester

... when we were kids.

Ben came from a broken family. My Old Man died, but Ben's father had left his mother when Ben was only three and his sister was five. They had to move in with his mother's parents and that wasn't very comfortable for any of them. The house was small, not really big enough for five people. Ben never knew his father and I think deep down inside he regretted that. But he'd never tell you so. He was too damned proud, sometimes for his own good. He had a tough time accepting that his old man would just up and leave him; that he didn't care enough about his family to stick around. I think Ben developed a deep, unhealthy hatred for his old man and I'm not sure he ever got over it. It wasn't the kind of hate that you get when someone does something bad to you. You might expect that kind of hate from Ben because his father did hurt him deeply by leaving him so young. No, I think it was the kind of hate you get when you want something so bad but you know you can't have it. It's a deep-rooted hurting that drives you mad. That pain turns into hatred or at least resentment. I think Ben wanted to know his old man so bad that he became bitter and that emptiness turned to hate. It ate him up from the inside out, and eventually consumed him.

Ben never did find his old man. It's a shame. A boy needs his father. I know that for a fact. You need your old man around when things are good and when they get bad. There were times when I could have used my Old Man, but he couldn't be there. Maybe Ben's father was unable to return to him for some unknown reason, but we never knew for sure. Sometimes the not knowing is the hardest part of the mystery when someone disappears. And other times the knowing can eat you up.

The fact that both of our fathers were gone allowed me and Ben to make a special connection. There was a bond there between us that I can't explain and that I didn't have with any of the other guys, not even my best friend Hank. It was as if we found in each other what we were missing from our fathers. That kind of deep brotherhood bond can lead people to do a lot of things they might not normally do. Me and Ben went through a lot because of that connection, some of which I treasure; some of which I regret.

Our serious adventures started when we were both nine. It was a warm day in September when hell broke loose for the first time. The night before, my Old Man had asked me to cut some wood while he was at work. He never thought, not for one minute, that I was too young to chop wood when he wasn't around. Back then, kids were expected to carry their end of the load. The Old Man had bought and made arrangements with one of the local foresters for a load of firewood to be dropped off a few weeks earlier, and now before the cold weather came it had to be sawed, split and neatly piled in the little lean-to shed the Old Man built next to our house. As usual, Ben had arrived early that morning and he offered to help with the wood. It was an offer I could not refuse since we had planned to go to the lake after lunch, if I got some wood split. We still wanted to swim before the weather turned cold, but there was no way I could leave until I had done what my Old Man asked.

We got to work shortly after eight o'clock. I intended to make a good dent in the pile that day hoping the Old Man would think I had done well. Ben took to piling the wood as I chopped it, and we made great progress for awhile. About an hour into the work, he complained of being tired and said he was going to take a break. "I gotta take a rest, Jack," he huffed, trying to catch his breath. "This here's hard work and I'm sweatin' like a pig."

"Not me. I'm not the least bit tired," I said, continuing to swing the axe. I figured if we stopped, we'd never get started again. I kept chopping, not paying much attention to what Ben was up to.

"Jesus, Jack, it won't kill you to take a break," he continued. "You'll wear yourself out if you don't pace yourself."

I was going strong when Ben came over next to me by the chopping block and insisted I should rest. It was getting warmer and we were both working up a good sweat.

"Okay," I said, and stopped swinging the axe.

I guess Ben must have thought I was finished for awhile because he was about to sit down on the chopping block when I struck the near-fatal blow. It was a stupid thing for Ben to do, but for some reason, as he was looking for a place to sit, he placed his right hand on the block at the very same time I brought the axe down.

It happened fast. There was blood everywhere. But Ben didn't cry out or scream like you might expect. Instead he looked at me blankly, as if in shock, and then, without a word, pulled the blade out of the back of his hand and threw the axe on the blood-splattered ground. The cut was deep and I knew he needed medical attention right away.

"Shit," I screamed. "Jesus, oh Jesus. Mama, come out here quick. I think I cut Ben's hand off."

Luckily this was a Saturday and it was one of those weekends that Mama wasn't at work. She came running out of the house at my first cries for help. Quickly assessing the emergency, she removed her flowered apron and wrapped it tightly around Ben's hand, but the blood immediately seeped through. Then she brought him inside the house where she laid his arm straight out on the kitchen table and packed it in damp towels.

"Go as quickly as you can and get Doc Halliday," Mama said. "Tell him what's happened and bring him to the house right away. Don't delay, Jack. Time is of the essence."

It was a good fifteen-minute run into town at normal speed, but my legs flew that day as if they had wings. It took me another five minutes to explain the emergency to Doc Halliday and another fifteen minutes for him to gather his things and get back out to our house.

"Such a serious cut can mean major trouble," he said following his initial observation. "It's especially bad if there has been a lot of blood loss." But following a careful examination right there in our kitchen, he reported that the axe had not cut any vital veins or tendons. "Luckily for Mr. Weaver here," Doc Halliday said in an upbeat tone, "the axe blade appears to have been dull. It hit in the fleshier part of the hand between the knuckles and wrist. That's a good thing. That's probably why it didn't go all the way through to sever the fingers." He also said Mama did the right thing by keeping the arm out straight and not elevated because it was important to keep the blood circulating to the fingers.

Despite the good report, however, he told Ben he would require several stitches. "It's still a nasty cut," he added. "We're going to have to stitch you good and tight. And it's too early to tell, but it's possible that you might lose the function of your middle finger. Other than that," the doctor said, "you're a damned lucky boy. A few more inches and we would have been picking your fingers up off the ground."

I shuddered at the thought.

Through it all Ben remained miraculously calm. He never reacted. He never even cried. He must have been in shock from the pain he had to be suffering, but he never so much as shed a tear. Some people never show emotion no matter how serious the situation. The doctor worked for almost an hour and a half on Ben's hand. In the end, it took twenty-nine stitches to close the wound I had inflicted upon my friend. As Doc Halliday began stitching up the cut, Mama sent me to bring Ben's mother to our house. "Until the swelling goes down," Doc Halliday said, "it's impossible to say for sure if there will be any lasting damage from the injury." But, he cautioned Ben's mother that while he could not tell if there would be any lasting effects, he didn't think it would reduce the hand's usage, except maybe for that finger.

When the stitches came out almost two weeks later, Ben didn't seem to have any serious problem with the hand, but in later years he would complain his fingers often went numb and sometimes felt cold. Naturally I blamed that on the childhood injury. I also experienced some guilt for what I had done. While it had been an accident, I still felt responsible. I can't imagine how I'd have felt if I had cut off his hand that day. And even after all these years, I can never stop thinking about what might have happened if Ben had gotten his head in the way instead of his hand. Another few inches and who knows?

Life is like that. You just never know. It's a good thing you don't, Nanny Vera used to say.

Charlie Henderson was another of my close childhood buddies. The Hendersons lived in a nice little house just off Main Street, directly behind the general store his family operated.

Liverpool survived through many hard times, but the town could never boast a large commercial core. We had one large general store and it was a constant hub of activity. It was called Henderson's after the owners, Sam Henderson and his wife Beatrice. They called her Beatty. They were very nice people. There were also a couple of smaller stores, but Henderson's was the biggest in Liverpool. It's the one I remember best. I spent much of my childhood there. They had everything you needed, even a fresh meat counter where people could bring in their critter in the fall to be cut up to get them through the long, cold winter. Sam was a good butcher, or a carnifex as some of the old people called him. Some said he was the best meat cutter on the whole South Shore and he got business from all around these parts.

Besides the meat counter Henderson's also had a place where you could get animal feed and most other dry goods. They had clothes, tools, candy and all kinds of preserved food. It was a real general store with everything you could ever need or want and they did a damned good business. Don't know if they were rich or anything like that, but I think they did all right. I believe they were successful because they were friendly. They treated all the customers with the utmost respect, even us kids. Happy customers mean good business.

Unlike some of the other businesses, the Hendersons didn't give us kids a hard time when we went into their store. I liked the place. It was comfortable and relaxing to shop there, not like the big-box stores we've got today. Old Sam was as crazy as a loon. He liked to talk and, man, could he ever tell a joke. His delivery was natural and brightened many days when most of the townfolk had nothing to smile about. I don't believe Sam had a mean bone in his body. I've never met anyone since then who could crack a joke as well as old Sam Henderson, or who could make me feel so comfortable and relaxed.

Charlie Henderson was a nice guy and it didn't matter that he came from the rich part of town. We called him Bunny, which seemed appropriate to us; for some stupid reason his mother made him eat carrots with every meal. No matter what they had at meal time, she always made him eat carrots - twice a day, every day.

"Carrots," Mrs. Henderson said, "are good for the eyes. We must eat carrots to protect the gift of sight that He has given us." To say she was obsessive about carrots would be like saying China is over-populated. Some people around town said she got scared about going blind after a close relative of hers lost his eyesight for some mysterious reason. Mrs. Henderson got worried after that and made Bunny and the entire family eat carrots as a preventative measure. "An ounce of prevention is worth of a pound of cure," she'd say whenever anyone in the family complained about having carrots. Don't know if it ever helped them much, but I don't suppose it ever hurt them either.

It's funny now when I think of it. Bunny was the only one out of us five who wore glasses. He had glasses from about the time he was twelve and he hated them with a passion. "They're a pain in the ass," he'd say. He'd tell us how much he hated having to wear glasses, especially when he was playing ball or swimming or doing anything physical. It had to be pure hell for an active young boy. Bunny despised his glasses. And eventually he grew to hate carrots just as much, almost as much as he hated his nickname.

I don't think Bunny was a bad name, but kids never like nicknames. We didn't mean him any harm with it. We were only having a little fun, like kids do, but he used to get pissed whenever we called him Bunny. He wanted us to call him Charlie or even Chuck, but we never did. We knew it made him mad when we called him Bunny. We did it just to spite him.

Bunny was two years younger than the rest of us, but he was a real scrapper. He wouldn't back down from no one or anything. It didn't matter how big you were. If you pissed him off, Bunny would be ready to fly into you without regard for his own wellbeing.

Ben was bigger than Bunny by at least twenty pounds, and he would razz Bunny all the time, constantly pushing and picking. I could understand how his persistent nagging would get under Bunny's skin. It got to me a few times too. I remember one day when we were playing ball and Ben was getting on Bunny's case. "Hey four-eyes, you look like a sissy in those cute little glasses," Ben teased.

Poking fun at Bunny had become a regular pastime for Ben. But on this day, the teasing didn't sit too well with Bunny and he wasn't prepared to put up with it. "I'm tellin' ya, Ben, you better shut your big mouth or else," he said.

"Or else what, you little weeny," Ben taunted. "What'cha gonna do, sissy? Go cryin' to your mama?"

That was it. With lighting-flash reflexes unlike anything we had seen before, Bunny hit Ben on the side of the head with a baseball bat. He hit Ben so hard in one furious motion that the blow knocked him off his feet and left him unconscious for a minute or two. Ben didn't move for what seemed like a long time. We thought Bunny had killed him, but it turned out he barely dented Ben's thick skull. We all had a good laugh after we knew Ben wasn't seriously hurt. We had a great time at Ben's expense. We taunted and laughed at him, saying he had a fat head and there wasn't anything in there he could hurt. But it did cost Ben a few teeth. From that day on, everyone had a different kind of respect for old Bunny ... but we still called him Bunny just the same and he came to accept it. But he never did like it.

Chapter 6

That was the five of us. We were an odd lot. A rag-tag group of young snots with piss and vinegar coursing through our veins. We were each unique with distinct personalities. We were all alike in many ways, yet different in many ways. We shared common likes, but at the same time had many disagreements. We were all too proud and pigheaded to give up our independence. I think that's what probably made the company work so well. We played off each other's strengths to compensate for our own weaknesses. You wouldn't have thought the five of us would have bonded so tightly, but our friendship was real and sincere. It ran deep like a swift, underground stream. Me, Hank and Ben had practically grown up together from our births on the hill. We met Levi and Bunny after we started school. The attraction was quick and the respect we all shared for each other was mutual, even if we sometimes disagreed.

As youngsters we did many things together, including almost getting ourselves killed more than once. When we were about eleven years of age, one of our favourite pastimes after school was to go down to the river bank and watch the ships coming and going through the front harbour. It was beautiful. Breath-taking. It's something this town will never see again. As kids often do, we usually threw caution to the wind, thinking we were invincible and that no harm could befall us, no matter the danger or risk. But that attitude almost ended in tragedy one January afternoon.

It was bitterly cold that day, with a wind-chill that cut to the bone and froze the little black hairs in your nose. The snow hadn't arrived yet, but winter had its icy grip on the land just the same. It was so cold that some parts of the river had frozen over. It has to be pretty damned cold for that to happen because the tide usually keeps the river ice-free.

We had grown up around the river and we knew it demanded a certain amount of respect. We also understood that we should avoid the ice. But what you know you should do, and what you do in the end, are two very different things, especially when you're young, stupid and think you're invincible.

It all started when Levi arrived at school that morning and told us about the new ship that had arrived at the wharf some time through the night. "She's a beaut," he said, describing the masts and elaborating on the ship's size. "I don't know where she's from, but wherever she's been they've taken good care of her."

I've always marvelled at the majesty of ships, particularly the old trawlers. I've been impressed with the idea of something so big and so heavy being able to stay afloat on the water. The ingenuity of man to construct such spectacular vessels has amazed me most of my life. That curiosity drew me regularly to the wharves, as it did the others. If there was a new ship at the dock, we were compelled to have a good look.

That's all it took to get us excited. After school, around three o'clock, despite the biting cold, we ran down to the river to see the trawler that had tied up at Tupper's wharf for a refit. We learned the ship had just finished a cross-Atlantic voyage from England. There was much excitement in Liverpool about the ship's arrival. Everyone was talking about her, and naturally we wanted to have a good close look for ourselves. We were a curious lot, and you could be sure if something was going on around Liverpool, the five of us would be nearby. Instead of heading home after school that day like we were supposed to do, we trotted off into town to check out this ship that was causing so much fuss. It was an impressive vessel, but the sight wasn't worth the price we almost paid for a look.

Where the shipyard met the edge of the town's modest commercial development, Tupper's had erected a fairly high fence along its portion of the bank to keep curious people, like us kids, out of the shipyard for safety reasons and for security. But to five stupidly-brave young boys who loved a challenge, that fence only served as an invitation. There it was, just daring us to find a way to get on the other side. Without hesitation we rose to the test, going up and over as quick as you could shake a stick. In search of a better vantage point, we slowly picked our way over the slippery rocks along the few hundred feet of icy river bank that had been fenced off. Our goal was to get to the wharf for a close look at the trawler. That we had to go over the fence and pick our way a few hundred yards down the ice-covered shores of the harbour where the Mersey River dumps in the Atlantic Ocean, only added to the test.

Despite the danger on the icy river bank we foolishly decided to take the risk. We thought we were invincible. "This will be a snap," Levi decided, taking the lead. "You guys follow me and I'll show you how it's done."

Obediently we followed. Initially it was pretty easy going along the slippery rocks. There wasn't much ice near the top of the riverbank, but closer to the water the rocks were threatening. Levi was showing us the way. I was directly behind him, about six feet away. It all happened pretty fast before any of us had a chance to react. One minute Levi was on the slick shoreline in front of me, the next minute he went flying head-first into the water. He slipped and plunged into the river before any of us could reach him.

The next thing I knew, I too had slipped into the cold water. But I had been more fortunate, reaching out and grabbing hold of some dormant shrubs which had been sticking out through the ice on the riverbank. Somehow they held my weight and saved me from also plunging into the freezing waters ... but not entirely.

My feet went through the slush lapping against the rocks and I slid in up to my knees. The cold was piercing, like hundreds of pins and needles sticking me all over. Then my legs went numb, like dead weights. I struggled to pull myself to safety, but the lower portions of my legs felt like sand bags. The harder I pulled with the upper part of my body, the heavier my legs became. Then, just when I thought I had no more strength left in my arms, I felt an unusual surge of energy. To this day, I still don't know how I did it, but somehow I managed to hold on and pull myself back up to shore. Actually it was more like someone had reached down and rescued me from the cold water. The adrenaline rush had saved me from sure death.

Hank was the first to reach me. "Jesus, Jack. Didn't you guys see how slippery the rocks were?"

I didn't need a lecture right at the minute. "Just shut up, Hank, and get me outta here," I screamed. "I ain't got any feeling in my feet."

"This was so stupid," Bunny huffed as he reached Hank and helped me up. "You gotta get outta them wet clothes right now before they freeze to your skin. We gotta get something dry for you to put on right away."

"I ain't gonna strip right here," I shot back. Vanity was one of my stronger characteristics. That would soon change, however.

"Here Jack, put this around your legs." Despite the frigid temperatures, Hank quickly removed his coat, offering it to me to use as a blanket.

Ben had now also reached us. "Here, take mine too. You're gonna need it."

By then Levi was in serious trouble. We were only young boys, but we knew we didn't have much time to save our friend. It would have only taken seconds for hypothermia to set in from such cold water. I quickly forgot about the numbness in my legs in my concern for Levi.

"We gotta find a rope or a branch or somethin' to throw out to him," Ben was ordering as he combed the shoreline. "He won't last long in there."

"This is useless," Hank replied. "It's probably already too late for him. We're never gonna find anything under all this ice."

"We can't give up," I screamed. "We gotta get him out. I ain't gonna leave him in there." I was panicked. I didn't want this to be the day I lost one of my best friends.

The four of us ran about the riverbank frightened for our own safety, while at the same time searching for something that we might throw to Levi and pull him to shore. As we scrambled about, one of the men who had been working on the wharf and had witnessed the entire incident, came to our aid. Basil Kohler, a black man who worked his entire life at Tupper's, had seen Levi slip into the icy water and quickly sprang into action. Without thinking about his own safety, he dropped what he was doing and came to Levi's rescue, plunging headfirst into that cold water like a polar bear in pursuit of lunch. Basil later described the icy water like thousands of little knives cutting him all over his body. But if he was experiencing any pain, he didn't show it during the rescue. I'm sure it was no more than a minute, maybe two, for Basil to get in the water and pull Levi back to safety. He was a real hero, even if he didn't think so.

The story of Levi's rescue made the newspapers. Even the provincial daily paper carried a story on Basil and Levi. People found it interesting that a black man would risk his own life to save a rich, white kid, particularly in a town that still had a bylaw on its books stating that all black people had to be off the streets by nine o'clock in the evening. We couldn't understand the fuss. I don't know what any of that had to do with saving the life of a kid who would surely have died that day, but people seemed to make a big deal over it back then.

After the story hit the papers, both Levi and Basil became reluctant celebrities, but neither cared too much for the notoriety. Basil dismissed the attention. "I only done what anyone would have done," he'd answer whenever anyone asked him about the incident. But even though he didn't see himself as a hero, I gave Basil lots of credit for his brave rescue. I was in that water that day too. I know what it felt like. Basil deserved every bit of recognition he got for saving Levi's life.

As for Levi, he didn't like to discuss that day at all. "Drop it," he'd demand whenever we brought up the subject. He said the fact that he had slipped on the rocks made him look stupid and clumsy. He only talked to us about the experience once over the years and only because he had been drinking. It was with a great deal of emotion several years later that he told us that when he was in the water he believed he was going to die. "I don't remember very much after I went through the ice," he said. "It all happened so fast and my whole body went numb right away." It was hard for Levi to relate the story, but he said, "I remember seeing Jack hanging onto the rocks, trying to get back on shore. And I remembered seeing Hank, Ben and Bunny scurrying around the river bank like chickens with their heads cut off."

Strangely, he said, although he thought he was going to die, he didn't recall being afraid. "It's a feeling I can't describe. I was scared shitless, yet I was really relaxed, like I was in a trance or something." Within seconds Levi had blacked out from the intense cold. The next thing he said he remembered was Basil pulling him up on shore and a large group of people standing around asking if he was okay. "That was such a stupid question. Of course I wasn't okay." He had just been plucked from the brink of death so how could he be okay?

That was only one of the many experiences the five of us shared growing up in this backwater town. If we learned anything from Levi's brush with death that day, it was the knowledge that life is precious. It should never be taken for granted. We saw firsthand how life can change in a matter of seconds, how your world can be altered in an instant. If not for the quick action of one brave man who defied his own fate to save the life of a helpless kid, Levi would surely have died. That's a sobering reality for youngsters to face and accept.

Did that revelation change our outlook on life or how we went through life? You might think so, but it didn't. Even when you gain such wisdom, most people don't know how to apply it. Such knowledge is not for the faint of heart or the weak of mind. Despite the knowledge we had gained from our experience, we bumbled along just like everyone else in Liverpool, oblivious to the reality that life hangs by a very precarious thread which can be broken in the blink of an eye. There were many other lessons to be learned throughout our lives, some good and some not so good. If only we knew then what we know now.

Not everything in Liverpool was a disaster when we were growing up. We also had many fun times, and the bond of families and friends was strong, I think even more so than what you find today.

One of my favourite stories from my youth took place in the spring just after my fourteenth birthday and only months before my Old Man died. On the second Saturday of every month, except December, dances were held regularly in town. Everyone went, no matter what your age or your social standing. It was the only time all the townspeople mingled, although the rich stayed to their side of the hall and we kept to ours. There wasn't much for entertainment around Liverpool in those days. You took advantage of the dances when they were held in the old Meeting House, a little hall that used to stand at the end of Main Street on the edge of town. The music wasn't great, but it was a chance to get out of your house and socialize.

It was important to be neighbourly in such a small town if you wanted to get along even if the classes couldn't find any common ground. Me and the other guys usually went to the dances. We knew the girls were always there. That was the only excuse we needed.

This Saturday night in April, Hank and me left the dance just after nine o'clock. It had started to rain hard and we wanted to get home before the storm got worse. Ben had left about half an hour earlier, just before the rain started. It was about a fifteen or twenty minute walk up hill to our homes, but we knew it would be even slower in the dark and in such heavy rain. We hadn't been as smart as Ben. We should have gone when he left for home. It was raining pretty hard when Hank and me set out. We were drenched by the time we reached the outskirts of town and decided to duck for cover in one of the three old barns at the bottom of the hill. The barns were built by the town's first settlers as storage for hay and other provisions. They hadn't been used in many decades and were ready to fall down. It was probably dangerous to go in there, but we took the chance.

As we were growing up, we had heard stories of the ghosts that lived in the barns, but Hank and me decided we didn't believe in such nonsense. Despite the real dangers from the falling-down structures and ghosts that could inhabit them, we were soaked to the bone and wanted to get in from the storm. Once inside we would wait out the heavy rain and then head for home again after it slacked off. We found ourselves a pile of musty old hay and made ourselves comfortable, prepared to stay for awhile as the rain beat down on the rotted roof above us.

We weren't in there long before Hank reminded me again of the ghosts that were supposed to live there. "Do you think they really exist?" he asked as his trembling voice betrayed his emotions. I'm sure he wanted me to tell him that they didn't.

I didn't let on that I knew he was scared. After all, we were fourteen, almost men. There was no way we were going to show each other that we might be frightened of such foolishness. "Naw, Hank," I insisted, trying to put on a brave front for his benefit. "There's no way that ghosts exist. It's all just a bunch of bullshit stories that somebody made up to keep people outta these barns."

"Yeah, I guess you're right, Jack. There's no such thing as ghosts."

"That's right," I insisted. We sat silent for maybe another five minutes and then the scraping began. It was a constant scuffing sound coming from the hay loft above us. "It's only rats," I assured Hank.

He didn't say a word, but I did feel him inch closer to me in the darkness. Then suddenly, we heard it ... a dry, mournful voice coming from right over our heads. "It's just ye and me!" the voice bellowed. "Leave this place at once and never return." Sure as I'm laying here in this hospital bed, that's what we heard.

Needless to say we weren't long getting the hell out of there. I don't know about Hank, but I damned near shit myself when I heard that creaky voice in the darkness. Years later, when we talked about that night in the barn, we reached the conclusion that Ben, who left the dance before us that night, had been in the barn and had played a trick on us. But try as we might, we could never get him to admit that it was him ... maybe it wasn't.

If someone is a true friend, they'll always be there when you need them and they'll be there to lend a hand when things get tough. That's how I looked at the guys from the company. I knew no matter what came along, we'd be there for each other. We had a special relationship, the kind of close-knit bond that nothing can break. Ours was the kind of friendship that could stand the test of time and many other tests along the way.

But in the end, when we were each tested to the extreme ... we all failed. Ever wonder what hell is? Hell is getting to see the results of your actions. Hell is getting to relive your mistakes, over and over until the pictures become a non-stop movie in your mind. Hell is wanting your life back and longing to undo all the wrongs you have committed. Hell ... that's been my life.

Chapter 7

Is it sane to continue pumping this shit into my veins trying to keep me alive? I should have been dead weeks ago. Is it sane to spend your whole life climbing and scratching your way to the top of the heap only to be knocked off again? You're going to end up six feet underground in the end, but you work your butt off just the same. Is that sane? If a crazy man tells you the world is out of control, should you believe him? We're too quick to judge and too willing to discard people because of how they look on the surface. The old and dying are easily dismissed. It could be that a senile old fool like me just might have something important to say.

Society puts too much stock into the words of "sane" people. The truth is, the lines between sanity and senility, fact and fiction, reality and make-believe have become blurred and fuzzy in this modern material world. Everything is slightly out of focus and off balance ... in my world, and in the real world. I often find it difficult to tell these two worlds apart, to distinguish between real and imagined. Sometimes, I even imagine there's someone in my room when, in fact, there's no one there. That sort of thing has happened often throughout my life. I've grown accustomed to it. It's my little piece of insanity.

I wouldn't have blamed you if you hadn't showed up here today. I would've understood if you hadn't come back.

What's that?

No, you didn't tell me you'd be on the late shift today. But it doesn't matter.

Can you stay awhile? I've had a rough day. The doctor was in this morning and delivered the final blow. My time's up. He said it's only a matter of days, maybe even hours before the cancer finally wins. I wanted to point out to the little shit that he wasn't telling me anything I didn't already know, but for some reason I couldn't find the words. But now I could use someone to talk to. The news of my imminent death has given me cause to think ... and remember. I've gained a new perspective and it's frightening. It's not the dying that bothers me. It's the being alone when I take my last breath that I fear. I don't want to be by myself when I die. I've been alone far too long.

I have to give the little shit credit, though, for having the guts to finally tell me the truth. I haven't thought of him as much of a doctor. I didn't think he had the courage to look me in the eye and tell me I was about to die. But when I told him I wanted to know it all, he held nothing back. That's as it should be. I have the right to know. It's too bad I don't have the right to make my own decisions.

My most recent round of tests confirmed the cancer has progressed through my spine. They can't treat it. The monster has stretched out its tentacles, travelling along my nervous system, and is now attacking most of my vital organs. "There's nothing we can do for you anymore," the doctor said, "but we will try to make you comfortable. We'll keep the pain under control as best we can."

I told him that was fine but I didn't want to be kept alive like some lab rat, with drugs keeping my heart pumping and machines breathing for me. That's not living. That's the worst kind of death sentence I could ever imagine. Maybe it was wrong, but I asked him point-blank if he'd help me die. It caught him off guard, but I had to ask.

He didn't know what to say. In turn, he merely shrugged his shoulders and pulled back from my bed. "I can't do that." His response was terse, as if scolding me for having such a notion. "It's against the law for doctors to help their patients die. It goes against everything I stand for as a healer," he tried to explain, but I didn't want to listen.

I wasn't interested in his by-the-book lectures. "I want relief," I shot back. "The kind of relief that only death can bring. You owe me that for keeping me alive like this."

"That is the most twisted thing I have ever heard, Mr. Webster," the doctor said. "I've tried to help you and give you a few more weeks to live. I'd think you'd be grateful."

"Grateful? For what?" I asked. "How is this helping? I didn't ask to be put in here to be poked and prodded every damned minute of the day. I didn't ask you to put this bag on my side for me to piss in. I didn't expect you to carve me up like a Christmas turkey. This isn't help. This is a punishment. The best thing you could have done for me is let me die."

"I'm sorry you feel that way, Mr. Webster," the doctor said. "But it's out of my hands. I have to follow hospital procedure. If it's any consolation, though, it looks as if you'll be getting your wish soon enough."

In turn, I replied, "Not soon enough. You just don't understand that my only escape is through death, but it was stupid of me to ask. You don't have the courage to do the honourable thing. But what about me? What about my rights? What about me having a say in how, or even if, I have to be kept alive? What about my quality of life? Doesn't any of that count for anything? Why don't you ask me if I want to be hooked up to all these machines, unable to move about or take care of myself? Thank Christ for the drugs. If you're going to insist on keeping me alive, that's the least you can do for me. Maybe you can get me so doped up that I won't realize what's going on. You owe me that much."

"I'm not going to argue with you, Mr. Webster. This is getting us nowhere and it's not helping you to be worked up like this. I have other patients to see. I'll check in on you later," he said. Then he left.

I wasn't surprised to finally hear the truth that I was about to die. People in my condition really do sense when their time is up. I've suspected for some time this disease had gone beyond help. I wanted to thank him for finally telling me something I already knew, but I couldn't find the words. They just weren't there. It's not easy to say how you feel when someone hands you the news that you might only have a few more hours to live. You always hold on to that shred of hope you'll be cured, even when you know the truth. Even when you think you want to die, it's still a shock. It's a hard pill to swallow. It forces you to take stock of what you've done with your life. When I do that, it makes me shudder.

I try to see this the way doctors see it. But I can't. I'm the one laying here like a rotting log. He isn't even sure if that crap you've been pumping in me for the pain will help, but he is going to keep it coming. Pain management isn't an easy thing to accomplish for someone in my condition, he told me. But with the right dosage, they can at least dull the sensations and still keep me conscious. Conscious for what, I have no idea.

The truth is, I just wish it would end right here, right now. I don't know if I can stand the pain much longer, especially if there's a chance it could get worse. It feels like someone's using a hot knife to scrape my skin off in thin layers from the inside out. What gives anyone the right to keep me alive like this and in so much pain when I could be out of my misery? The money they're wasting on me could be spent on something more worthwhile. Why is it such a crime to let me die? It's no secret I want to die. I've told them all, the doctors, the nurses, everyone. I've also signed a do not resuscitate order. It's right there on my chart, but still they keep insisting that I must fight this losing battle. For what? God only knows.

If I could stop this foolishness right now, I would. I'd blow my brains out. I've seen that done and it's most effective. After everything the doctors have put me through, this body is like the discarded shell vacated by a Hermit crab once he's moved on. It's useless. I have no other choice but to lay here and suffer, and hope the good Lord decides to make it quick. He may not do that, however. He may not be through with me yet. He may figure He still has to get even with me before He puts me out of my misery. If that's the case, then there's nothing I can do about it. Unless I could find someone to help me and that's not too bloody likely, is it?

What's that?

Who was Ruby Todd?

Now how in the hell did you know that name?

Oh!

Well, I guess I ought to be more careful what I say when I'm talking in my sleep. It's probably all that medication. Makes me higher then a kite and gets my head all screwed up. It makes my thoughts all muddy like the bottom of Brier Lake after it's been churned up on a stormy day. It also makes me say crazy things that you'd never say if you had your head on straight.

Chapter 8

Ruby Todd. I haven't heard that name in a very long time and it has been many years since I spoke those words, but now it looks as though I can run no more. She's caught up to me after all these years. Perhaps the time has finally come to set the ghosts free.

It isn't easy to speak the name Ruby Todd, but I'm going to tell the story like I remember it. Be warned though, it may not be exactly like it happened. I might get a few of the minor details mixed up or even get off track every now and then, but you must forgive a senile old man. For the most part, the story goes something like this.

It begins with that desperate first breath of life. It ends with a last gasp before death enters our bodies. Everything in between is mostly filler. Our hopes, dreams, aspirations, successes, failures are nothing more than illusions. My greatest fear is that reality as we know it is actually someone else's dream and when that dreamer wakes up, we will all cease to exist.

Where do we fit in?

Who can say for sure? Do we really know anything for certain?

I've learned some tough lessons along the way and now I'm near the end of my journey. Looking back over it all, there is much I liked about my life. But there are also many things I'd change if I had the chance.

What will people remember me for? I don't know. Furthermore, I don't care.

You say you want to learn everything there is to know about me, both the good and the bad, but are you really sure you're prepared for what you may hear? You should be careful what you ask for. You just show up here in this hospital room and expect me to tell you everything. I've never seen you before in my life, but yet you want to know all my personal secrets, all the intimate details of my life. Why should I tell you? No one else around here has ever bothered to listen to anything I've had to say. What makes you different? Why do you care about me?

And maybe there isn't too much to tell. What can a dying old man tell you about life?

I love baseball. Some people find it dull. I see it as the most competitive team sport on earth. Life is like a ball game ... you go up to bat when it's your turn, and then, strike three and you're out. Sometimes you get lucky and get a hit. When you make it to base, you're experiencing success, the same as when you overcome a hurdle in life. It's challenging. It's not supposed to be easy. It's meant to test our fortitude, our persistence and our resolve to survive. Life is about putting your past into perspective and struggling to overcome adversities in beating the odds. You only get a few chances to bat. You better make them count.

My life has been an interesting and eventful journey filled with many ups and downs ... more downs. Ruby Todd was one of the high points and, unfortunately, one of the low points.

There was nothing fake or phony about Ruby Todd. She was honest and caring. She got along with everyone in Liverpool. She had a great sense of humour and liked being with people. Her warm personality came naturally and her pleasant ways seemed very sincere. Everyone in this introverted, backwater town immediately took a liking to Ruby Todd. It just felt right. I remember well the first time I met her, almost as if it was only yesterday. It was over sixty years ago, but she left an impression, in more ways than one.

The day began with a heavy mist shrouding everything, but gradually the day warmed and the sun burned through. You knew it was going to get hot. The first item on the agenda that morning was to find the rest of the guys. If it was going to be hot, I intended to spend the day at Brier Lake. Liverpool could be like Hell itself under such smothering temperatures and I wanted out of there as quickly as possible.

It's long gone now - nothing left but the foundation following a fire more than twenty years ago - but our favourite haunt was the local drug store. It had a small soda counter in one corner and a few booths where we would sit for hours and talk in private. We called the place J.P.s because it was owned by a Mr. J.P. Harnish, an immigrant from some place over in Europe. He was married to Judy, a wonderful woman. Together they were a warm and inviting couple. There were no Harnish children, but they were good to the local kids.

Like Sam Henderson, Mr. Harnish used everyone very well. He was the druggist and he hired several young people to look after the soda shop. Those who went to work there were thankful they had a chance to help their families. Mr. Harnish had a knack for selecting the kids who needed his help the most. He touched many lives in a positive way with this gesture. It made a difference in those days when kids could help their family. Five cents an hour may not seem like much nowadays, but when I was young, a few cents went a long way. You'd think you were rich when you heard those few pennies jingle in your pocket. I remember it well.

It was the summer of 1940 when Ruby Todd entered the picture. The five of us - Levi, Ben, Hank, Bunny and me - were stationed in our regular booth down at J.P.s. We were talking about the war, as was everyone else in Liverpool. The fighting in Europe was getting worse with each passing day. That morning we were talking about the German U-boats near our coast. It was a scary time filled with fear and nervous anticipation, but there was also a certain flair of excitement in the air. It was almost electric. Reports in the paper claimed two enemy submarines had been spotted about a hundred miles out from our coast. That news sent a shock wave through this little community. The reality was driven home. Our freedom was lost. The very idea that the enemy might dare to come so close to our shores emphasized just how real the war was. It's one thing to read about it in the papers or to see clips in the newsreels before the movie, but we never expected the war to reach out and touch our part of the world. We thought our distance from Europe would protect us. But the arrival of German submarines was all the proof we needed that the entire world was in a fight for survival.

The town was humming that hot, hazy morning when Ruby Todd first bounced into J.P.s along with her mother and two sisters. Their names are easy to remember because they all start with an R. The others were Ruth, a year older than Ruby, and Rose, the youngest. They were both cute, but not like Ruby. She was, by far, one of the prettiest girls I've ever seen ... kind of like you in many ways. But Ruby wasn't stuck up like some of the other snooty Liverpool girls, and they didn't have half of Ruby's looks. Her sincerity and wholesome appearance were, I think, part of her charm. It was a lethal combination. She caused many young men's heads to turn. Beyond her appearance, Ruby was outgoing and seemed genuinely interested in people. There was nothing shallow about that girl. She laughed a great deal and after she got to know us, she became a good friend, someone I would remember for the rest of my life.

After Ruby and her family arrived in J.P.s that morning, the conversation shifted gears as the talk centred on them. Strangers in a town like Liverpool have a way of attracting attention like hungry ants to a picnic. The arrival of the three pretty young girls was a welcome change of topic from the war. The Todd women had come for some party supplies and decided to stop at Mr. Harnish's shop. They had heard his store carried such things. Ruby's mother was planning a small get-together for several of the girls in Liverpool. She wanted Ruby and her sisters to meet some friends, seeing as the family had arrived only a few days earlier. We had heard new people had arrived in town, but hadn't seen them until that morning.

I liked the Todd women from the start. They didn't seem pretentious in any way. They appeared to be nice, down-to-earth people. They should have been the kind to fit right into our close-knit, social conscious society. They arrived with no fanfare. In fact, Ruby and her mother and sisters came waltzing into J.P.s like nobody's business. It was as if they'd been there a hundred times before, talking to all the people they met, like they knew everyone.

The Todds had been in the store about five minutes when Ruby waltzed over to where the five of us were seated. She sauntered up to the booth and introduced herself without hesitation. She wasn't shy in any way, even though she had never laid eyes on any of us before that day. The fact that we were perfect strangers didn't seem to bother her one little bit.

"Hi," she said. She had a sweet voice unlike any I had heard before.

"My name's Ruby. That woman over there's my mother and those are my sisters, Ruth and Rose. We're just new to your lovely little town, but I have to say I already like it very much. From what I've seen, it looks very quaint and comfortable. I think we'll like it here." Pausing to survey the collection of assorted and eclectic young Liverpool citizenry we represented, she then asked, "And just who are all you gentlemen?"

Her openness caught us off guard, but it was refreshing to meet a young girl so full of life. However, I admit, I was surprised at how forward she seemed. In those days, girls were not usually open and friendly to the boys - it just wasn't proper. But Ruby wasn't from these parts. She wasn't aware of all that societal crap we'd been exposed to since we were kids. Besides, it was clear she wouldn't have been the type to easily fit into any slot our society might have designated for her. It was most intriguing and a welcome change of pace. As Ruby continued to speak, we hung onto her every word, but we really didn't know what to say to her. We were dumbfounded, as if our brains were in neutral. I'm sure we didn't make a very good first impression. Who would be impressed by a bunch of rag-tag hoodlums in dirty jeans with their mouths hung open and drool dripping down their chins? We were shell-shocked by her beauty. We had watched the Todds come into the store, but we hadn't been expecting Ruby to come over and introduce herself. She caught us totally by surprise. But she was particularly friendly that way, and somewhat brash too, as we'd soon find out.

Finally, after gathering his tongue back into his mouth, Hank spoke up on our behalf. "Hi. Nice to meet you. I'm Hank. This is Ben, Jack, Levi and Charles, or Bunny, as we like to call him."

"Stop it Hank," Bunny interrupted, annoyed that Hank had told the new girl his nickname. "What the hell you have to go tell her that for?"

"Bunny, is it?" She immediately jumped in, quickly defusing the tension. "That's very cute. Someday you'll have to tell me why they call you that." It worked. Bunny gave up, overcome by Ruby's charms.

The exchange between Hank and Bunny didn't faze Ruby. She seized control of the conversation once again. It was a lesson in tactfulness that we should have all noticed.

"My mother's planning a little get-together for some of the girls in town this Saturday afternoon. She wants my sisters and me to meet some of the local kids. I'm sure she wouldn't mind if some of the boys decided to show up. I'd like to get to know everyone around here. I don't see any reason why we can't all be friends. You all seem nice. Why invite only girls? I'll expect to see you all there, okay?"

It was a welcomed invitation, if not somewhat of a surprise, since it was clear Mrs. Todd had not sanctioned the proposal. We would have gone in a minute, had we been sure Ruby had gotten her mother's approval beforehand.

But it would not have been proper if Mrs. Todd had only planned to invite the girls. We knew all the boys in Liverpool would be hot after Ruby once she began to circulate. That party would give us a great opportunity to get to know her. We wanted to go, but how could we without Mrs. Todd's invitation? We didn't want to give the Todds the wrong first impression about us. We wouldn't want them to think we were some small-town hicks from rural Nova Scotia, even if that's exactly what we were.

Despite this reality, though, Ben didn't hesitate making the first move. "What's brought you and your family to Liverpool, anyway?" he asked, looking her over. He was sizing her up from head to toe, like a butcher eyes a fresh rump roast. He wasn't exactly frothing at the mouth, but it was easy to see Ben had already been taken by the girl's good looks and charms. That deer-in-the-headlights look gave him away, betraying his feelings.

"Well, my dad's found work here at the shipyard. We just arrived three days ago. We bought that big house down there by the courthouse ... you guys probably know it, the Haddon House."

Just then her mother called to her from the door, ready to leave.

"Listen, I have to go. Please think about the party. I'd just love to see you all there."

"Well, I'm sure we'd all just love to be there," Ben piped up, continuing to eye her up and down. His common sense had melted away, lost in the girl's enchanting personality. "But what would your mama think if we all showed up there for your nice party?"

"Oh, Mother won't mind," Ruby quickly shot back, turning on her heels to acknowledge her mother's departure. "She told me to invite anyone I wanted and I want to invite you. I'd like to see you all there. Please do try to make it. I'm sure you'll have a wonderful time. Us Todd women are known for throwing great parties."

Following their departure, Ruby became the main topic of our conversation for the rest of the afternoon. The war was forgotten as testosterone invaded our brains, to say nothing about the other parts of our bodies.

"That sweet little thing's gonna be mine and you can take that to the bank," Ben bragged in that typical self-assured, cocky style we expected from him but found repulsive most of the time. Despite Ben's infatuation, the rest of us weren't so sure Ruby was going to be too quick to take up with anyone in Liverpool. She was young but seemed sophisticated for her age. She probably wasn't ready to be tied to one boy especially if he came from the hill like Ben. Anyway, I had picked up a weird feeling about the Todd family, but I couldn't quite put my finger on it. That's probably because I had just only met the girl. I'm usually quite good with first impressions though, and something was telling me this little girl was going to be trouble.

"And just what makes you think she'd want to have anything to do with a freak like you, Ben?" Levi taunted, knowing full well how to pull Ben's strings. "I watched her while she was talking to us and Ben, my friend, I'm afraid she didn't pay much attention to you. In fact, I'm not sure she even noticed you were here. I don't really think you're her type. Hell, old Bunny here is more her type than you'll ever be. You just don't make a perfect match and you can take that to the bank, Ben old boy." It was clear Levi was up for the challenge as well.

"What the hell do you know about it, Levi? You think I'm not good enough because I come from the hill? You got money so you think she'd be more interested in you? Is that it? Money ain't everything, Levi. She's only been here for a god-damned minute and you're already an expert on her ... you don't know nothin' about it." Ben was prepared to do battle and it was obvious he was pissed by Levi's suggestion that because he came from a different social class than Ruby Todd she wouldn't find him acceptable.

"Don't get your ass all tied up in a knot, Ben. I don't care who she's interested in. She seems too immature for my taste. I don't really give a damn who she ends up with. I'm just saying that she didn't seem too interested in you, that's all." Levi was a shit disturber with a capital S and a capital D. Normally, he would've argued with Ben for hours over who was best suited to chase Ruby Todd, but for some reason he cut off the argument before it could escalate. That wasn't like Levi, but from where I sat, that was just as well since we'd only just met the girl.

We later learned that the Todds had moved to Liverpool from some place up in New Brunswick after Ruby's old man took a bookkeeper job at Tupper's. Mr. Todd was not a likable man. The first minute we met him, we found out just how strict he was with his girls. He didn't even bother to get to know us. He immediately passed judgement and decided he didn't like us. If we had dicks between our legs then we couldn't be trusted. He figured we were trouble from the start and didn't want any of the boys talking to his girls, especially his precious Ruby. We learned that lesson the hard way when we showed up at the Todd house that Saturday afternoon just like Ruby had asked. However, when Mrs. Todd greeted us at the big front door of their fine house, we could tell she was surprised to see the five of us standing there in our best worn-out jeans and T-shirts. We probably looked like a bunch of thugs to her, but she was gracious and eventually invited us in, although I'm not sure she liked the idea that the local riff-raff had just arrived to crash her lovely party.

"Well, hello there," she said in a friendly, but slightly hesitant tone as she greeted us on the doorstep. "And you boys are ...?"

"They're my friends, Mother," came Ruby's soft voice from somewhere within the house before Mrs. Todd had a chance to continue the question. Obviously Ruby had been watching the door, waiting for us to arrive. "I met them the other day at the malt shop and invited them over. This is Levi, Hank, Ben, Charles and Jack. I told them you wouldn't mind. They really did seem very nice."

First there was silence between mother and daughter as they exchanged glances, then gradual acceptance. "I don't know, dear," Mrs. Todd paused. "This might not be a good idea."

"But Mother, I told them you wouldn't mind," Ruby continued. "We can't very well send them away now. What would people think?"

Mrs. Todd paused for a few minutes, then gave in to her daughter's wishes. "Okay, sweetie. It's fine by me, but I just wish you had told me you had invited boys. You know how Daddy is about these things." Turning back to the five of us, she became a very gracious hostess, welcoming us into their large and obviously expensive home. Clearly the Todds had culture, and money to back it up. There were about half a dozen girls from town at the party, but we were the only guys, just as I suspected we would be. That made me a little uneasy, but despite my reservations I tried to make the most of it.

It was a nice party, as far as parties go, but I've never been too comfortable with that socializing thing. It's not for me. We stayed until about seven o'clock and we got to meet the entire Todd family, getting to know them better ... especially the father.

Mr. Todd made it crystal clear that we weren't welcome in his home. We knew he didn't like having us there from the minute we crossed his doorstep. As we entered the large sitting room, his agitation visibly rushed to the surface and exploded in anger. "Ruby, I thought you told me only girls would be invited to the party," he bellowed, ignoring us and speaking directly at Ruby and Mrs. Todd. It was as if we weren't even there. He didn't care if he offended us. We were only young. We weren't important people in this town.

Then he quickly pulled Ruby into the next room and while he didn't think we could hear him, we heard every word he said. He wasn't very nice. "What are they doing here? If I'd known they would be here, there would never have been any party. You know I don't like boys hanging around. I'd prefer that they leave this house right now, but because your mother and me will be here, they can stay. But listen young lady, I don't approve. I want you to know that I don't like this ... I don't like it one bit that you invited them behind our backs and we're going to talk about this again later. Do you understand? We're not done with this."

Then he and Ruby came back to the sitting room where he turned his attention to the five of us standing there dumbfounded with our mouths hanging open in surprised embarrassment. "I'll be watching," he barked. Then he left the room. That's all he said to us, but it was enough. We got the message.

A few minutes after Mr. Todd's stormy departure, Ruby pranced over to make us feel more welcome. She looked real fine that afternoon, with her strawberry blond hair all down in curls. She was wearing a green frilly dress that clung to her every curve. God, she was pretty. Beautiful, like none of us had ever seen before. She lit up the room with a radiance that would make most young men quiver with anticipation. "Don't worry about him. His bark's worse than his bite," she said, smiling at the five of us standing there like little boys who had just been caught with their hands in the cookie jar. Leading us into the party room, she said, "He's a pussy cat, really. Daddy's a bit worried about how well we'll all fit in here and the pressure's getting to him. He doesn't mean any harm, honestly. It's just that sometimes he's a little over-protective of me and my sisters, which makes him say things he doesn't really mean. Give him a chance. Once you get to know him and he gets to know you better, I'm sure you'll all like one another. Now, let's just forget about Daddy and have a good time. After all, that's what you're here for, isn't it?"

We stayed, but I'm not sure if the others had a good time or not. I certainly didn't. While I wanted to get to know the Todds better and make them feel welcome in Liverpool, her father's cold reception put the fear of God in me. Mr. Todd was a small-featured, bespectacled man with a receding hairline, hell bent on protecting his Ruby no matter what the cost. He didn't care if he insulted the feelings of a few small-town hicks. That was the least of his worries. The family had big plans for Ruby, and that future was paramount to everything else. His attitude was insulting and repulsive. I wished I hadn't come.

"What's the matter, Jack?" Hank whispered as we made our way to the well-stocked refreshment table. "Somethin' botherin' you? You look like you just been kicked in the guts. You gonna be all right?"

"Yeah, Hank," I answered. "I'm just great."

"Well you sure don't look like it."

"No, really," I insisted. "It's just that somethin' doesn't feel right."

"Whatcha mean? Don'tcha like Ruby?"

"Yeah, I guess. I just can't shake this weird feelin' that somethin's gonna happen ... and that bothers me."

"Don't know what ya mean, Jack. It's all in your head. What could happen at a party like this?"

"Don't know, Hank. But whatever it is, I don't like it, and besides, her ol' man has made it clear he don't want us here. I'm not stickin' around long."

"Suit yourself, Jack. But I ain't goin' nowhere till I get somethin' to eat. That's a pretty good lookin' spread they got here."

We stayed, we ate, but I never could shake the feeling that something extraordinary was about to happen. It was like a dark storm cloud had suddenly descended over Liverpool, but it appeared strongest around Ruby.

It didn't take long for talk of Ruby's good looks and her over-protective father to spread throughout Liverpool. People here loved to gossip and they began talking about the Todds everywhere. No matter where you went, everyone agreed Ruby Todd was just about the prettiest little girl that ever graced the streets of Liverpool. The word around town was that her parents hoped someday she would become a stage actress or something like that, and she probably could have with that reddish blond hair of hers and that nice, wide smile. She would have been beautiful up there on the stage or in the movies. Although the family had been in town only a few days, Ruby had already started taking piano and voice lessons from one of the old women, Mrs. Henley, who lived across the bridge on the other side of town. Nurturing the girl's talent was an obvious priority for the Todd family. Yup, they had big plans for Ruby Todd, but you know what they say about making plans. Nothing ever works out like it's supposed to.

Me and the guys were out of school by the time the Todds came into town that summer. At the Todd house that evening we learned Ruby was fifteen and entering grade nine in the fall, too young for the five of us. Three or four years may not seem like much of an age difference when you're an adult, but it's like a wide canyon when one of the parties is still in school. Besides, most of us were out looking for work and hoping to settle down and start raising families of our own. We all thought Ruby would be a nice catch, but we knew she was out of our reach. However, that didn't mean we couldn't be friends.

Levi was getting ready to go off to college. He would soon be leaving Liverpool. In the fall he'd go to some big fancy medical school in Halifax where he would study to become one of those know-it-all, hot-shot doctors and earn all the big money. As for the rest of us, we didn't have any plans and we sure as hell didn't have the money to go off to college or any fancy school, not even Bunny even though his family was considered to be well off. We would have to make do with whatever we could find right here in Liverpool. I could accept that. Liverpool was the only place I ever knew and it didn't bother me that I'd have to stay here. I would be perfectly content, just like my Old Man had been and his Old Man before him.

The summer the Todds arrived in town was the last year the five of us were going to spend together and we were having a good time when Ruby entered the picture.

The truth was, we didn't know what to make of Ruby Todd. We all thought she was fine looking with a nice personality to match, but after the party, none of us felt comfortable around her. It was clear Mr. Todd didn't want us near his daughter and I thought it was smart to avoid trouble. It's sometimes better to leave well enough alone than to tempt fate, but that's not always easy, especially around here. In a place the size of Liverpool you can't avoid anyone for long, even when you're trying. Somehow, over the next few weeks, we got talking to Ruby again down at J.P.s and before we knew it, we all became good friends. She fit right in with the guys. She even sometimes came out to Brier

Lake with us for a swim.

Ruby had also made friends with several of the girls in town and they would often come along as well. Even though Patty Fergusson was our age, she and Ruby grew close. She came with Ruby on many occasions. Patty was dating Bunny, a mismatch if ever there was one. They were about as different as two people could get. But that was fine by me if they wanted to date. Me and Patty had gone out a couple of times and had some fun, but we never got serious. I couldn't see myself spending the rest of my life with a girl who was more interested in partying than having a family. But I was glad she and Bunny were getting serious, if that's what he wanted. Although, I have to admit, out of the five of us Bunny was the last one I would've picked to be the first to have a steady girlfriend.

We all knew that taking Ruby Todd out to the lake with us could mean trouble because of her old man. It was risky. He was strict beyond reason when it came to Ruby hanging out with guys. He'd be pissed if he ever found out she was with us. But it wasn't just us. She wasn't allowed to be around any guys, period. He didn't trust anyone with his little girl, and maybe he was right to be afraid for her. These were tough times. The Second World War was raging and there was a constant stream of strange men coming into Liverpool. Tupper's was getting busy with the new war contracts, especially with work on the corvettes. Those little ships were probably what put Liverpool back on its feet after the Depression. With the war came contracts. With the contracts came more jobs and good money. While the older men were back to work, most of us young ones were lining up for jobs. I was still getting a little time at the newspaper office, but it wasn't enough if I was ever going to settle down with a wife and family. I had to keep looking for something steady just like everyone else.

It was a strange time around Liverpool, as it was everywhere else in the world. You didn't know what was going to happen next with the war and you didn't know when you were going to get a letter saying they were sending you overseas. Although they didn't draft men to go to the war to fight for this country, we had heard about conscription and we were confused by it. We didn't understand what it meant to us. That lack of knowledge contributed to our feelings of anxiety. Especially the young men. Many volunteered to go fight in the war, but those of us who stayed behind at home became reckless. It was as if we figured we didn't have much to lose. Since we didn't know what the future held for us, we thought we might as well have a good time while we could. As for the strangers coming into town, we were seeing many of them in those days; men from all over the world, but mostly England and Norway. I'm sure that's part of the reason Ruby's old man was so worried about his girls. He knew some of those fellows were only in town for a few days and he believed that made them dangerous predators. Mr. Todd didn't trust any of them. He thought they'd zero in on a pretty little girl like his Ruby. Truth was, he was right. All the men did zero in on Ruby, but it wasn't only the sailors. The locals also found her very attractive and that drove the little man crazy.

Ben was really taken by Ruby. He fell head over heels for her the first time she walked through the door at J.P.s. The sad thing about it, though, was that she didn't seem to care about him as much as she did some of the other guys, especially Levi. Oh, she was friendly enough to Ben. She'd talk to him and laugh with him, but it was clear to me and the other guys that she wasn't really interested in Ben the same way he was interested in her. I don't think Ben ever understood why she felt that way and I'm sure he never asked Ruby why she didn't return his affection. Ben wasn't usually the kind of guy to get hung up on a girl, even if he had a real thing for her. He figured if she wasn't interested in him, then screw her, there were plenty of other young girls around Liverpool who would love to be his girlfriend. In those days, girls got married young. Ben never had a hard time finding a date. But I think he would have settled for Ruby in a heartbeat in spite of the age difference. It just wasn't meant to be, however, and it wasn't anybody's fault.

I do remember though, that with time Ben became upset at Ruby because she didn't return his interest. It was clear to his friends that Ben found it hard to be nice to her because it reminded him how much he really liked her. Eventually, the more Ruby came around, the more he started ignoring her and giving her the cold shoulder. He'd be rude to her for no reason. Sometimes he'd be hateful and short-tempered. It was clear that if they couldn't be more than friends, Ben didn't want any part of her. The two never argued that we knew of, but I think it bothered Ruby that Ben became so openly mean and nasty towards her. And I know it bothered Ben that she rejected him. You could see the longing in his eyes every time she came around, especially when she seemed to cling to Levi. That show of affection towards Levi made Ben jealous. I remember he kept saying how pretty she was and how he'd be really good to her if she'd only give him a chance. Infatuation would be a good word to describe what Ben was feeling for Ruby.

Truth is, I don't think Ruby was interested in any of the boys. Even though she seemed to like Levi, it was an innocent friendship. She mostly stuck to the other girls. Actually, it was probably more to the truth that her old man had her terrified of boys. She was most likely too afraid to become interested in anything other than maybe being friends.

Despite Ben and his girl problems, we were having a good summer enjoying each other's company. It was just as we had planned. Me, Hank and Ben would go down to Tupper's or up to the sawmill every day in search of steady work. Bunny worked six days a week at his father's store. His old man wasn't feeling too well by then and we figured Bunny would end up running the shop after Sam died or got too sick to take care of business himself. As for Levi, he didn't work and he didn't bother looking for a job. His old man was taking care of all his needs. He'd paid Levi's way into college and was getting him ready to leave Liverpool by the end of August. In return, he expected Levi to give up his friends to spend time with his family since he wouldn't be seeing much of them after the fall. Levi had long figured out how to manipulate his old man. He took every cent his father dished out but continued to follow his own agenda. If he hadn't played along, his old man might have made him go out and find a job. He couldn't have handled that. Levi wasn't capable of doing a hard day's work if his life depended upon it. He really had grown into an arrogant piss-ant.

That was Levi. We still tolerated him, but some of the guys had grown to dislike him. They were tired of his holier-than-thou attitude. Ben and Bunny even tried to push him away, but I didn't think that was right. I had my problems with Levi as well, but I didn't hate him. After all, he'd been around since we were all kids and we had been through many things together. He belonged with the company, especially if this was to be our last summer together. Me and Hank decided it was easier to put up with him than to send him away. We didn't have the heart to tell him he wasn't welcome. We figured he'd be leaving town by September and we wouldn't be seeing much of him anymore, if ever again. There was no need to hurt his feelings. Besides, his old man still hated us, and the idea of getting under the old man's skin gave us a few laughs. There was something about pissing off Levi's old man that never grew old.

We did some regrettable things that summer, but mostly we spent the days looking for work or doing odd jobs. Then in the evening we'd go out to Pine Grove and spend most of the night there, drinking and smoking and talking and enjoying the friendships that would soon only live in our memories. Pine Grove was still a magical place to us. We felt close to nature and at peace there, despite the madness in the world around us. The woodsmen hadn't arrived yet. The trees were still standing big and graceful, reaching towards the sky as if guarding our special sanctuary. I may never get to the real Heaven, but that place was about as close to Heaven as you could get. It was spectacular. Now it's nothing more than a sawdust pile, and the little lake's a cesspool, all polluted and filled with shit from those homes they built up on Wildcat Rock. They've turned the crystal water into a sewer bowl. It's a damned shame we didn't try to stop that from happening, but when Liverpool started growing after the war, everyone thought it was a positive thing ... it was called progress, they claimed. Progress, hell. It was destruction, pure and simple. Now they're talking about spending millions of dollars to clean up the mess and restore the lake. Don't that beat all? If they would have just left well enough alone in the first place, they wouldn't be looking at these bills now.

Chapter 9

It was close to the end of August when we heard the news about Ruby Todd ... news that would change our lives forever and set this entire town on its ear.

The five of us had been up to Pine Grove the night before. We stayed late, well into the next morning. When we left the Grove, we departed together and we all went home. This I know for a fact. But when we headed for home that night, we had no idea what trouble was brewing ... no idea that by the morning light Liverpool would be turned upside down. We had no idea of how the events of the next few weeks would impact upon our lives.

Me and Hank were sitting in J.P.s drinking coffee and smoking cigarettes early that Friday morning when Bunny burst in like some maniac who had just busted out of the insane asylum.

"Have you heard?" he blurted out, struggling to catch his breath, nearly unable to contain his excitement.

"Have we heard what?" we asked, somewhat put out that Bunny had interrupted our morning ritual.

"Ruby Todd's missing," he said.

"Jesus. Are you sure?" we asked at the same time.

"Yup. It's true," he answered. Bunny had been at the store when he heard the news. Police Chief Bert Frasier had been there asking Sam Henderson questions about Ruby Todd. Her parents had come to him the night before saying she was missing. Bunny said the chief wanted to know when his old man had last seen the girl? Was she in the store yesterday? Was she with anyone the last time he had seen her? Was she doing anything strange or unusual? Was she acting peculiar? Did he notice if anyone was with her or if anyone was following her? Bunny pointed out to me and Hank that these are the type of questions police ask when they're looking for a missing person.

"No kidding," we said. Bunny must have thought we were stupid or something.

"Are you sure he said Ruby?" Hank asked. "Maybe it's someone else."

"I'm sure. That's what he said."
"What do they think happened?" I picked up the questioning. "Does he think she's hurt or something?"

"Don't know," Bunny replied. "And the police don't know anything either, the chief said so when he was in the store."

"Jesus, this could be bad," I continued. "I don't think old Chief Frasier's cut out for this. About the only thing he can find is the hole in the middle of a doughnut. There's going to be trouble if they don't soon find her."

"You know, Jack," Hank said, "sometimes they never find missing people. They just disappear and are never heard from again. It's like they fall off the face of the earth or something. Some of these mysteries are never solved."

"What are you saying, Hank?" I asked. "Are you saying something's happened to Ruby?"

"How would I know that, Jack? All I'm saying is that strange things happen sometimes ... and sometimes there are no answers. It's happened before, remember?"

"Yeah, I know that. But let's hope they find her soon or, like I said, there's going to be trouble around here."

Liverpool didn't have a big police department in those days, just the chief and two other officers. It was big enough though. We didn't have much trouble back then except for the few major cases that came along every so often. But when we did, somehow Chief Bert Frasier would take care of it, or at least he'd go through the motions. If there ever was a cranky old man, he was it. He was a hateful son-of-a-bitch ... and I'm being kind. None of us liked him. He seemed to have it in for the five of us for some reason. He was mean and irritated all the time as if he had a permanent hair across his ass and it was rubbing him the wrong way. Not many men would stand up to Chief Frasier even though he was never respected as a police officer. He was tall and big with broad shoulders and a huge belly that hung down over his belt in an obscene way. We wondered how he could ever do any police work with a gut like that. Seems to me he was in that job when the town decided to get rid of the local police and go with the RCMP. After that, Chief Frasier moved away to Ontario where he eventually died of a heart attack. It's a sad story really but I can't say I feel bad for him.

Word of Ruby's disappearance spread quickly through Liverpool that morning. Then again, it didn't take long for any news to circulate in this backwater town. As a matter of fact, it still doesn't. If you want other people to know your business before you know it, then you must live in a small town like Liverpool. By early Friday afternoon, rumours about what could have happened to Ruby Todd began spreading like a swarm of hungry mosquitos at a nudist camp. Talk about a buffet.

When Ruby failed to return home by nine o'clock the night before, Mr. Todd had gone directly to Chief Frasier. Because we didn't have a whole lot of trouble in Liverpool in those days, old Chief Frasier should have realized immediately that something was wrong. It's just that he was too lazy to do anything about it. Even though Mr. Todd insisted that Ruby wasn't the kind of girl who would stay out past her eight o'clock curfew, Chief Frasier didn't like anyone suggesting that he should get off his fat ass and start looking for her. Obviously, it didn't occur to the stupid son-of-a-bitch that the young girl might be in some sort of trouble in a strange town with people she didn't know. Instead he made Mr. Todd go home to wait for his daughter. He pointed out he'd been in the police business a long time and that he'd seen this kind of thing before ... many times, he said. He assured Mr. Todd that Ruby would show up with some half-baked, hair-brained excuse for making her parents worry. The way he saw it was that, being new to town, Ruby had probably made some friends and was having a good time getting to know them. When she realized how late it was, she'd be home. Of that he was sure.

But she never did come home and there was no word from her ... ever.

No one had seen or heard from Ruby that night. By seven o'clock that next morning, a frantic Mr. Todd was back in Chief Frasier's office in the town hall. He insisted that the chief stop stuffing his fat face and do something to find his missing daughter.

"I know something's wrong," he said. "I can sense that my little girl is in danger. I know there's been some kind of serious trouble." The man was near hysterical as he insisted some terrible tragedy had befallen his precious daughter. "It's not like Ruby to stay out overnight. You must start looking for her right away," he insisted.

Chief Frasier was now getting worried as well. It finally occurred to him that something didn't seem right. So much for detective work. He wasn't much of a police officer, that we've already established. Sometimes I think the town would have been better off without him. That morning, however, after seeing how distraught Mr. Todd had become, the chief finally accepted the man's concerns. He too was beginning to think things appeared to be a little off-kilter in Liverpool, as if the universe was doing loops instead of spinning in even rotations. That morning Chief Frasier and Liverpool's two other police officers combed every inch of town, particularly the wooded and grassy areas. They went into every business and knocked on every door of every house in the downtown area but still they couldn't find hide nor hair of the missing girl. There were no clues about what could have happened to Ruby Todd.

By the time Chief Frasier waddled into J.P.s just before lunch, he appeared pretty worn out and ragged. He was panting and puffing like a dog locked up in a car on a hot day. He was flushed. I figured he'd never make it through the rest of the day if he kept up the hurried pace. It was a scorcher for the end of August and he was soaking wet from sweat. It wasn't healthy for a man of his weight to be chasing around town in such heat, but that didn't seem to bother him much. He may have been an ignoramus, but concern was now written all over his sweaty red face. Better late than never, I suppose. It was clear that morning he desperately wanted to find the missing girl, and fast.

He was now on a mission. Once inside J.P.s, he assumed command, eyeing up all the customers. As soon as he spotted me and Hank, he charged over to the booth like a bull in a china shop. We had nothing to tell him. As a matter of fact, we were hoping for updates. Bunny had gone back to the store to get more news but me and Hank were still perched in the booth like two mother hens on their nests. I can only imagine how we must have looked to the chief as we sat there waiting for the next juicy tidbit of gossip about our missing friend. We probably looked guilty as sin. But then again, everyone in town was doing the exact same thing. We had been planning to go down to Tupper's to see if anything had come open, but we hadn't left yet. The job picture was starting to improve but you pretty much had to be there when an opening came up or else you'd lose it, kind of like standing in the line-up at a busy bathroom ... you step out of place and you go to the back of the line. But on that Friday, we stayed in town the entire morning. J.P.s was central. We knew if we waited there, we'd be able to keep up on the latest news. As soon as Chief Frasier came over, we knew he was on serious business. He wanted answers wherever he could get them ... and he wanted them fast.

"S'ppose you boys heard what's been goin' on 'round town this mornin', haven't ya?" he wheezed, fighting to catch his breath through clenched teeth. His lips were turning purple from the lack of oxygen.

"Sure." We answered matter-of-factly, like the cocky little brats that we were.

"You'd have to have your head stuck in the toilet all morning not to know what's goin' on." It was a brazen comment even for me. "What'd you expect? It's all everyone's talkin' about. It'd be pretty damned hard not to know, Chief." I hated it that he still called us boys. But he knew it bothered us when he talked down to us. He did it just to pull our strings and it worked.

There wasn't much love lost between the members of the company and Chief Frasier. The old bastard liked to drive the wedge in a little further every time we crossed paths, and this morning wasn't any different. He didn't like us much. He knew we had gotten into some trouble when we were kids and didn't like the idea that we'd basically gotten away with it. Maybe he figured we'd never amount to anything and that we'd always be trouble for this little town. For some reason, he always seemed pissed at us. But that didn't really matter on this day. There was more serious business to discuss. I got the distinct feeling that he thought we knew something about Ruby's disappearance. That made me uncomfortable. It didn't take much to make me squirm, particularly since I didn't know how much Chief Frasier really knew. He may have been trying to trick us up, or trying to get us to say something that we didn't really mean to say, and that made me uneasy. But we were ready for him.

"So ya know they can't find Ruby Todd. She's been missin' all night and her mama and daddy are real upset. I'm sure you boys can appreciate that. Her daddy's given us a list of people she's met since they moved here and you boys are on it, along with your friends. We're tryin' to talk to everyone on that list ... you know, cover all the bases just in case you might know somethin' that can help us. Don't s'ppose you boys know anythin' about where she is, now do ya? Have any of ya seen her 'round since yesterday afternoon? Have ya talked to her? Her mama and daddy are gettin' real worried that somethin' terrible has happened to her ... and 'ya know, boys, I'm startin' ta think that too. It don't look real good and that means we got a whole bunch a trouble on our hands."

Then he stopped and glared down at us for a few seconds, the sweat dripping from his forehead. I got the distinct impression he was waiting to get a rise from us. It was as if he was throwing us small, bite-sized morsels and then looking for a reaction, wanting us to bite. Maybe he wasn't outwardly accusing us of anything. He could have been working us over and looking for clues wherever he could find them, but I didn't feel good about the conversation. "I'd hate for somethin' terrible to happen to that sweet, young girl here in Liverpool," he huffed. "Ya know boys, things like that aren't s'ppose to happen 'round here. I don't know how folks would handle it if somethin' happened to that little girl, not after what happened the last time."

It was strange that Chief Frasier had confided in me and Hank that morning, even if he was fishing for information. We weren't fond of each other. Truth is, we hated the old bastard's guts as much as he disliked us. That morning I think he liked showing his authority by questioning us in such a manner. But I wondered if, without coming right out and saying it, he was trying to tell us that he felt something bad had happened to Ruby. He looked worried. Actually, panicked would have been a good word to describe Chief Frasier that day. He stood there next to the booth all sweaty and panting. He was in rough shape and I didn't think he'd make it through the rest of the day. I kind of felt bad for the old son-of-a-bitch ... for a few seconds at least. But the feeling didn't last long. It was then that I knew Bert Frasier was out of his element. It was clear he wasn't cut out to be a policeman. He'd gotten the job through a friend of a friend of the mayor and wasn't really qualified for it. Now he was being tested and it was obvious he couldn't handle it. I didn't feel bad for him for very long but for that passing minute I almost sympathized with the old bastard. He seemed almost human.

Actually, Chief Frasier was probably right. People in Liverpool weren't likely to do well if another young person had gone missing. The fear went back to almost three years earlier when the five-year-old Tupper twins were lost. Don't remember the boys' first names but I know they were connected to the same Tupper family that owned the shipyards. Anyway, they lived close to the woods and they went missing one day without a trace. Their mama had put them outside to play in the yard and within a matter of minutes they were gone ... just disappeared and were never seen again. The town had a major search that day and for the next few weeks after that, but they never found any sign of those two little boys. It was the strangest thing. People had all kinds of ideas about what had happened to them. Some believed bears had eaten them and some thought travelling gypsies had stolen them away. People can be stupid sometimes. We don't get many bear attacks in these parts or gypsies passing through Liverpool.

The local people never got over the tragedy of losing two small children. It was a sad thing. It must be twenty years ago now since the truth finally came out about what happened to the twins. A hunter was out in the woods not far from the old Tupper homestead when his leg went down through some underbrush and trapped him in a burrow. As he pulled his leg out, he discovered some bones hidden down in the bottom. When he looked closer, he found two little skeletons and he knew right away they were the remains of the little Tupper boys. He had helped search for them years earlier. Everyone concluded the boys had gone into the woods to play and become lost. When it started to get dark, they must have crawled into that burrow where they huddled together for warmth. That's where they died.

It's a strange thing that searchers hadn't heard the boys when they were looking for them. That place had been combed from top to bottom but there they were. The mystery was finally solved. Police ruled there was no foul play but I don't know. It kind of makes you wonder when someone goes missing like that. How would you ever know what really happened? After all, the only witnesses were dead.

As for whatever happened to Ruby, no one had any answers on that hot summer day. There didn't appear to be any clues anywhere in town as to the missing girl's whereabouts. But there was lots of speculation. Chief Frasier was in a real quandary. He looked like a fevered dog chasing his tail, going round and round, and getting nowhere fast. "Now if you boys know anythin' 'bout Ruby Todd or where she might be, you gotta tell me even if it don't seem all that important to ya," he said, still struggling to catch his breath and swiping away at the sweat as it ran down his gritty forehead. Carrying that extra weight was making his job all that much tougher in such heat. I remember thinking that if the fat son-of-a-bitch didn't take it easy, he'd have a heart attack and die right there in J.P.s. He didn't look good. His skin was grey and his eyes were sunken, but he was too freaking pig-headed to keel over in our presence. He wouldn't give us the pleasure of seeing him crumple. Regardless of how we felt about him, however, we would have helped him that morning if we could have.

"Chief, I know you got to ask everyone on that list of yours but do you honestly think we would hide her from you? What would be in it for us? We haven't seen Ruby Todd since she was in here yesterday morning," I told him, slightly raising my voice to let him know we didn't appreciate any implication that we knew more than we were telling. Just in case he had gotten any ideas from Mr. Todd, we wanted to be perfectly clear on how we stood on the matter. "Besides, we don't see the girl all that much, only when she comes here once in awhile for a soda with some of them girlfriends of hers. Did you ask Patty Fergusson if she saw her yesterday? They're pretty good friends. I'm afraid that's all we know, Chief. It really isn't much help. I wish we could do more."

Hank added, "I can tell you, though, that she wasn't with anyone else when I saw her in here yesterday. She was alone, at least as far as I can remember. Is that important?"

"Could be," the chief responded, jotting it down in his notebook. "Anything else?"

"Come to think of it, Chief," Hank continued, "I ain't seen Ruby around town very much for the last couple of days. S'ppose that means anything? Maybe she's got a secret hideaway somewhere."

"I doubt that," Chief Frasier answered sharply. He stood motionless for a minute or two, not saying another word, glaring down at us over his porked-out cheeks. Finally, he spoke again. "Don't get me wrong, boys. I'm not suggestin' anythin'. I just gotta ask everyone who might have come in contact with the girl. That's all. I'm sure we'll be talkin' again." Then, with an air of arrogance like only that old bastard could muster, he turned on his heels and waddled over to talk with Mr. Harnish at the drug counter.

He hadn't directly accused us of anything but I didn't feel comfortable about the conversation. Neither did Hank. We knew the police had a job to do which meant they had to talk with everyone who might have had some contact with Ruby but it's not easy to go toe to toe with someone like Liverpool's chief of police and feel good about the outcome. He had a certain way about him that made you feel inferior. I'm not certain if Chief Frasier suspected us of something but his behaviour that morning made me and Hank feel ... well, kind of weird.

"Think he knows anything?" Hank asked as Chief Frasier moved from hearing distance.

"What's to know?"

"You know, about Ruby and us."

"You mean that she sometimes comes to the lake with us?"

"Yeah. Think he knows?"

"Does it matter if he does?"

"Maybe. He might try putting two and two together and come up with his own answers."

"He can't do that. He's not smart enough."

"I wouldn't be too sure. I don't think we should underestimate him."

"Maybe you're right. But even if he knows about her coming with us, that's all he knows."

"That could be enough to keep him asking questions."

"Let him ask. Who's going to talk to him? Bunny? Levi? Ben? You and me ain't gonna say anything so let him ask all the questions he wants. He won't get answers from us."

"I don't know, Jack. Sometimes it only takes one question, and a little slip up could lead to trouble."

"There's nothing we can do about that, Hank. We've got to cooperate with him or else if he thinks we're hiding something he'll keep prying. We don't want that."

"I guess you're right. All we need is for the chief to think he's got a lead that points straight to us. If he thinks he's onto something we'll never get him off our backs."

"Little pieces at a time. That's all we'll give him. Little tidbits just to keep him thinking we're on his side. But we've got to be careful. Let's hope the others are just as cautious."

"Yeah. We can only hope for that."

Chapter 10

We finished our coffee, and after the chief left, so did we. I went to Tom's Barber Shop, even though I wasn't in need of a hair cut. I knew if there was one place in Liverpool where they'd have all the latest news, it would be at that gossip central.

Most of the men in town hung out at Tom's Barber Shop and Pool Hall. Tom cut hair in the front part of the building, and out back, down a dimly lit corridor, was a pool hall with six pool tables. That little shop drew a large crowd every day, and not only for hair cuts and pool. It was where the men exchanged the latest news.

The barber, Tom Winchester, was the ringleader. He was a likable guy who looked like a character out of some pioneer picture with his coal-black, handlebar moustache. Tom loved conversation. He had the gift of gab. I swear he could talk to anyone about anything. If he got wound up, there was no stopping him. He'd keep talking until the last customer left and the lights were turned off. Tom was well suited to lead the gab-fest. The men would congregate at Tom's every morning to exchange the latest. That was the place to go if you wanted to get caught up on the town news. Every little town has them and Tom's was Liverpool's place for all the juicy updates on who was doing what with whom, who was sleeping with whom and who was about to lose their job for stealing from the company. Life and death topics. It was actually nobody's business but it made for some good talk, I'll give them that much.

When I arrived, Tom's was abuzz with talk of the missing girl but no one, not even Tom, had any real news to share. There were seven men in the shop that day and they were all talking about Ruby, saying how terrible it was that Chief Frasier had made the Todds wait a whole night before he took them seriously.

"A couple'a hours can be the difference between life and death when someone's in real trouble out in these woods," one of the men observed before suggesting the mayor ought to take away the chief's badge and give it to a "real" policeman.

I chuckled at that suggestion. I knew that's how most people in Liverpool felt about our police chief. The problem was, who would they get to replace the old son-of-a-bitch? There probably wasn't a qualified police officer for miles around who could do any better. For better or worse, Liverpool had to make do with what we had. In short, we were stuck with the fat, lazy bastard, whether we liked it or not.

"That'd be great, Dicky," Tom answered. "Who would you suggest they hire to take the chief's place? Would you do it?"

Dick Hubbard wasn't a smart man but he played along. "Yeah, I could do it. Couldn't do any worse than the lazy bastard they got wearin' the uniform now. Probably could do a lot better."

"Sure, Dicky," Tom prodded. "And I could walk to England on top of the Atlantic Ocean."

The exchange drew a small, reserved chuckle from the other men gathered at the barber shop that day. It was obvious Ruby's disappearance was weighing heavy on their minds. Concern for the girl's well-being was visible on all their faces.

"What da'ya think happened to her, Tom?" Dick asked, turning serious.

"Haven't got a clue," Tom answered, reflecting on the possibilities. "But the longer she's lost, the worse it gets. A young girl like that don't know how to survive out in the woods ... if that's where she is."

There were many rumours about what could have happened to Ruby Todd, and the men at Tom's discussed them all. Some theories were actually plausible. Most were pure nonsense, the figments of overactive imaginations or mass hysteria. When you're confronted with a possible tragedy such as the loss of an innocent young person, your mind tends to work overtime and forces you to consider all the possibilities, most of which always suggest the worst. But of all the conjecture I heard at the barber shop, nothing intrigued me - or frightened me - more than the theory put forth by another of Tom's regular customers.

Winston Fisher - they used to call him Winnie - was one of Liverpool's oldest and most endearing characters. When he wasn't drinking he was actually quite likable. He was probably around eighty years old, give or take a year or two, and most of the time, when he was sober, he was a hoot. He told wild stories that would make most young men dream of faraway adventures. I liked him for that ... for giving me an opportunity once in awhile to escape from this backwater town. I loved to sit on the front steps at Tom's and listen as Winnie told of his exploits on the fishing boats and triple-masted schooners as they traded in the Caribbean and other exotic places. I especially enjoyed hearing him tell about his times with the beautiful young women in the South Seas. I often thought it sounded like paradise and fantasized of seeing it someday.

That was when he was sober. It was another story when he was drunk. The day Ruby disappeared, it was still early, but Winnie was already well on his way to oblivion. Through that alcoholic haze he forecast doom and gloom in Liverpool for the days that lay ahead.

"Ain't no doubt about it." He was a frail old man with a quivery voice. "I'm tellin' ya that young girl's a goner," he said. "She's either far away from this town or she's dead by now." For some reason, the others believed just about everything old Winnie said, no matter how drunk he was or how foolish he sounded. If he would've told them they struck oil in the middle of Liverpool's dry, dusty street, they would have lined up with their oil cans to get their share. That was Winnie. Most of the time you knew he was talking bullshit but you believed it anyway. It seemed like the right thing to do. In truth, he was a senile old bastard. In the end, he died broke and alone at the county poor farm. That's the place they used to put people when they got old and crazy and didn't have any family to fall back on. The place doesn't exist anymore. They've turned it into a special care home for seniors.

That was old Winnie. Crazy to the bone but people still listened when he spoke. "I ain't nuts," he'd say, hoping to get your attention. Then he'd launch into a tirade. "Ain't none of you have to believe in nothin' I'm sayin' but I know what I'm talkin' about. I think Amber's got her. You know they say you could never trust yer young'uns 'round him. I bet he got her as she was walkin' home last night and took her away to his cabin out there near the Head. God only knows what he did to her once he got her out there. Probably cut her up to use for fish bait!"

I knew old Winnie could spin a wild yarn when he had a few drinks and was cranked up, but I didn't like where this one was going. I didn't think Winnie would be cruel but then I remembered something that I heard a few years earlier about Winnie and Amber becoming bad friends because of some stupid bet over fish. At one time, the two men were good friends but by this time they hadn't spoken to each other for many years. That rumour about the fish feud might explain why Winnie would accuse his former friend of some terrible crime.

Amber was short for Ambrose. His last name was Payzant and his family was among the original settlers of Liverpool back in the seventeen-hundreds. Amber had a long, but mostly sad, history in this town. He lived to be one hundred and three and he saw a lot go down in that time but he was destined to live a life of unhappiness.

He died in 1976 but his troubles began when he was just a young lad. His parents died in a fever epidemic. He was orphaned and homeless by the time he was nine. The other townspeople sent him to live with a mean old witch of an aunt in Lunenburg, another small town further down the coast. People said she was horribly cruel to Amber. He had no formal education and when he got old enough to run away from his life of slavery, he did just that. He found himself down on the Lunenburg wharves where he met Winnie, who was about twenty years his senior. Age didn't matter though. The two quickly became friends. Amber learned fast. He soon developed a reputation as a reliable, hard worker on the boats and he got steady work. Amber finally seemed to have a decent life. The two men remained close for several years until a wager over who could fillet the most fish in an hour, of all the stupid things, broke up the friendship. Winnie was a seafaring man with saltwater in his veins. It was a matter of personal pride that he be the best fish filleter on the coast. He didn't take too kindly to losing to Amber, a young snot of a kid, and questioned the legitimacy of the contest. Seems there was some dispute over filleting fish with their heads on or with them off. Whatever difference that makes, you be the judge. In the end, the dispute was never resolved and the two friends parted ways. As far as anyone knows the two never spoke to each other ever again.

The failed friendship probably caused Amber some grief but some said a woman totally destroyed him.

At some point in his twenty-first year, Amber returned to Liverpool where he met and fell madly in love with a beautiful young lady named Agatha Buchanan but their love could not survive Liverpool's unforgiving social structure. Agatha was the daughter of the owners of The Lodge, one of two boarding houses in town that survived mostly off the crews who needed a place to stay while their boats were in refit at Tupper's. The girl was said to be an exceptionally pretty woman who, although she may have initially returned her young suitor's affections, knew the relationship could never win her parents' approval. It is said the two held secret rendezvous for several months, then Agatha grew frightened of her parents' retaliation if they learned of her secret. Fearing they would be angry, she promptly broke off the arrangement. Only weeks after calling off her affair with Amber, Agatha began seeing another young Liverpool man, Roland Snow, who came from a better background. His father was a local merchant who dealt primarily with imports from the south. Eventually, the two married and moved away to Toronto. Amber never saw his beloved Agatha ever again.

Within days of Agatha's departure from Liverpool, more misfortune befell Amber. While out fishing the Grand Banks on a square-rigger one fine July morning, he became so distraught about the loss of his ladylove that he broke his concentration ... something you can never afford to do when you're working the lines. As his mind drifted, his right hand became entangled in some of the rigging and within seconds his fingers were pulled into the block. Like a hot knife gliding through soft butter, the pressure from the block and ropes completely severed Amber's little and ring fingers along with a portion of his hand down almost to his wrist. It was touch and go for awhile as he lost a great deal of blood on the two-day return trip to port. Doctors in Halifax, where the trawlers tied up for such emergencies, did what they could but the fingers were gone and there was no way to repair such serious damage. The grotesque hand became a useless club, and eventually it came to resemble a hook as the ligaments and nerves retracted, causing his remaining two fingers to curl inwards. Because he had such a hideous appendage to carry around, the youngsters in town came to fear old Amber as a monster. Kids can be cruel ... people can be cruel.

Injured, heartbroken and alone, Ambrose became a recluse, building a small, one-room shack from bits and pieces of discarded lumber in the dense woods out near Hell's Point, not far from where the ocean and the river meet at the place we call the Head. From that point on, he never worked again but somehow managed to survive. He didn't need much money but he did make a few cents by trapping and selling rabbits to the townspeople. I remember as a kid seeing old Amber in his long, black scruffy overcoat sauntering up and down the streets and back roads of Liverpool, casually selling his rabbits to whoever was in the market for that evening's supper. But I don't ever recall hearing the grizzly old man speak ... don't know what his voice sounded like.

It was there in his lonely cabin that he lived out his sad, desperate life and there he died. But not before his story became legend and his reputation became tarnished by the likes of long-lost friends such as Winston Fisher. Over the years, the story of Ambrose Payzant has been twisted and blown out of proportion until it has become nothing like the way I remember him. At one time, the parents of Liverpool would frighten their mischievous young children with tales of old Amber coming to steal them out of their beds in the middle of the night if they didn't behave, much like the way today's parents threaten children with tales of the Boogie Man.

But old Amber didn't deserve that reputation and he didn't deserve to be dragged through the mud back then, especially on a day when everyone was already fired up and ripe to find a scapegoat. People were looking for someone to blame as if that would absolve the town of any guilt if it turned out something bad had happened to Ruby. I didn't believe what I was hearing and I was relieved when Tom finally quashed Winnie's wicked words.

As much as people became caught up in the old man's stories, they listened to reason when Tom spoke. "Winnie, you crazy ol' fool. You and me both know that ol' Amber wouldn't hurt a god-damned fly let alone a helpless little girl. How in God's name can you sit there chawin' on that hunk of tobacco and bad mouth him about somethin' so serious? Ain't you got any common sense, ol' man, or has that brain of yours shrivelled up with age just like everythin' else on that wrinkled ol' body of yours? Now my advice to you is to stop spreadin' such nonsense before someone takes you serious and goes off half cocked after an innocent ol' man who has never done you - or anyone else in this town - any harm 'cept beat you in some stupid fish contest."

Winnie quickly left, most likely to search for another bottle of wine.

I was glad someone in the barber shop that day was still capable of common sense and was able to reign in old Winnie before things got out of hand. I know what can happen when a mob-mentality sets in. If the other men at Tom's had believed that Ambrose Payzant could have done something to Ruby Todd, then we would have had a heap of trouble on our hands. As it was, Tom nipped that foolishness in the bud. But the town still didn't know what happened to the missing girl.

Chapter 11

That day I stayed at Tom's for about twenty minutes listening to the bullshit, then decided to get out of there. It was clear I wasn't getting any new information from anyone in that place.

I met up again with Hank, who had just come from talking to Bunny, and we went to my house to wait for more news. We didn't have to wait long. We weren't even there half an hour before Ben came flying in with an update. He told us Chief Frasier was organizing a search party to comb all the woods and waterways around town. They were asking everyone to help, even the women and children.

"People in town are gettin' pretty aggravated," he reported. "They want to do something to help the Todds. Maybe we should go see if there's anything we can do to help."

We agreed that would be the right thing to do.

Ben said Chief Frasier was anticipating a large turnout for the search because that's what people in small towns do. They're a real nosey bunch and they like to spread other people's gossip, but when the chips are down, they'll come running to lend a helping hand, without fail.

Everyone now figured that, for whatever reason, Ruby had either gone out of town on her own and got lost or was taken out of town by someone else. They all knew that it was important to find her trail as quickly as possible. A strong, easterly wind had begun blowing in off the ocean. We had to act fast. Such a breeze might carry away clues and it would be particularly bad if the winds brought rain with them. Time was of the essence ... that everyone was sure of.

Ben also told us that we should be prepared, as more rumours had already started flying around town. People throughout Liverpool were guessing at what could have happened to the missing girl. There were many theories and much speculation, some believable, some pure rubbish. Everyone seemed to have their own idea about what happened that night, even those people who never knew Ruby or the Todd family.

The theories were wild and strange and filled with innuendoes. One of the most common suggestions was that Ruby had been afraid of her father and had run away from him. After all, he did have a reputation as a tyrant when it came to his daughters. People believed Ruby couldn't live under his strict rules any longer. They thought she just up and left home. Maybe, some people speculated, her father was abusing her and she ran away to be safe. I didn't believe that, not for one second. I'd seen Ruby with her parents and her sisters many times. That wasn't a girl who was living in an unhappy home. It's true her father was strict and overbearing, but that didn't mean he was hurting her. It's also true that we can't know what goes on behind the closed doors of other people's homes, but there was no proof of anything suspicious happening at the Todd house. Why would a young girl leave a warm, loving home in the middle of the war years to go God-knows-where? It just didn't add up. But some people believed it. They said Ruby had met a young sailor on one of the boats and had run away with him. They figured she didn't leave a note or anything for her parents because she knew her father would come after her, like any other concerned father would.

Then there was the popular gossip that her parents were putting on a hoax; that they really knew where their daughter was. Some people believed the Todds had cooked up this big elaborate scheme because Ruby had gone and gotten herself pregnant by one of the guys in town. Instead of raising a bastard kid and having Ruby looked at as a whore for the rest of her life, the Todds sent her away to hide their shame. I had heard stories about places where unwed mothers went to have their babies. Mama used to call them "homes" and she said the babies were usually adopted - sometimes even bought - by rich, out-of-the-country people, mostly from the States, who couldn't have their own children. While she thought it was a disgrace that any young girl would find herself in such a predicament, she tempered her judgement with the suggestion that it was probably better for the child in the long run, and the mother as well. After all, she reasoned, what kind of life would a young, unmarried girl be able to provide her bastard child?

Maybe the idea that young pregnant girls would go to such a place to save their family's face and avoid their own disgrace was not so far-fetched. Supposedly there had been several girls from Liverpool who had sought such refuge. Many people believed this theory, even Chief Frasier. He grilled the Todds many times about that possibility. He was coming up short on answers and grasping at straws. Why do police rely on such tactics? When they can't find the people responsible for a crime, they have to find someone to blame. There was no evidence to support the idea that Ruby's folks would ever do something so mean to the people of Liverpool. It is true that back then having a baby out of wedlock was a major problem for young girls, especially in a socially structured town like Liverpool, but there was no proof that the Todd family could be so devious. What would they have gained? There's no question though that, if Ruby had gotten pregnant, she would have been an outcast and her parents would have been cut off from the rest of the town, so many people around town bought into the idea.

So if she didn't run away and she wasn't sent away, then what could have happened to her? There were more theories. Some people suggested she was taken away. That seemed possible, didn't it? After all, Liverpool was crawling with strangers at this point in its history.

It became common talk in town that Ruby Todd had been seen "flirting" down around the wharves with some of the men from the boats. People now speculated she had been stolen away by sailors off one of the boats that had been in port when she went missing. According to the people at Tupper's, however, that wasn't possible. They explained that before any ship left port it was carefully checked for stowaways and contraband. The jerquers were sent in before each ship sailed and they searched the vessels from stem to stern. If Ruby had been on board any of the ships, she would have most certainly been found.

And since the Tupper twins, who had disappeared three years earlier, hadn't been found yet, people began wondering if someone had taken Ruby just like they did the two little boys. Most people found that a frightening possibility since, if it was true, it would have meant other children could also be in danger. As a result of such talk, people grew scared and paranoid. Naturally they became protective of their kids. Some even kept their youngsters home from school because they feared there was some sort of madman prowling Liverpool whisking away young boys and girls. But there was never any proof that somebody in town was stalking the children, and no more kids ever went missing after Ruby.

It was known that Ruby took piano lessons from Mrs. Henley on the other side of town. To get there from where the Todds lived, she would have had to walk over the small, wooden bridge that crossed the river. It wasn't much of a bridge, just big enough for a carriage or one of those small cars that had just arrived in town. People mostly used it for walking. Since we didn't have many cars back in those days, most of us travelled by foot everywhere we went. It was suggested that maybe Ruby fell off the bridge and then was swept out to sea by the strong current that fed through to the ocean. People thought this scenario was the most sensible one yet, even after the police took a close look at the bridge and couldn't find any clues that might indicate someone had fallen off. It was a stupid suggestion anyway. How could anyone have fallen over the high railings that ran along the sides of the bridge? You could jump or be pushed, but it wasn't likely you could fall ... so if she went over the bridge, then she either killed herself or someone helped her. Those were two more possibilities that ran their course around town, but again it was all speculation.

The most probable theory was that Ruby had gone for a walk and become lost in the woods somewhere outside of town. Because she was new to Liverpool it was possible she could have decided that, since it was a nice day and she wanted to see more of this new place she now called home, she'd do some exploring. Maybe she got turned around in the strange woods. Being from the city she wouldn't know her way around the outdoors.

When I heard they were organizing a search party, I went right down to the town hall and volunteered to help. Hank and Ben came as well. Bunny had to stay at the store to help his old man. And Levi, well, he was just too lazy. Furthermore, he acted like he didn't care about Ruby.

The town's people searched for days. They looked everywhere in the weeks following Ruby's disappearance, but came up empty-handed. Me, Hank and Ben volunteered to look around Pine Grove and Brier Lake since we knew the areas well. Chief Frasier sent two other men with us and we looked around there for several days. It was tough going back there. We hoped that we wouldn't find anything there that would spoil the magic of that place we had come to appreciate so deeply. It's hard to think that something could have happened there to tarnish all those great memories we had created over the years. We turned that place upside down and inside out, but didn't find a thing ... not a clue about what happened to Ruby Todd.

The rumours and speculation didn't stop after the search was called off. It was impossible to continue looking after nearly three weeks, although Mr. and Mrs. Todd kept insisting that the searchers do more. Everyone sympathized with the pain the Todds were obviously suffering over the loss of their precious daughter, but it wasn't likely that Ruby was going to turn up after being missing for such an extended time. That stark reality became clear to the searchers after a couple of days, but everyone felt they had to keep looking for the benefit of the Todd family.

It must be a terrible thing to lose a child like that, not knowing if they're dead or alive; if they're injured or suffering somewhere, calling out for help; or if they just don't want to be found. I'm sure the Todds had all kinds of emotions and questions running through their heads. They weren't the only ones.

Mrs. Theresa Jones also had lots of questions and she used "The Crier" to ask them. Strongly believing that a conspiracy surrounded the girl's disappearance, most likely a cover-up involving someone in a position of power, Mrs. Jones offered a $100 reward - a lot of money back then - for information on the whereabouts of Ruby Todd, but nothing ever came out of it. For some reason, she took Ruby's disappearance pretty hard, almost personal. Maybe she saw Ruby as the daughter she would never have with Mr. Jones, or maybe she felt sorry for the Todds' loss or didn't like the idea of a cover-up. Whatever the reason, she pushed the police and town council to keep doing something, even after it seemed everyone else had given up. In the end, I remember Mrs. Jones saying how very sorry she was that she couldn't do more to help the Todds, but there wasn't much anyone could do. Ruby's disappearance was another Liverpool mystery and that was how it was going to stay.

But Mrs. Jones wasn't convinced it was such a mystery. I remember an editorial she wrote in "The Crier" about Ruby and how very sad the town was that another young person had been taken under such mysterious circumstances. She knew it might make her very unpopular in our small, closely-knit town where people look out for each other, but she came right out and said what everyone else wouldn't say or admit - that someone or some group of people in Liverpool knew exactly what had happened to Ruby Todd on that hot summer night and in the end they would pay the ultimate price for what they had done. She refused to believe Ruby Todd had gotten lost. Something more sinister surrounded the girl's disappearance, she thought.

"Some day," Mrs. Jones wrote, "those who were responsible for whatever happened to Ruby Todd will have to answer to a higher power for what they have done. God help them when that day comes."

She continued, "People in a position of power think they can manipulate the public agenda, and for the most part they can if they have enough money and connections in the right places. Let there be no doubt. Someone in this town knows exactly what happened to the missing Todd girl, and while you think you have gotten away with your crimes, you must not be too smug. Someday you will be judged and punished."

Reaction to Mrs. Jones's comments was mixed, but for the most part, the people of Liverpool seemed to agree. However, the editorial didn't sit too well with town officials, especially Mayor George Keddy, a crusty old coot who seemed to be at the centre of every controversy. Some said Mayor Keddy liked to drink while doing town business and that he was too pigheaded to properly execute his duties. Everything had to be done his way or not at all, and many people didn't like that autocratic approach. Whatever the case, he kept getting returned to office every time we had elections. In all, he spent twenty-one years there making him the longest-serving mayor this town has seen so far. I honestly don't think anyone else wants the job, and no wonder. The pay is dreadful, and it comes with a heavy workload with very little thanks from the townspeople.

Poor old Mayor Keddy was a hard looking ticket. He had arthritis so bad that the fingers on his hands were curled up like hooks, all twisted and bent. Got so bad in the end that he couldn't use his hands any more, not even to sign his name. I pitied him for that, but the man was a mean old shit and didn't like anyone fussing over him. He was the kind of man that could tell you to go to Hell and you'd say thanks all the way there. He was crafty, but he seemed to get the job done and that's all that's important when there's business that needs doing, especially for a town which faces a constant struggle for survival.

The morning "The Crier" hit the streets, Mayor Keddy stormed into the newspaper office like a full-force hurricane blowing up the Eastern Seaboard. The old man was pissed, that was obvious. Frothing at the mouth as he slammed the paper down on Mrs. Jones's cluttered desk, he called the editorial a bunch of bullshit and demanded that Mrs. Jones print a retraction in next week's issue. He also insisted she apologize to the people of Liverpool for insinuating someone in this town would be party to such a dreadful conspiracy.

"To suggest a cover-up around the disappearance of a young girl is preposterous," he huffed. "No one in Liverpool would do such a thing and to say otherwise is near slander."

I was in The Crier's office talking to Mrs. Jones that morning about getting more work when the mayor blew in. She was expecting him. They had previously locked horns on several occasions. "Now Mayor, how can you say it's slander? I didn't name names. I was merely stating the facts. Furthermore, I didn't say anything that wasn't on the minds of most people in Liverpool. It's just that no one else has the courage to say it." She refused to be intimidated by the powerful man. She would not back down. "I do not have anything to apologize for and I will thank you for not raising your voice in my office. This is my place of business and I do not take kindly to being bullied by you or anyone else. I don't care who you are. I'll do my job the best way I know how. Besides, they say the truth is hard to swallow. You must admit, Mr. Mayor, that the circumstances of the girl's disappearance are more than suspect. Surely you cannot expect this newspaper to sugar-coat the truth. People must be told what's going on around them, even when it's not pretty. Maybe that's the way it used to be done around here but it's not going to be like that anymore."

"I don't know who in the hell you think you are, coming into town from up there in Toronto, missy. But you better learn how things are done around here. We ain't lookin' for any hot-shot big-city newspaper reporter to tell us how to do things. We were gettin' along just fine before you showed up, thank you very much." This was not the kind of talk you'd expect from a gentleman addressing a lady but then again Mayor Keddy was not exactly a gentleman. "This town has a reputation to protect and it won't help us any if you go printin' this trash in your little paper and spreadin' rumours that you can't support. Surely you can't believe someone in this town would do anything so despicable?"

"Excuse me, Mr. Mayor, but this 'little paper' has a job to do and I will not be intimidated ... not even by you," she fired back. Like I said, Mrs. Jones never backed down from an argument, especially when she knew she was right. "And why wouldn't someone in this little town do something so horrible? People are people, and some of us do terrible things, even people here in Liverpool. Yes, Mr. Mayor, I do believe that someone has something to hide. I really don't care if you can accept that or not. That's really your problem. If you don't like the truth, then I'm afraid you'll have to stop reading because there's no way that I'm backing down."

"Listen, missy, you don't know what you're doing ... who you're dealing with. I may not be the only one in Liverpool who stops reading this garbage ... if you know what I mean."

"Are you threatening me, Mr. Mayor? Are you saying that you'll have other people in Liverpool boycott my paper because I'm not afraid to print the truth?"

"You're damned right I am, missy." The old man seemed pleased that she had gotten the point.

"Well, Mr. Mayor, then I guess we're done here for today. But before you leave, I want you to understand one thing. We're in this business for the truth. If that truth hurts, then so be it. I know this may be hard for you to comprehend, but the mayor, of all people, should understand that truth is paramount to a properly-functioning community. If we stick our collective heads in the sand, the truth will kick our asses. If you want to try and boycott me, then do your best.

Oh, and by the way, my name is not missy."

I stood dumbfounded as the mayor left the cluttered newspaper office. He was still steaming as he departed. I could tell Mrs. Jones was shaken by her confrontation with the most powerful man in Liverpool, but she was not about to buckle in front of him. She wouldn't give him the satisfaction of seeing her cave in to his pressure. I respected her for her integrity and her guts. That's why I wasn't surprised to see in the following Wednesday's paper a full recounting of the conversation that had taken place between the newspaper editor and the mayor. It was all there in black and white ... his demand for an apology, her refusal and his threat. She had balls, I'll give her that much. And despite all the mayor's blustering that day, he could never convince others in town to stop buying "The Crier," or advertising in it, for that matter. If anything, I think the people of Liverpool became more supportive of Mrs. Jones and her newspaper for sticking to her guns.

Sadly, though, none of this helped the town find Ruby Todd. About two months after Ruby went missing, the Todds finally decided they could no longer stay in Liverpool. It was too painful to think that something terrible had happened to their little girl in these parts. There were too many reminders. They had to get away. Who could blame them? I'm sure many people in their position would have done the same thing.

The Todds didn't bother to sell the house ... they just abandoned it. They packed up everything they owned and left the house sitting there, empty. Actually, you know the house. It's the one up there behind the courthouse. It's a mess these days; fallen down the last time I saw it, with all the windows broken out and boarded over; all the paint worn off and the trees and tall grass growing up around it. Over the years, the town had its work crews put boards over any broken glass in the windows and that's all that's been done since the Todds moved away. Shame really. It was such a big, beautiful home but no one ever lived there after the Todds left. It just sat there and rotted. It's gone too far now. You could never fix it up. It would cost an arm and a leg to get it back into shape.

Somehow, though, that big, empty house seems like a fitting memorial to the young girl that went missing all those years ago. It's a reminder for this town that some mysteries should never go unsolved. As for the rest of the Todd family, no one really knows where they went. We never heard from them again. They never came back to Liverpool or had any contact with anyone back here.

There are many mysteries in life, that's a fact ... especially in little backwater towns like this one. Ruby Todd blew into Liverpool and in only two months left a legacy that still haunts this town after more than sixty years. I knew Ruby Todd and I liked her a great deal. She wasn't around long, but she left her mark.

Chapter 12

Come in, come in.

I'm surprised to see you here. I didn't think you were working today.

You weren't supposed to be on duty today, were you?

I guess that's what being on call is all about, never knowing when you'll be working. It must be difficult to have a relationship under these conditions but you do have to work, don't you? Is there anyone special in your life?

Too shy to talk about it, eh? I understand. But you don't have to be shy around me. God knows, I've told you enough about me in these past few days ... more than I've told anyone in all my life. After all that's been said, you should realize there are no secrets between us ... well, okay. Maybe just a few.

I promise I won't pry. I know it's none of my business. But I want you to know if there's anything you need to talk about, feel free to run it past me. I've got nothing better to do than lie here and listen. You might say you've got a captive audience.

I am a good listener. That's one of my best qualities. It's one of the things people used to say about me. They'd say, that Jack Webster, now he's a good listener. And the best part of it is that I can keep a secret. I know when to keep my mouth shut. My friends knew they could tell me anything and it wouldn't go any further. Maybe that was my downfall. Perhaps I kept too many secrets.

Listen to me ramble. I'm glad they called you in today. I've got so much to tell you. Don't suppose that before I get started you could fix this damned bed so I'm not lying out so straight. I'm not dead yet, but they seem hell bent to keep me laid out like a corpse. It's dreadfully dull looking up at the ceiling all day, every day. It's not a pretty view from here on your back day after day.

Thanks! That's much better. You really are an angel. You're too kind to me. I want you to know how much I appreciate what you've done for me the past two days. It's more than I deserve.

What's that?

Don't be foolish. You have no idea what you've done. All I could have hoped for in these dying days of my life is to have someone beside me who will listen; someone who won't pass judgement. When you're as close to death as I am, you don't need someone standing over you preaching that "you should have done this or you should have done that." I know what I've done wrong. I understand the misguided turns I've taken but I am not looking for salvation. All I want is to be given the chance to set the record straight. It's as if you were sent to me for this special purpose.

Don't be saying you haven't done anything for me, young lady. You have no idea what you've done. You may not fully appreciate the role you're playing in a dying man's life but believe me, it's a significant one. Perhaps someday, after I'm long gone, you'll understand. And when you do, maybe you'll think of me and remember this tormented old man who wished for his life to be over but got no redemption in death. Someday you'll put it all into perspective ... I know you will.

Now enough of that. It's time to get down to business.

Chapter 13

Life went on, but it was never the same here in Liverpool after that August night when Ruby Todd disappeared. It was as if the entire town was submerged in a long, dark period of mourning. Everyone suspected that something was terribly wrong, that the girl's disappearance was more than an accident. The entire town understood the tragedy of a young girl going missing with no apparent explanation. Everyone in town wanted to solve the mystery, but no one could figure out what could have happened to Ruby. In fact, the mystery haunted some people so deeply, they never quite got over it.

The mystery gnawed at the very fabric of Liverpool much like a mouse nibbles on a chunk of cheese; small bites, until finally the whole piece is gone. Eventually it consumed this entire town and everyone in it. That's how it was for many people in Liverpool.

For us - me, Hank, Ben, Levi and Bunny - things never got back to normal; whatever in the hell normal was. We grew apart by the end of that summer. It probably wasn't supposed to be like that but we became distant strangers, drifting in our own directions. We all followed our own destinies and, in some cases, never saw each other again. People do that. Even good friends. But this was different in many ways. It was as if we could no longer tolerate being near each other, as if we were dirty. And it wasn't only the five of us. Many people in Liverpool experienced the same sense of separation from close friends and, in some cases, family. For whatever reason, there seemed to be a deep vein of guilt and remorse coursing through this town and it left many relationships in ruin.

I didn't want to lose touch with any of the others. We were all such good friends for so long, especially me and Hank. And even Ben. Their companionship was important to me. I couldn't stand the idea of trying to go on without them. It tore me apart inside to think of my world without them in it. For some of us, the guys were the only close family we had.

It isn't easy to get over losing a good friend. Some of the fellows were more like brothers to me than friends. We relied on each other to get us through some pretty bad things. They made the tough times more palatable. Now it was as if that history didn't mean anything to them. Maybe, as the summer was drawing to a close and the entire town was in such turmoil over Ruby's disappearance, the guys figured it was time to get on with business and live our own lives. Maybe Ruby's disappearance was a wake up call telling us to move along. You can't live in the past forever. They say it isn't healthy to do that but it isn't always easy to let go.

Whatever the reason, our previously tight-knit group was breaking up and I was feeling bad about it. I think much of what I was feeling had to do with me believing I didn't have much to live for. Fall was fast approaching and I was still searching for a better job. I liked working at the newspaper very much but the pay was terrible. And I still hadn't found a steady girlfriend either. That bothered me too. Was I inept in some way? Some of my friends were leaving in pursuit of their dreams while others were settling down to start a family. But in my world, it seemed as though everything was coming apart at the seams. I became depressed for awhile. I wondered what was going to become of me. I began pitying myself and that isn't healthy.

My life seemed to bottom out for a few months that fall, until I finally found some part-time work down at Tupper's. After that, things started to look up. It wasn't a great deal of work, mind you; about three hours a day, but I figured that was good enough for starters. I hoped eventually it would turn into something more steady or even full-time if I was lucky. The work wasn't strenuous. They hired me and three other fellows to help hose down the ships after they went up on the dry dock so they'd be good and clean before the welders started working on them. But there was a catch. If I wanted the job, I had to be available seven days a week, even Sundays. The shipyard was extremely busy at that time with the war raging on. They never took a day off. In those days, it seemed there was a steady parade of ships into the harbour. Mr. Morash, the wharf foreman, told me and the others that if we did a good job, then maybe he'd see what else he could find to give us more hours. I worked my butt off to impress him. I wasn't going to mess up any chance of getting a full-time job, no matter if I had to work around the clock. I'd do whatever I had to do and any kind of work they assigned to me ... they'd get no argument from me. I probably could have found something else if I would have looked for it but I wanted to work on the wharves. That's where all the excitement was. Besides, the money was better in the shipyard during the war, and the work was steady. I was glad something finally seemed to be going well for me after the rough time I had that fall.

Chapter 14

Levi was the first member of the company to leave Liverpool. He boarded the train the first of September in 1940 to go off to school in Halifax. I remember the day very well. Me, Hank and Bunny went across town to the train station to see him off. Ben didn't come. He hadn't been the same since Ruby's disappearance. We hadn't seen much of him. It was like he was avoiding us, like a wall had been built to keep him on one side and the rest of us on the other.

The day Levi left town was wet and cold. The leaves had started to change colour, signs of an early winter. The train station is gone now. It burned down in the late eighties but it used to sit next to where they built that big grocery store. A portion of the parking lot is where the main station building used to be. Biggest mistake this country ever made, tearing up those train tracks. Someday they're going to wish they'd left them alone. Someday maybe we'll all recognize our mistakes but by then it'll be too late.

The day Levi left I went to wish him well. I'm glad I did. We never saw Levi much after he went away to college. It was an emotional day at the station for his family, especially for his mother. But through her tearful goodbyes, he and I did manage to steal a couple of minutes before he boarded the train. Surprisingly, while Levi had always tried to come across as a hard ass, he seemed quite nervous and apprehensive about leaving Liverpool. That's understandable. He was, after all, setting out for the first time, embarking on his future, and he was doing it all alone. But this was Levi's destiny and he knew it. He just had to accept it.

"I can't stop thinking about her," he said as we stood on the boarding platform, keenly aware that this could be our last time together.

"Who?"

"Ruby Todd."

"Why bring her up now?"

"I don't know. It's hard to get her outta my head."

"I know what you mean, but you can't let her haunt you this way. She's gone. You've got to let this go. She's got nothing to do with your leaving."

"But she does, Jack. Her disappearance reminds me of how fragile we are; how we can be here one minute and gone in the blink of an eye. I can't help but wonder if anyone will remember me when I'm gone."

"I will."

"What if I can't do this? What if I can't do what he expects of me? Failure is not acceptable."

"You can, Levi. I know you can if you want to. But you have to promise me that you'll go in there and do well for yourself. Of the five of us, you have the best chance of doing something special with your life." I remember saying that to him as we handed his luggage to the train attendant. "You've known all along this day was coming. Don't worry about it, you'll be fine. You know it isn't going to be easy but I know you can do it."

"I don't know, Jack," he said. His voice conveyed apprehension. "I've never been away from home before. What if I can't do this? What will my father think?"

There was the crux of the matter. Levi was afraid of failing because he feared his old man. "Don't think that you have to prove yourself to anyone back here, especially your old man," I told him, trying to sound reassuring. "You know he's an asshole, and he expects you to be at the top of your class. But don't do it for him, do it for yourself. You can do it. You have the brains to be a success but you have to have the determination ... you have to have the guts to show him. You have what it takes. You just have to believe in yourself."

"I'm not sure I can, Jack."

"Sure you can, Levi. Just do your best. That's all anyone can do. That's all anyone should expect. If your old man can't accept that, then to hell with him."

"Yeah, right, Jack. To hell with him." Levi laughed, trying to be brave but he didn't fool me. "I'm glad you came down to say goodbye. I think, that of everyone I'll miss back here, I'll miss you the most. I do feel bad that I'm going away to the city while you'll still be stuck back here in this shit-hole of a town. Why don't you come with me? We'll have a great time."

"I can't do that. What would I do in the city? Don't feel bad for me, Levi," I said. "Liverpool is my home and I'll be perfectly happy here, especially now that I have a chance to get a good job down at the shipyard. It's honest work. I can be content with that but you couldn't stand it for long. You were never cut out for this small-town life. I was born here and I know I'm going to die here but I can accept that. I'm going to make it work for me. I have no regrets that I'll spend my life in Liverpool. It's not so bad if you accept things as they're meant to be. But even though you're moving on, try to keep yourself grounded. Don't ever turn your nose up at this little place, Levi. Remember that no matter how bad - or good - things get in the outside world you should know you will always have a place to call home back here in Liverpool. No one can ever take that away from you, except you."

Climbing on board the train Levi tossed me one final comment. It's been rolling around in my mind for all these years. "I don't know, Jack," he said. "I'm not sure that I'll ever consider this place my home ever again, not after everything that's happened. I have this nagging feeling in my gut that once I leave here things will change forever."

And they did.

Life is about change. I learned to accept that a long time ago.

For the first couple of years Levi made it a point to come home for Christmas and other holidays, but when he did he spent most of his time visiting with his family. The other guys didn't seem to care but I regretted that Levi and I hadn't made time for more visits when he returned to Liverpool. I think in the end, I probably got to be the closest to Levi. It's a funny thing. No matter how long you know someone, when they go away and then return, they're never the same person they were before they left. It's like they leave town as the person we knew and come back as someone completely different, almost a stranger. They go off to some foreign place where they meet new people and have different experiences that you can't understand. That changes them in some way and you naturally grow apart. I don't think you can ever get back to where you were before. You stay friendly but you're no longer close.

Or at least that's the way it was with Levi. I remember the first Christmas he came home for the holidays. He seemed different from how I remembered him. When he got back in town, he came down to the shipyard to look me up but it wasn't the same when we got together for a few drinks that night down at Joe's. We talked about how things were changing around Liverpool, the war and the other guys, but he seemed distant somehow ... so far away from here. It was like his body had come home for the holidays but his mind and everything else about him had stayed behind. Hank and Ben said the city changed him. They thought Levi had gotten too big for his britches, that he seemed stuck up on himself. But I didn't get that impression at all. In fact, to me, it felt as if Levi was more vulnerable and weaker than before he went away to college. It was as if he was reaching out for someone or something but he couldn't quite connect with anyone. He was searching for something but I didn't know what. Actually, I'm not sure Levi even knew what it was. But I'm not sure that Hank and Ben could handle the fact that one of us was going off to better himself while they might have to stay in Liverpool. It didn't bother me, though. I figured if someone had a chance to make a good life for himself, then why the hell not?

It's funny how that works in a small town. It doesn't matter who you are or what you do, there's always someone out there trying to knock you down. For every step you take forward, there's three other people trying to kick your legs out from under you and hold you back. They think you have no right to find success because you come from a place like Liverpool.

I don't see it that way. I try to give people credit for what they do.

Instead of making people regret their success, we should get behind anyone local who goes out in the world and does something great. I don't think people in Liverpool would ever appreciate what Levi could do. He knew he could never come back here to practice medicine because the locals wouldn't accept him. You can't do a good job if people don't respect you. People here were too jealous to make Levi feel welcome as a doctor. Sure, Levi had a lot more breaks than most of us kids his age because his old man had money and influence, but you couldn't hold that against him. And yes, his old man rode him pretty damned hard to do well in school, but was that such a bad thing? But even with all that Levi had going for him, he still had many problems. He was working his ass off to live up to his father's expectations and that wasn't easy. His old man always wanted more. In truth, Levi should have been working hard for himself, instead of doing everything to please his old man. But that's the kind of relationship they had. Levi was trapped. He didn't know how to escape his father's clutches even though he was miles away in the city.

That Christmas Levi told me school wasn't going well. No matter how well he had done here in Liverpool schools, he was struggling in college. But he felt he could handle the studies if he could only find a way to concentrate.

"It's hard being away from home," he confided. "It's pretty tough. You have no idea what it's like. You think Liverpool is busy because of the war, it's worse in the city. There's so many strange people coming and going. Sometimes I feel lost. It's like I can't find a way out of the dark haze that seems to hang over me."

I'm sure it must have been overwhelming, even for a well-bred boy like Levi, but he seemed to accept that he had no choice but to succeed. "I know I have to go back to school and make the most of it," he said. "My father expects me to do that. He has spent hundreds of dollars to send me there and I don't dare let him down. Truth is, I really do want to become a doctor."

He seemed determined to succeed. "I'm going to find some way to make it work, even if it kills me," he said.

I figured his feelings of isolation were nothing more than good old fashioned homesickness. "I don't know what to tell you, Levi," I said. "It sounds pretty tough but I'm sure you'll get over it if you get out and find some friends, maybe even a girlfriend."

"Once you get a new life everything will change for the better," I said, even though I wasn't sure if I believed it myself. "You'll soon forget about Liverpool; about everyone and everything that happened here." I knew it wouldn't be easy but I tried to sound convincing. Some things you can never forget but I told him if he didn't stick with it, he'd be like the rest of us back here in Liverpool, and I knew he didn't want that. Besides if he dropped out of school that would be giving people exactly what they wanted. Many people were waiting for Levi to fail and fall flat on his face. They would have embraced that failure, making it Levi's noose. It's hard to imagine, perhaps, but there were some locals who wanted him to buckle. But that night after our talk I think Levi found a new determination, some kind of inner strength, to make it work. It would have been a terrible waste if he had dropped out of college. I don't think he wanted to give those assholes the satisfaction of seeing him quit.

That night down at Joe's was the closest me and Levi had ever been. I know for certain it's the most serious talk we ever had with each other. Maybe it was because the others weren't around to distract us. I don't know but it was intriguing after all those years to finally get to know Levi on a different level. Even though we had been friends most of our lives, there was still much I didn't know about him. Maybe it was the beer talking, or that he was glad to finally be home again with a familiar face, that he dropped his guard.

"No matter what I do, who I meet or where I go," he said, "I find it hard to stop thinking about Liverpool and the past. Sometimes I lie awake at night remembering our lives as they were and thinking about the things that happened here ... the good and the bad, but mostly the bad. I see her face everywhere I go, in everything I do. I see her in everyone I meet."

His words were deep. It was more than the normal growing pains of a boy gone away to college for the first time. I remember he was determined to make me understand it wasn't homesickness he was going through. "My memories of Liverpool are like ghosts that keep coming back to haunt to me," he said. "Sometimes it's impossible to shake them, even while I'm awake. I've tried to accept them and go on with things but it's too difficult."

I understood what Levi was saying. I knew exactly what he meant. I shared many of those memories. But, I said, "You can't let this eat you up. What's done is done. Some memories are made not to be forgotten no matter where you go or what you do. There is nothing you can do to escape them. Some things get into your head and they stay there. Sometimes you meet people and you do things that you can never undo. These are the things that you can't forget. These are the things that leave an impact on you, as if touching your soul. But somehow you must manage to go on with your life, and those memories, over the years, will eventually blend into the passage of time; they will contribute to the kind of person we eventually become. All you can do is allow them to evolve and hopefully fade away. But sometimes some memories don't slip into the background so easily, and when that happens, they'll eat you up. You can't let this win. You've come too far to back out now."

"How do we go on, Jack? How are we supposed to keep living and pretending that nothing happened? I don't know how long I can keep living with these lies."

"We just go on one day at a time. That's all we can expect." I told Levi he had to make a conscious effort to push aside his bad memories. If he didn't, they'd surely take over his life and control it. They'd consume him if he didn't keep a tight grip on his senses. "It isn't easy," I said. "I struggle every day. Some days I have to push to get myself out of bed but I know I can't let this beat me. I know I have no choice. I keep fighting because if I didn't, I'd go insane. Life is very unpredictable," I remember telling Levi. "If you let it, life will overwhelm you, and when that happens, my friend, you lose control. If you let them, your ghosts will consume you. The key is to focus all your energies on your studies and your future. Try to block out those memories, or you'll destroy yourself. You can't undo anything that has already happened. Don't get trapped in the past ... move on ... put the past where it belongs - behind you."

I was usually good at throwing advice around like it was yesterday's dirty laundry. It's too bad I never learned to listen to my own words.

After that night down at Joe's, I only saw Levi briefly on two other occasions that Christmas. His family kept him busy. Or should I say, his old man kept him away from his friends.

Levi returned to school in the new year, and me and the other guys went back to our own business, seeing each other every now and then. They never had many good things to say about Levi but I came to respect him better after our talk, even though I'll be the first to admit I hadn't always liked him. That night down at Joe's it didn't seem to matter that he had been a bratty, self-centred kid. Even though he seemed vulnerable, there was something about how he was facing the challenge and working hard to achieve his goals that made me see Levi in a different way. I learned to respect him for his fortitude, even if he would eventually grow too arrogant for his own good.

He came home once in awhile after that Christmas but on each visit he grew more distant, mostly keeping to himself. Eventually he stayed in Halifax to study and work. He was making a new life with new friends and didn't have any need to come back to see us. I didn't hate him for that. I know that's how life goes and you must move on. That night down at Joe's was the first and last time me and Levi had an honest heart-to-heart talk, but it left its mark on me.

With time we finally fell out of touch like most childhood friends do but I did manage to keep track of Levi over the years. He did become a respected doctor and I was sincerely happy for him but he had a most unhappy life. Maybe that was his fate. After college and medical school he went out west for a few years, then eventually settled down in southern Ontario where he set up a practice. He was quite successful there, at least as far as medicine went. But he never married. He came close once but it wasn't meant to be.

It was a sad story. The way I heard it, Levi had met an attractive nurse at a Toronto hospital. Her name was Margaret. I never met her. After a few months, the two decided to marry. It was going to be a grand affair with all the trimmings befitting a successful doctor from a rich family. Naturally Levi's family made the trip to Toronto but none of us were invited. We weren't important enough obviously. It was to have been a July wedding to remember but it never happened. Fate had other plans. As Levi waited on his wedding day in the church vestry for his bride to arrive, a police officer bearing bad news came instead. There had been a terrible accident three blocks from the church. A drunk driver had crossed over the line and ploughed head-first into Margaret's car. Her father had been driving and he was unharmed. But the bride died instantly from the impact. Crushed, the official police report said. The drunk driver walked away without a scratch.

Levi must have been devastated. He never again gambled on love.

I last saw Levi when he came home for his old man's funeral. That was at least thirty years ago. We talked briefly after the burial but he didn't have time for me. He was only home for three days and he kept busy tying up loose ends around his father's death. After that, Levi's mother moved to Halifax to take care of some elderly relative. She never came back. Too many painful memories here for her, I suspect. Or maybe she was too embarrassed over her husband's indiscretions to face the residents of this town alone. Pride is a powerful influence that guides the actions of many people, sometimes to regrettable results.

I have always thought it ironic that even though Levi's mother knew about his father's affairs, she stayed with him until he died. That's how they did things back then. Look the other way while everyone else in town gossips over tea. It certainly wouldn't happen like that today. Now they'd go for a quick divorce or someone would end up being killed. I'm not sure if Mrs. Taylor stayed with her husband out of some die-hard love for him, a deep devotion for the father of her children, or if it was some sort of misplaced loyalty on her part. But for whatever reason, Levi's parents stuck it out to the bitter end. I think she was too scared to leave him. Women didn't do that sort of thing in those days. It wasn't acceptable. He didn't deserve her love or loyalty after the way he treated her, but she remained committed to him.

With his father's death and his mother gone, Levi and his brothers and sisters finally sold that big house. It was the last connection Levi had here in Liverpool. He had no reason to come back. I never laid eyes on him again after his old man's funeral. He became only a memory from my youth, like a figment of my imagination that never actually existed. It's sad when good friends become so distant. I sometimes wish I had seen Levi more often as we grew older, like all my childhood friends. But I know you can't hang onto your youth by clinging to those who shared it with you. The reality is that life moves on and so do people.

Levi kept working until he got sick and finally died of brain cancer. He died young, in his late-thirties. People said he was in a great deal of pain, as the cancer had been eating away at him for many months. They first found that Levi had a tumour when he began having constant headaches along with eyesight problems and dizzy spells. He ended up in the hospital for about two months until he died. It was a miserable death, slow and drawn out. I know what he went through. The cancer moved slowly, causing him to gradually lose his mind. In the end, they said, it's as if he went crazy, slipping in and out of consciousness and losing all control of his body. It isn't very flattering when that happens. Believe me, I know. Eventually, he fell into a deep coma that lasted four days. Then he was gone. Just like that. After everything he went through. After all the hard work he put into being somebody, he was history. And that's what we all have to look forward to. It's all very final but that's all some of us deserve.

About a week after Levi died, I received a letter with an Ontario postmark. I knew right away it was from Levi, although I was puzzled as to why he would contact me after all the years with not so much as a Christmas card between us. I was surprised to hear from my old friend out of the blue like that. As I held the envelope in my trembling hands, wondering what secrets ... confessions ... or lies ... it could contain, I was almost tempted to throw it away. But I couldn't. If he had taken the time to write, I, at least, owed him the courtesy of reading what he had to say. It was weird holding that letter. It was almost as if my long lost friend was reaching out to me from the grave. I had a similar experience once before and the memory gave me goose bumps.

I opened the letter, cautiously, holding my breath as a feeling of deep regret swept over me. But, as I read Levi's note of reconciliation, my apprehension drained away. It was replaced by a deep, deep feeling of loss and isolation. The letter contained a sombre message from Levi and I could tell almost from the first words that he had written it out of guilt.

"Dear Jack," it began. "I know I am the last person you could ever expect to hear from after all of this time but if you're reading this letter, I'm already dead. I have asked my good friend Barbara, who has worked with me for the last twelve years, to send this note off to you after my death. I hope you will read it and understand the humility and deep regret with which it is written."

"Writing has become a major chore for me these days. If I sound confused, please understand and forgive me. Now that the cancer has progressed, I find it difficult to remember all the words I need to complete a sentence but I felt compelled to make contact with you this one last time. I have asked Barbara to help me find the words and, as always, she has come to my aide like the precious angel that she truly is. I don't know what I did to enjoy such a good friend but she has been a God-send. Her friendship is much more than I deserve. I am writing this letter with the loving support of my friend. Please read it with the sincere affection that comes with it. It is one of my last wishes that you receive this letter as a way of making up for lost time. Perhaps it comes too late for me to expect or deserve your forgiveness but you must understand that it comes from my heart. I know that as a friend, I have let you down in many ways. However, I hope that you can find it in your heart, as a friend - no, as a brother - to forgive me for running away from Liverpool and hiding from the past like I did. I thought I had no choice. Now I know that was wrong. Those memories followed me. No matter where I went, Ruby was there. I saw her, heard her, even smelled her, and, on occasion, could almost touch her. I should have faced my ghosts years ago. I know you cannot condone my decisions but please try to forgive me."

"I cannot begin to tell you how many times over the years I picked up the phone and started to dial your number. But I could never complete the call because I would not know what to say to you, except that I am sorry for everything that happened between us. Jack, I know it has been many years since you have heard from me but I was afraid you had grown to resent me as some arrogant son of a bitch. Or even worse, that maybe you had come to hate me. Perhaps you would be right to view me in such a way. You would have every right to despise me. Maybe I did become a big shot who thought himself too important to accept his past. I regret that we lost touch after I left Liverpool. If things could be undone, I'd go back and change all of that. In fact, if I could, I'd go back and change many things but once the dice are thrown, you have to roll with them."

"Jack, my friend, this is but a brief note to say how very sorry I am that our paths became separated. Of all the people in Liverpool, it is you I have missed the most. Of all the guys in the company, it was you with whom I felt the greatest kinship and the strongest bond. Even though one may consider me to have been successful, whether by luck or by chance, in reality, my life has always contained a void for our lost friendship. My life has been empty in many ways because of what I did. I know that I was considered something of an outsider in the company but you always made me feel a part of everything. I have learned much too late how valuable true friendship really is. Jack, it is for that reason that I feel compelled to tell you that you were the closest friend I had in Liverpool and you had a profound impact on my life. You didn't know it but you made a difference. When things got tough, I recalled your sincere words of encouragement, and somehow I got through the bad times. Now that it is too late for a personal reunion, I hope these few simple words will at least convey my deep appreciation for what you have meant to me even though we were hundreds - sometimes thousands - of miles apart."

The letter was signed, "Your friend forever, Levi." It was dated one day before he slipped into the coma from which he never woke. I kept that letter all these years as a reminder of what true friendship is all about. I regret that I did not get to see Levi again after he left Liverpool and, although I hate to admit it, he was right. I did grow to resent him for his holier-than-thou attitude but his letter removed the time and space that had kept us apart. It was as though the words in that letter jumped off the page and embraced me, erasing all the negative feeling that had evolved around our friendship. It was then that I felt the deep loss of a true friend but I took some comfort in knowing that for Levi at least the dance was finally over. Don't get me wrong. It hurt knowing he was gone. It was a deep pain I had already experienced once in my life, and it hurt all the way to the bone.

You see, Levi wasn't the first member of the company to die. That unfortunate distinction went to Hank and it wasn't long after that summer when Ruby Todd went missing.

Chapter 15

It was a terribly cold day in February 1941 when Hank came down to the shipyard to tell me he was leaving Liverpool. He had volunteered to go fight in the war. It was the right thing to do, he said. "There isn't anything in this town to keep me here. I might as well go some place where I'll be more useful. I have to try to make things right after everything that's happened. I feel I have a debt that needs to be repaid."

Hank didn't have much to do with his family, except for his younger brother Jimmy, and the local job prospects didn't appeal to him. They were looking for employees most places around town but he said he wouldn't have liked working at the shipyard or the mill. Going to war seemed like the only suitable option to Hank and as much as I hated to see him go, I understood. Now, however, I know that like Levi, Hank was running away. But I'm also sure Hank's ghosts followed him just as they did Levi.

Maybe Hank was answering a deeper calling when he volunteered to go overseas. He said he wasn't scared of getting killed or hurt over there. In fact, he said, he had not given that much thought since he had already made his mind up and that was all there was to it. He felt he had to do it, as if some deep inner voice was telling him to go and do something he could be proud of. He was quite frank and candid about the whole thing. If anything bad was going to happen to him, then he considered that to be an act of God. If that was his fate, to die overseas, then it would just have to happen.

"If it's meant to be," he told me point blank, "then it's meant to be. I'm not going to lose any sleep worrying about it." He looked me square in the eye and said he wasn't scared, and I believed him.

The only advice I could think of to pass on to him for when things got ugly over there was to wish on a falling star as we used to do on those hot summer nights when me and him would go up to Pine Grove and sleep out under the open sky next to Brier Lake. That way, I told him, he could remember the good times we had together before life got complicated.

Anyway, I'm sure it wouldn't have mattered what I said. Once Hank made up his mind to go, it was too late to do anything about it. Before he left, he refused to talk about the dangers he would face in battle. He believed talking about it would jinx him. Instead we spent his last couple of weeks in town down at Joe's shooting pool and drinking beer. We tried to have a good time and forget that he was soon leaving and maybe never coming back again. For me, though, it was like I was losing a brother and I hated the way that made me feel. It hurt to think about going on without having Hank around. I never told him how I felt. He didn't like it when people became sentimental but I hope he knew how much I cared about him.

It was the first week of March when Hank finally left Liverpool. Bunny and me came down to the train station to see him off, just like we did when Levi left for college. But again Ben never came. Guess he didn't like goodbyes. Hank was shipped out to England through Pier 21 and that's where we met him three months later after boot camp just before he left.

It was spring when Hank came back to Halifax for the ship-out. He had written to Jimmy that he was only going to be there a few hours and we decided to surprise him. We took the train to the city to see him off. He was surprised to see us when he got off the train from Ontario but he was pleased we had come. He looked great in that soldier's uniform. He was no longer the inexperienced young man who had left Liverpool only a few months earlier. I hardly recognized him at first. It seemed like Hank was fitting in real well with the army life. He was proud to be going off to the war. He said he felt it was his duty and that he had to get away from Liverpool. He needed to do this for many reasons most of which I could understand. Hank always had to do the right thing even if it meant he might be laying his own life on the line.

He was in Halifax for only one night. We found a small bar down on the waterfront where the three of us shared a few drinks and remembered old times, but only the good ones. There were some things better left unsaid. Hank and I upheld our part of the bargain. We talked about what Hank was going to do when he came home from the war and he insisted that he didn't want to make any long-term plans.

"My philosophy is to take life one day at a time," he said over a beer. During the war years, there was no other way to cope. "After everything that's happened I now know that's the best way."

They were shipping the men out on board a converted luxury liner and I remember me and Jimmy kidding Hank about how he was finally going to be travelling in high-class style. He thought it was great and he never showed any sign of sadness or remorse to be leaving. Me and Jimmy were actually more emotional than Hank when it came time to say goodbye. We had a couple of fun hours together that night but the time passed too quickly. Then, just like that, he was gone and me and Jimmy were back home in Liverpool.

For some reason though, I knew that when Hank sailed out of Halifax that day at the end of May, I'd never see him again, and I never did. I still remember the last conversation we had as he boarded the ship. "Don't think you have to go over there and be a big hero," I warned him. "Keep wishing on that star and watch your butt."

"Jack, you worry too much," he shot back. Then he looked me square in the eyes like he had done many times over the years when he wanted to make a point. His words were stern and his strong posture proved that he had the courage of his convictions. "I'm not sad about going, Jack, and I'm not afraid about what awaits me over there. Please don't be afraid for me. Whatever happens is the way it's meant to be. There's no stopping our destiny, Jack. You should know that by now. I have to do this for me."

I didn't answer him. I didn't know what to say. I stood quietly and watched as the best friend I ever had boarded the ship that would take him to meet his destiny.

I only heard from Hank once after he left. Almost two years passed before I received a letter. It was a strange piece of correspondence. In hindsight, it was more like someone else had control of his pen. Over the years I had often thought that Hank had missed his calling. He could have been a writer, and a good one at that. He had an incredible way with words.

Hank had so much to tell me that it seemed as though he had thrown it all together in this long, rambling letter. His thoughts were deep, but disjointed in many ways. I knew Hank well enough to know that he was under great distress when he wrote the letter. In the time that Hank had been gone, I did keep up to date on what was happening with him through Jimmy, who had received three letters. Jimmy liked to share the news about his big brother. I wasn't surprised to hear that Hank seemed to be fitting into the army routine. Jimmy said he could tell from the few letters he had received that Hank seemed to like it over there. He said he was doing hard, dirty work and some of the men couldn't take it. But Hank could handle it. He was never the kind of person to shy away from hard or dirty work. I wasn't surprised to hear that he was taking to army tasks like a duck to water. But I also knew that Hank had only told Jimmy part of the truth. He didn't want the kid to worry. He told him he was okay over there. I'm sure Hank didn't want Jimmy knowing the hell he was really going through ... but I knew.

Hank hadn't come right out and said so in that solitary letter, but I knew the truth. It was clear to me that more than the Atlantic Ocean and a war had come between me and my lifelong buddy, a friend that was my only brother.

War, I've since been told, was a chaos of noise, mud, blood, vomit, shit, broken bodies and death. It was the carnage of men having limbs blown off and dying on the bloodied battleground while holding their guts in their hands and crying out for their mothers. There was the rain; the cold; the lice and all the blood. The battle ground was a sea of red ooze like the ground was bleeding. I'm sure the blood would have bothered Hank. There was blood everywhere out on the battle grounds ... and dead men by the hundreds ... brothers, husbands, fathers, sons ... all dead. They were scattered everywhere. Lifeless corpses of once vital young men lying in the muck where they fell. The death toll was staggering ... disgusting ... casualties of war. Today we forget what the men and women sacrificed over there for us.

Hank was short on personal details but he said he had seen many battles and he knew he was lucky to still be alive, although he understood that luck was purely the right mix of good timing and intuition. Men all around him were being killed every day ... dropping faster than a whore's pants, he said, from the gunfire and the land mines. I can only imagine the hell he was in. The images were frightening. Hank told me about a fellow soldier, walking a few yards to his right, who accidently stumbled into a minefield and was blown to bits right before his eyes. Hank said they picked up his pieces and put them in little bags much like a butcher packs hamburger.

Hank confessed he counted his blessings every day. He knew it was a miracle and by the grace of God that he was still breathing and that all four limbs remained attached to his exhausted body. He wrote that when he left Liverpool he hadn't believed in God but after a few months over there fighting for his life in the ditches, he learned to gain a new respect for God and his own mortality. He admitted that he asked God every day to help get him through the hell, to make sure he got out alive and in one piece. He didn't figure God owed him any favours but he was hopeful. Hank had never been much of a church-goer and he had done some things in his life he wasn't proud of but he had started praying everyday and asking for forgiveness. He knew he'd need help from a higher power if he was going to crawl out of those trenches alive.

Hank said you couldn't even begin to imagine how sick and grimy you felt after being in the mud up to your ass for days, sometimes weeks, on end. He said you even had to sleep in it ... when you could sleep that was, with all the bombing and gunfire that broke the darkness throughout the night. The fighting never stopped, he wrote. I knew the mud would bother Hank. Even though he didn't mind getting dirty doing an honest day's work, he still had to get cleaned up right away when the job was done. That's the way he was; almost fanatical about it. No matter what we did when we were kids, Hank couldn't stand being dirty, especially his hands. Having dirt on his hands was hard for him to deal with.

Hank told me he decided it was time to write because he hadn't heard from me and he figured someone had to make the first move. He also said he wasn't sure when, or if, he'd get the chance to write again. He was being sent back from the battlefield to England, where troops were training for some great Allied assault that would end the war, and he'd be tied up for months. He said he couldn't tell me too much about what was being planned because the mission was top-secret but he could tell me the troops would be rehearsing their landing strategy and combat tactics. And, he added, the Allied Forces were building up materials and munitions for an assault that would change the course of the war. He said it wouldn't be long before the war was over and he was excited about being part of history. I didn't know it then but in that letter Hank was talking about the invasion of Normandy that took place in June 1944. He was glad to be going back to England to join the 3rd Canadian Infantry because he said he had seen his fair share of death and dirt. He was looking for a break even if it meant he had to do some heavy-duty training. He knew he was up for it. He said he could handle it.

Hank did manage to find some positive things about being oversees in the midst of the dirt, death and destruction. He went to England when he was on leave. The countryside was beautiful, even if London was being levelled by

German bombs. He had met the family of an English soldier he had befriended when his unit visited the Red Cross hospitals set up behind the battle lines. The soldier, Edward Thatcher, and Hank became quite close. Edward's family lived just outside the city of London and they apparently took in Hank like their own adopted son. They were nice people Hank said. They would give him anything he wanted even though they had a hard enough time getting by themselves on short rations. I'm sure it was comforting for Hank to have a family over there. In many ways, he said, they were nicer to him than his own family had ever been. While I feared for his safety, I was happy Hank could find some comfort in the middle of that hell.

At times, Hank could be the strangest person I had ever known. In the middle of all of his talk about the carnage and destruction he had witnessed, he also told me he liked the food they cooked over there, even though food was in short supply. He especially liked something called National Rosehip Syrup which they made from rosehips, the pods that form after the flowers. It didn't sound very appetizing to me but Hank sang its praises. He told me rosehips were prized possessions in Europe but especially in England where they made the syrup extract. Apparently they also made teas and soup powders from them, as well. He said the people over there knew exactly how to make these tasty treats and how to prepare rosehips. You gather the rosehips when they are fully ripe but not over-ripe. If they are orange, Hank explained, it is too early. If they are dark red, then it is too late. It was amazing to me that in the middle of the war, Hank had the time to write about roses, while at the same time writing about the mud and blood. It was an unusual mix. But that was Hank. He could always find the silver lining in any dark cloud, even when things seemed to be at their worst. I had seen him do it many times before, and I think that's one of the things I liked about him ... that and his uncanny ability to step up and take charge in a crisis.

The war was raging and Hank told me he didn't know when he'd be getting out of the army but he figured he'd stay there until the fighting stopped. When he got out though, he said, he had already made up his mind that he wouldn't be returning to Liverpool. There wasn't anything for him here, he believed, except for bad memories. The only thing that bothered him about being away from Liverpool was that he felt he was losing touch with me. And he was of course. There wasn't much happening around here but we were all moving on with our lives just the same.

I never did answer Hank's letter and I came to regret that. Through the years, I felt as though I had let him down. I kick myself for not writing and telling him everything that was happening, even if it seemed trivial. To me, it all seemed insignificant but now, when I think about it, I'm sure Hank would have enjoyed a letter from home. He was reaching out to me, his friend, across the ocean from the battlefields and I didn't recognize his needs. What kind of friend am I?

I wasn't much for letter writing. I never knew what to say in them, so I didn't bother. But now I know Hank was looking for anything that would have helped to keep him going over there. He was reaching out to me for anything that might help him keep his sanity, anything that he could cling to. And I failed him. I let my best friend down when he reached out to me. I've felt guilty all these years about not answering his letter. Sometimes you wish you could put a halt to your life, and then back up and undo some of the things you've done, or didn't do ... even little things like not answering a letter from a friend. But you can't. You have to live with the decisions you make along the way. You better be damned well sure that they're the right ones as you go.

That emotion-packed letter was the last time I heard from Hank and I treasure it to this day. In fact, I still have it stashed away along with Levi's in a strong box at home. Ironically, the letter is there safe and sound but my friend is long gone. His dance ended many years ago. Hank was one of those soldiers who never got back home from the war. But he didn't get killed on the beaches of Normandy or in any other battle for that matter. Hank was killed while on leave in England. During the height of the conflict, the Germans launched a series of bombing raids on England. Over time, the city was devastated by what they called "flying bombs". The British army tried to issue warnings in time for people to take cover but mostly the citizens never knew when the flying bombs were coming over. The bombs did irreparable damage to the city and killed thousands of innocent people, mostly women and children since many of the men were off fighting. The bombs would be sent out over the city by the Germans and when their engines stopped, they dropped wherever their fuel ran out. They never had specific targets. Thousands of Brits were killed indiscriminately in their homes, schools, churches, marketplace or in the streets. They were the truest casualties of war. Hank was one of them.

One sunny spring day in April 1944, as Hank was waiting at a bus stop to go back to the base, a flying bomb, guided by the hand of death, dropped from the bright blue sky directly on top of a crowd of innocent bystanders. By all accounts, it was an horrific mess. Women and children were killed, along with Hank. They said the people never knew what hit them and they only had a couple of seconds to react once the bomb was spotted. But it seems that's all the time Hank needed to do something good for someone else.

I don't know what happened for sure but witnesses said when Hank saw the bomb dropping he courageously reached out, pulled a little girl to the ground and threw his body over hers, covering up the youngster and protecting her from sure death. Using his body to shield the little girl from the deadly blast, Hank saved her life but he was killed when pieces of debris fell on him. At least Hank died a hero, and that made me very proud of him. Hank would have been happy knowing he had saved the little girl's life, that he had done some good in the world before he died. He had evened the score. His debt was repaid in full.

I don't cry much but when I received the news that Hank was dead, I cried. That was one time I couldn't hold back my emotions. I didn't cry when the Old Man died even though I was only fourteen. But it didn't mean I didn't think anything of him. I really did care for the Old Man and I missed him deeply when he was gone. But I cried when my mother died. I finally realized she was out of her misery and I was relieved for her in an odd way. I knew she was finally at peace. After she died, I think I only cried two other times, maybe three. I know it's okay to cry but it's hard showing my emotions.

Does that make me a hard old bastard? Maybe. But hearing that Hank had been killed over there was like learning that my own brother was dead, and that made me terribly sad. To make matters worse, they never brought Hank's body home to be buried. He's planted in the ground overseas somewhere. That made it even more difficult to believe. It was hard accepting my good friend was dead. Seeing the body allows you to come to terms with a person's death. It's a final goodbye. Putting the person in the ground is the last favour you can do for them. But we didn't get that opportunity with Hank. I never got the chance to say goodbye the way I should have. I had wished to see his grave before I died but that's not possible.

Over the years since Hank died, though, I've said goodbye to him many times. Every Remembrance Day, on November 11, I wear a poppy to remember my friend. I wasn't sure if anyone else would do it. Jimmy left Liverpool a long time ago. I don't know where he is. For all I know he may be dead. Hank's parents died many years ago. I don't think he has any family left here in Liverpool except maybe a distant cousin or two but they wouldn't know who he was. It's sad that a person could be born and live a life - even a short one like Hank's - and then be gone without anyone remembering that he was here ... that he even existed.

That was one of my biggest fears when I was younger. Would anyone remember me after I was dead? If they did, what would they remember me for? I wasn't famous and I didn't do anything special to change the world. I was just an ordinary man who lived a not-so-spectacular life. But I no longer worry about such things. I've gotten well beyond that. Now I don't give a flying fart if people remember the name Jack Webster or not. I'm going to die. We're all going to die, and that's all that matters. I figure the time has come to get on with it.

At first, since Levi was already long gone from Liverpool, me, Bunny and, surprisingly, even Ben would go to the Remembrance Day services every year down by the cenotaph in front of town hall. But in the end, I was the only one who kept going year after year to remember Hank and all those other men who died in the wars. I never forgot what it was like in those dark years. I think it's a terrible thing that the kids today will never know what those brave men and women did for all of us. Many people died so we could live the kind of life everyone now takes for granted. That's a major sacrifice and that's reason to remember someone. I always tried to remember Hank; as a friend, as a brother I never had, as a soldier and as a hero.

There's an old saying that sums up how I feel about Hank and all those other brave men and women who died over there in the wars, "Greater love has no one than this, that he lay down his life for his friends."

I think those words describe Hank and the sacrifice he made. He didn't die on the battle grounds but at least he did his part. He made a difference in someone's life. But above all that, he made amends for what we had done. That's more than I can say for some of us lazy sons-a-bitches. I can be honest about it. I was scared as hell that I might be sent over to die and I was too much of a coward to volunteer, so I stayed behind. I let people like Hank go over and take my place. I'm an old man now but I still miss his friendship. Actually, if the truth has to be told, I miss them all very much. I'd love to see them all one last time before I go. There are many things we should have said and done but they're gone and it's been left to me to do everything. I've been left to carry the entire burden and I'm getting tired from the weight.

Chapter 16

    Bunny was someone we all took for granted. He was a good friend but also the type of person you never thought much about until he was gone, kind of like your shadow. Bunny seemed to be constantly under foot, yet he would largely go unnoticed. When we were kids, then as we got older, he was always there for me but I didn't realize how important he was to me. I was twenty-seven years old when Bunny finally announced he was leaving Liverpool. His father had died a few years earlier and he had taken over the general store to help out his mother. That's what she wanted. That, and the fact that he felt it was expected of him, his duty ... a family obligation to continue the business. But it wasn't something he wanted to do with his life. I know he didn't like it much. That made him miserable. He felt he should like his job or he wouldn't do his best at it. Bunny wasn't happy in the family business. He felt trapped. He hated being stuck in the store. He wanted to work outdoors and he couldn't handle dealing with the people, especially those who thought they knew everything, like many of those small-minded people who inhabit Liverpool.

    A few years after Ruby disappeared, Bunny and Patty Fergusson got married. Don't ask me why. He was the first of us to get married but the union was destined for disaster from the start. They were not meant to be together. It lasted less than two years. One day, out of the blue, Patty told Bunny she couldn't stand it in Liverpool any longer. She needed more excitement in her life, she said. This small town was suffocating her. She told him she was leaving town and him. And that's what she did. There was no room for debate. As far as Patty was concerned, it was over. Just like that. Fortunately, their coupling hadn't produced any children. That wasn't a concern. If there would have been, however, I'm sure she would have left them with Bunny like she did the house and all the bills. She walked away from everything, leaving him to pick up the pieces. That wasn't easy for Bunny. Like the rest of us, our lives were kind of in limbo. We could never be happy. We had no right to expect happiness.

    After Patty left, Bunny broke down. He became deeply depressed and withdrawn, pulling back from his family and friends. He tried to work at the store for a few months but his heart wasn't in it. He needed a change. The day Bunny told his mother he was leaving she broke down and cried right there in the middle of the store. She was getting older and not feeling well herself. She didn't think she'd be able to handle the business on her own. Without Bunny's help she would have to sell the store and that's not what his father had worked so hard for, she argued.

    Despite all the pressure she applied, Bunny held his ground. He didn't want to see the business sold to a stranger any more than Mrs. Henderson, but he couldn't continue to live a life that was strangling him. He needed to move on and he wanted his mother's blessing. But I'm convinced he would have gone even without her support. He loved and respected his family very much but it was clear Bunny had reached his limit. He had to get away from Liverpool before the ghosts suffocated him.

Mrs. Henderson eventually came to understand that her son's heart wasn't in the business and to have forced him to remain there out of family loyalty would have been wrong. It would only have hurt him in the end and maybe he would have resented her. They eventually sold off Henderson's to someone named Mitchell who ran it into the ground in no time flat. He was partners with several other local businessmen we called the Main Street Mafia. There were five altogether and between them, they owned most of Liverpool. People thought they were crooked but I pointed out they did a lot of good for the town. No matter what you thought of them personally or their sometimes suspect business practices, the partnership did create jobs for the local people through their many operations. And no matter what I thought about that Mitchell fellow ruining the Henderson's business, he was still probably a good businessman. But he didn't know general merchandise from shit.

The first thing Mitchell did at Henderson's was to get rid of the fresh meat counter even though it had regularly brought people into the store when Sam was there. Big mistake. He lost many customers as a result. Then he did away with the bulk animal feed. Times were changing, he said, and people didn't need dry goods anymore. That was another big mistake. There were still many people around these parts with critters and if they had to go some place else to get their feed, they'd get the other supplies they needed while they were there. Mr. Mitchell paid for those bad decisions in the end. He lasted less than three years; then we saw a "closed" sign go up in the window. Old Mr. Henderson probably rolled over in his grave that day. Henderson's had been a fixture on Main Street and an anchor of commercial stability for many years. Now it was gone. Sometimes that's part of a town's aging process. Things change, old businesses close and hopefully new ones open. There haven't been many new businesses in Liverpool in recent years, particularly not good ones like Henderson's. The town hasn't been the same since they put in that highway bypass back in the eighties. I'm not sure what the future holds for Liverpool anymore than we knew what it held for us that summer when we were all so young and stupid.

With the store gone and his marriage over, Bunny had no more ties with Liverpool. He went to Toronto in search of a new start. There were too many painful memories in this town and he wanted to put his past behind him. His failed relationship with Patty had taken a terrible toll on my friend but now he seemed to be determined to turn the corner. That was a good thing. As much as I hated to see him leave, I knew he needed to make a clean break. Other than his family and a few friends, there was nothing holding him here. Mrs. Henderson was to stay at his sister's. She had finally accepted that her boy was leaving home. She understood that he was a grown man and had to get out from under his mother's thumb. That's not always easy for some men, especially when the father has died. Usually the oldest son feels compelled to carry the load, and in Bunny's case he certainly felt that way. He made sure all the loose ends were tied up with the sale of the business and he made certain his mother was taken care of, then he headed off to Ontario, to what he hoped would be a better life. Bunny didn't figure he'd have any problem landing a job in the tobacco fields or in construction. But whatever he found, he told me before he left, it wasn't going to be anything where he had to work inside. He'd had enough of that. He was ready to find an outside job so he wouldn't be cooped up all day.

It was a sad day for me when Bunny left. It was one more lost friendship for me and by now I understood that in my life, goodbye usually meant forever. With Bunny gone, that left only me and Ben here in Liverpool. And as for Ben, now that was a different story, altogether. By this time I hated going to the train station. Every time I went there, I had to say goodbye to someone close to me, and I was getting tired of sending people away. It seemed whenever they got on that train, they left Liverpool and never came back. After Bunny left, I never heard from him again. He never bothered to write but neither did I.

I often saw Mrs. Henderson and his sister with her kids around town. I would ask how Bunny was doing and they were quick to brag. It was obvious they were impressed with him and very proud, as they should have been. He was doing very well, something they were naturally glad to see after the rough time he had with Patty. It only took Bunny a couple of weeks to find a good-paying construction job building skyscrapers. And he had found a nice place to live and was meeting new people.

Although I missed him very much, I felt good that he was doing better. He deserved to be happy after what happened that summer and after the shit Patty had put him through. Finally, I thought, Bunny was enjoying the kind of good life that he had always wanted. Anything would be better than the life he had with that slut, Patty Fergusson. I didn't know it when she and Bunny broke up but the truth eventually came out ... as the truth usually does. Patty was sleeping around with many of the men in town while she was married to Bunny. It's a good thing he went away. He never would have been able to face people after the talk started. If they could have gotten their tongues around that story with Bunny in ear-shot, they would have had a field day. For some, the story would have been sweeter if Bunny had been here to torture. Yes, that would have been cruel and mean but many people in this town are like that.

But Bunny wasn't around to hear the talk and I was glad. I'll be the first to admit that I said my share of nasty things about Patty, the little whore, but I could never blame Bunny for what happened to their marriage. Some claimed Bunny was terribly cruel and mean to her, that he drove Patty to the beds of those other men. Bullshit, I said. I didn't believe that for one god-damned minute. I had known Bunny Henderson since we were kids and I knew he wouldn't hurt another living thing. His parents had raised him to be good to people and respect the feelings of others. In all the years I knew Bunny, I never saw him do or say anything bad against anyone else or raise his voice in anger toward Patty. Truth was, he often stood up for others. There was no reason to think he treated Patty any other way.

Actually, the way I saw it, Patty liked to flirt with the men. She had a reputation as an easy woman who would drop her pants for anything with two legs and a dick. From what I heard, she gave new meaning to that old saying "busier than a whore on a battleship." That's the reason I never got serious with Patty. She was very pretty and liked having a good time but I couldn't tolerate the games she played with other men. Even though I had warned Bunny early in their relationship what she was like, he ignored me. He hoped he could make her happy and if he did that, then she wouldn't have to look at any other men. It didn't turn out that way, though. Those kinds of stories only have happy endings in fairy tales. Reality is a much harsher truth.

I figured Patty had married Bunny believing he had money because his parents owned their own business. After they were married, she found out that wasn't the case. The Hendersons weren't starving but they weren't exactly rich either. They were decent, hard-working people trying to make an honest living. Patty made Bunny's life miserable from the start of their marriage and I was glad he was doing so well in Toronto. He deserved it. If nothing else, going to Toronto gave him a chance to purge her memory. At first, I knew, it was hard for him to accept but I believe getting rid of that little tramp was the smartest thing Bunny ever did. If they'd stayed together, God only knows what would have happened.

After they broke up, Patty left Liverpool and stayed away for a couple of years but she eventually came back. Most of them do. When they're young, they're hot and horny to get away from a place like this. When they grow older and get a taste of the real world, then it's a different story. Then they come crawling back with their tails between their legs. In Patty's case, it was someone else's tail.

Patty thought the world owed her something. She believed life was going to be better, more exciting in the large cities. But when she got there, she was surprised by the reality she found. She got her eyes opened. Patty stayed in Calgary for a few years. She had a tough time out there, going from one man to the next. She was even forced to work as a prostitute on and off to make ends meet. Eventually she slithered back to Liverpool and brought two small kids with her for the welfare to look after. She hadn't changed much in the three years she had been away, except that she looked much older and worn out.

Patty had been home less than two weeks when she wound up with one of the regulars who hung out down at the tavern, a real tough guy named Ronnie Cunningham. He was a big, ugly son-of-a-bitch known for getting into trouble, fighting, drunk driving and other small-time crimes. Ronnie was a lazy bastard. A no-good bum. He didn't work much; just enough on the fishing boats to draw unemployment, which he pissed away on booze and drugs. He couldn't give Patty and her kids much of a life. He had nothing to offer. The four of them lived in a small, two-bedroom mobile home on the outskirts of town. Patty and Ronnie became well-known for their wild parties. Those two small kids saw more in their young lives than most adults have ever seen. It was a sin for the youngsters but Patty didn't think of anyone else but herself. She never did.

After a few months, word got around that Patty was neglecting her children and the welfare people stepped in, placing them in foster homes. I was glad to hear they rescued the youngsters from their tormented lives. God knows what would have become of them if they hadn't been removed from that trashy environment. But losing her children didn't bother Patty. It gave her the freedom to party all the more without having kids to get in the way.

They had to break up the two kids - a boy aged four and a girl almost three - but they both ended up in good homes. When the kids grew up, they went on to do well for themselves. For once, the system worked. Sometimes when kids are taken from an environment where they have been abused and neglected, their lives are all screwed up. I'm glad that didn't happen to those two kids. For some reason, I think Bunny would have been proud of the youngsters even though they weren't his. But I want to share a secret with you that I have never told anyone before. I have a few of those secrets and here's one. I always thought the oldest kid, the boy, looked something like Bunny, especially around the eyes. He had the same colour hair as Bunny and the same dimple on his right cheek. The children looked nothing alike. But Patty denied the boy was Bunny's. She maintained both kids' father lived in Calgary. But if you do the math, from the time she left Liverpool and then returned home, she could have been a month or two pregnant when she and Bunny split up. At times, when you looked at the kid in a certain way, he looked an awful lot like Bunny. It was sort of spooky. But we'll never know the truth. Patty took that secret to the grave with her. Many of Liverpool's secrets were buried in that way.

As for Patty, she got what she deserved in the end. It was no secret I didn't have much room for the bitch after she made Bunny's life so miserable. I didn't care what happened to her and I sure as hell didn't shed any tears when I heard she had been killed. Patty and Ronnie died like they lived - the hard way. Their deaths caused quite a stir around here. It gave people something else to talk about, as if they needed help finding gossip. Perhaps I shouldn't appear so pleased that someone was killed in such a terrible way but she didn't deserve to be happy after the way she used others, especially Bunny and her children. I couldn't stand to see her running around partying all the time. I especially hated when she used the welfare money to buy booze and cigarettes for herself and Ronnie while her kids didn't have decent clothes to wear or food in their bellies. That wasn't right and it turned my stomach to think that a parent could do something so terrible.

Patty and Ronnie had been partying hard that night - it was the Christmas Eve of 1962. They were drinking heavy and doing lots of drugs until they passed out. The next thing we heard was the fire trucks racing out of town to Miller's Point. By the time the trucks got there, that little mobile home was fully engulfed in flames and black smoke. Nothing could have survived in that inferno.

Although the firemen arrived in record time, nothing could be saved. Rescue crews knew Patty and Ronnie were both still inside but they were out of reach. It was so cold that night that the water froze in the hoses. All that was left to do was stand by and watch the flames burn themselves out. There probably wasn't anything the fire fighters could have done to save them anyway. The idiots were most likely dead long before the fire department got there. The next morning, Christmas Day, the firemen and policemen had a most unpleasant job. They had to leave their families to go out in the freezing cold and dig out what was left of Patty and Ronnie. It was a gruesome task. It must have been hard sifting through all those ashes and burned junk. It had snowed shortly before sunrise leaving the ground covered, just to make matters worse. It wasn't a pretty sight. The pair had been burned to a crisp. Maybe it's mean to say, but people weren't shocked or even sad at what happened to Patty and Ronnie, except that everyone was glad the kids had been removed before the fire. If anything, people said they were surprised it hadn't happened sooner. Patty and Ronnie had been heading for trouble for many years. They finally caught up to it that Christmas.

Poor Old Bunny. I'm not sure how he would have reacted if he'd still been alive to hear of Patty's death. I know he would have been sad that she had died in such a terrible way. He would have felt sorry that Patty's life had turned out so miserably. Despite the pain Patty had caused him, I never heard Bunny speak one bad word about her in all the years I knew him. He always kept a special place in his heart for her, even if she didn't deserve it. For some reason that I can't understand, he never held a grudge against her. That was the Bunny I knew. That was typical of how he treated others. But Bunny wasn't alive that Christmas. He had died a few years back when he fell from a scaffolding while working on a high-rise apartment building.

According to the official report, Bunny and the other men weren't wearing safety harnesses. They didn't have a chance once the ropes let go. You couldn't get away with that these days with all the government health and safety regulations but back then they weren't too strict with all that red tape. They were only interested in making as much money as they could and it cost dollars to be safe - so people died; casualties of another war - a war for dollars. And on the battlefield of money, greed is a powerful adversary. Bunny and two others had been welding about nine stories up when the scaffolding gave way. Authorities said it was a terrible accident. It happened fast. Supposedly there wasn't anything that could have been done to save them once the ropes came undone. They plunged to the pavement and two of them were killed instantly. Bunny was one of them. Every bone in his body was smashed from the impact. They said his body looked like jello. I hope he died on the spot, as people said. I tell myself that God wouldn't let him suffer as He has some of us. Bunny did nothing to deserve such a fate. Of the five of us, he bore the least blame. But in an instant, his dance had ended.

I can't imagine taking a fall like that. What would you be thinking on the way down? Who's face did he see? I wonder if it's true that your life flashes before your eyes when you know you're about to die? I wouldn't want to see my life again. Living through it once was hell enough.

As for the third guy that took the fall, he lived, although he probably should have died that day too. It was quite a mystery how he could have ever survived such a fall. Apparently he landed on a grassy area and that broke his fall. The grass cushioned his impact. Maybe he was luckier than Bunny and the other guy, or was he? Living for the rest of your life paralyzed from the neck down doesn't sound lucky to me. The poor fellow might have been better off if he had died there on the pavement along with the others. Instead he was forced to live the rest of his days on his back hooked up to dozens of machines. After being trapped here in this hospital bed for the past few weeks, I know what that's like. Death probably would have been a welcome respite for the poor fellow.

Sometimes you have to wonder why a compassionate God would allow such a tragedy. I've wondered about that many times since the summer Ruby Todd went missing. It's better to die quick and get it over with, rather than laying around suffering like a vegetable. Just look at me. This cancer has left me in a mess and there isn't a damned thing I can do about it. I'd sure as hell be a lot better off if I'd died right away when they first found the cancer but that didn't happen and now it don't matter how much I want to die or how much I beg for an end to this suffering. Modern medicine is a wonderful thing when you still have hope for some quality of life but when they keep you alive so you can die a slow, agonizing death, what's the use? If society has become so compassionate, why are they keeping people like me alive?

Mrs. Henderson and his sister had Bunny's body brought back home to Liverpool so they could lay him to rest next to his father in the family plot. I was glad of that. It was important for them to give Bunny a proper burial in order for them to be close to him, even in death. It wasn't a fancy funeral, simple but nice. Me and Ben were asked to be pallbearers along with four of his cousins from out of town. I've done that a few times, and I never like it. There's something unsettling about carrying one of your childhood friends to a six-foot deep hole in the ground where they'll spend the rest of eternity. That's not going to happen to me. I've asked to be cremated. That way there's nothing left to rot. It's more final, and when I'm dead I just want to be gone once and for all. I want it over and done with. I don't deserve to be remembered.

Even though I never liked being a pallbearer, I'm glad I did it for Bunny. It was the last gesture of friendship I could make toward him. We had all been such good friends, even if it seemed like a lifetime ago. For Bunny it was. Along with a few of the townspeople who remembered the Hendersons from when they ran the store and some of those bastards in town who go to every funeral for something to gossip about the next morning over tea, there wasn't any more than twenty or twenty-five people at Bunny's funeral. The poor turnout for his funeral made me think that Bunny hadn't had much of an impact when he was alive. Could it be that such lives are wasted? I felt bad for his mother and sister. I'm sure they would have been expecting to see more of the townspeople there. The Hendersons had lived in Liverpool all their lives. The family had been an important part of the town's fabric for many years. In a way, the town let the Hendersons down and that's unforgivable.

I was glad, though, that Mrs. Henderson had insisted on bringing his body back to Liverpool so we could say goodbye. I remember how hard it was to let one friend go without a proper funeral and I didn't want to have to do that again. As the six of us stood beside the open grave next to the casket containing Bunny's body, I couldn't help but think about Hank. I remembered the pain I felt with losing such a close friend, and now I was doing it all over again. When I attend a funeral, my mind wanders, trying to block out the reality of the moment. I'm sure most people do that. My thoughts drifted that day in September. My eyes scanned the small group gathered there around the grave site. Hypocrites, I thought. Most of them were at the funeral more for gossip than to pay their final respects to a grieving family. From the mourners, if you can call them that, my eyes rested on Bunny's mother and sister. I was shocked to realize how old Mrs. Henderson had become. Her hair was nearly all grey and her eyes were shallow. I couldn't help but think she wasn't long for this world. A revelation such as that during a funeral drives home your own mortality and I shuddered at the very thought.

A funeral is the last place you want to be when thoughts of your own death start invading your mind. I get goose bumps just talking about it. The cemetery was dreary and quiet that day. I remember wondering why there were no birds, other than a single crow on a nearby branch. The Henderson family plot wasn't far from where my parents were buried. As I was thinking about how badly I missed them I saw a movement in a distant corner of the graveyard. At first I couldn't tell who it was but as I stared at the dark figure leaning up against a large, old oak tree, I could feel a cold, icy wave wash up over my entire body from the tips of my toes to the very top of my head. It was him. It took me a few seconds to realize it but the dark figure was him; the same man I had seen standing at the foot of my bed the night before my Old Man died. My heart skipped a beat and my breath caught in my throat. I leaned over to ask Ben if he saw the man in black over there by the tree but when I turned back, the mysterious figure was gone. I had only taken my eyes off the tree for a second to get Ben's attention but the man in black had disappeared.

"What's the matter?" Ben asked. "Are you all right? You look like you're about to pass out. Did you see a ghost? You'd better be careful. You don't want to end up in that hole before Bunny gets in there."

The morbid bastard. I didn't bother to answer. What would I tell him? That I had seen a ghost? That I had seen a forerunner? Maybe he didn't believe in such things but I sure as hell did. Did it mean someone else was going to die? Was it a message from my past? When I left the cemetery after the funeral that day, I was exhausted. I sensed some disaster was going to strike. It's a feeling I've experienced many times in my life.

With Bunny in the ground, some of the small group of mourners returned to his sister's house for tea. An intimate group of people gathered, giving us a chance to talk casually. We didn't dwell on the way things had gone for Bunny in his short life. That would have been too hard on Mrs. Henderson and his sister. People talked about the "good old times," whatever in the hell they were.

But that day was also an important one for another reason. After Bunny's funeral, me and Ben found the chance to step outside for a few minutes. We needed to catch up on each other. It was long overdue. Neither of us should have allowed our friendship to deteriorate the way it had but life moves on and sometimes people fall out of touch. Ben and me were like that, even though we still lived in the same small town where you'd think it would be impossible for good friends to become strangers.

Chapter 17

Despite our common pasts and shared memories, me and Ben grew further and further apart in the years after that summer Ruby Todd went missing. Nothing was ever the same between us. He became very distant and grew angry at everyone. Bunny, and Hank before he went to war, hadn't seen Ben all that much after the search for Ruby Todd was called off. As for Levi, he had gone away. They couldn't - or wouldn't - keep in touch. You never knew from one minute to the next how Ben was going to react in any given situation. He had an explosive, mean streak that ran deep and a quick temper that cut to the core when he got pissed off. You add liquor to that mix and it was spontaneous combustion. When we were young, we learned to deal with Ben's unpredictable personality. Ben could be nice and friendly one minute and then, in the blink of an eye, he could turn on you, sometimes for no good reason. He had a volatile disposition and didn't take kindly to being pushed against the wall, even if it was often only in his imagination.

Ben was nasty when he got in such a foul mood. It was better to avoid him when he got like that. It was useless to argue with Ben because he always thought he was right. He would never concede an argument. When Ben couldn't beat you with words, then he'd turn violent. I didn't like that. Maybe that's why we drifted apart despite our childhood friendship. The fact that we were the only ones left back here in Liverpool didn't seem to count for much. That would not have been a good excuse to stay friends, anyway. That day following Bunny's funeral, however, Ben wanted to talk and I took him up on it. I recognized it as a chance to get caught up. Maybe it was the death of our mutual friend but he seemed vulnerable; almost like a small child after a scolding from his parents. I was surprised when he opened up. He wasn't known for his conversational skills or for expressing his feelings but he did that day.

"It hasn't been easy," he said. "I've got a pretty good job down at the yard. The money's good but I'm still having a tough time making ends meet with all the bills. I don't know how other people do it."

I could have suggested he could save some money by laying off the booze but I kept my opinion to myself. Despite his financial hardships, though, Ben considered himself lucky to have found such a wonderful woman to make his home with. It was evident from how he spoke that Ben was unhappy, and I didn't know what to do about it.

After the summer of 1940, Ben started a fulltime job at the shipyard working on the boats. It was honourable work and Ben threw himself into it. There was no doubt that he was a dedicated, hard worker. Everyone said so. The shipyard's the only place he ever worked. They kept him on even when they had mass layoffs after the war ended and contracts slacked off. He was such a good worker that no one could ever argue anything to the contrary. Ben laboured at Tupper's for over twenty years and some of the men down there said he never missed a shift in all that time. That's an amazing record once you understand what Ben was really like.

Ben was no angel. In fact, he was far from it. As hard as he worked, he liked to play hard too. How many people can get off work at five o'clock, go straight to a bar and drink until the place closes at midnight? Ben did that at least four times a week. But somehow he always managed to pull himself up and off to work early the next morning. You'd think after a few years, his battery would have run down. I don't know how he ever kept pushing himself day after day. I'm sure such a pace would have killed most people but not Ben. Although, come to think of it, perhaps his hectic, carefree lifestyle might have contributed to his self-destruction. Maybe he wanted it that way. Ben could drink all weekend and still be at work Monday morning on time and ready to give his all to the job at hand. Obviously the management didn't care what he did on his own time, just as long as he showed up for work and did what they paid him to do.

Some people can consume great amounts of alcohol but yet you can't tell they've been drinking. That was Ben, unless he got mad. If he lost his temper, then you had trouble on your hands. Ben was a major hot-head when he got pissed. I sometimes wonder how he managed to stay alive as long as he did. But Ben would never admit he had a drinking problem. He had been picked up a couple of times over the years for drinking and driving but the police let him off easy. He never lost his license even though he should have on more than one occasion. But drinking and driving wasn't such a big deal back in those days, so he kept getting away with it. I'm sure Ben would never survive in today's world with these tougher laws. I wouldn't have any sympathy for him. This zero-tolerance approach is the right way to deal with drunk drivers and I'd feel the same way if they caught one of my friends or one of my family. Anyone who gets behind the wheel after they've been drinking deserves the toughest penalties available and I don't care who it is.

After Ben went his own way, I'd see him about town every now and then. Sometimes we'd talk, most times we didn't. Usually, he wouldn't even let on he'd seen me. We were never close again after that summer of Ruby's disappearance. He mostly kept to himself and I got busy with my own life. So we drifted apart but I still managed to keep track of him. I heard stories from people who knew what Ben was up to. Liverpool was a small town and it wasn't hard to know somebody else's business. Usually, you didn't even have to ask, particularly with someone like Ben. He always provided the townsfolk plenty to talk about. Knowing Ben, he probably did some of the shit just to keep the rumour mill turning. That would be his style.

Ben eventually moved in with a girl by the name of Rachael Woodsworth. It's hard to picture such a nice young girl with a heavy drinker like Ben had become but for some reason she was attracted to him. Rachael was six or seven years younger than Ben but she grew up here in Liverpool. She was a hometown girl who never lost sight of where she came from. She was pleasant and content with life in this small town. People said she was too good for Ben and maybe she was. I don't judge that sort of thing and I wish others wouldn't either.

I don't know how Ben and Rachael met but somehow they ended up with each other. Maybe it was love or something else like it. Maybe it was destiny or fate but through some quirk in nature they found each other. Despite Ben's drinking and the way that made him behave, she fell for him. They never got legally married but lived together in common law. That arrangement may have contributed to the problems in their marriage. That, and the fact that Ben was an alcoholic with a short fuse. Their pairing didn't sit well with Rachael's parents. The Woodsworths, who made their money by selling timber off the family woodlots - and they had a great deal of property around the county - weren't one of Liverpool's richest families but they weren't one of the poorest either. Naturally, they had hoped Rachael would find a nice, respectable young man, settle down and raise a family. They never expected Rachael to end up with a bum like Ben, as they were so fond of calling him. It surprised me too that the son-of-a-bitch could attract such a sweet, innocent girl but who can say what attracts people to each other? Rachael's family let it be known they didn't take kindly to the pair shacking up together. They refused to accept Ben into their family. Their relationship was doomed to failure from the very beginning. It was hard on Rachael that her parents wouldn't have anything to do with Ben. Maybe if they would have made him feel more welcome, things might have turned out differently. It shouldn't have mattered who she ended up with, as long as she was happy. But parents only want what's best for their kids and, of course, parents always know what that is.

There's no question Ben wasn't the best thing for Rachael but her parents should have tried to make the most of it instead of becoming part of the problem. On the surface, the two seemed as though they were getting along. The truth is, you never actually know what goes on behind closed doors of someone else's house. Back in the sixties you never heard much talk about wife abuse and domestic violence. It wasn't proper to talk about what other people did in the privacy of their own homes. That was their business. We foolishly believed it was best to mind our own affairs and let everyone else take care of themselves. We soon found out it shouldn't always be that way.

Ben and Rachael had been together for a few years when the rumours started that he was beating her. People reported seeing black and blue marks on her body. She always said she hit herself with a door or fell down the stairs or something like that. It was the typical response. She always had an explanation or excuse for the bruises or the limping. Everyone believed what she said, no questions asked. Besides, who would have ever thought that a husband would inflict such injuries on his wife? But when Rachael began pulling away from her friends and family, especially her sister Martha, those close to her finally recognized something wasn't right. Still, she wouldn't talk to anyone. Despite their suspicions, no one knew how bad things had become between Rachael and Ben. And I'm not sure what anyone would have done about it anyway, even if they had known.

Ben and Rachael had one child, a son, named Billy. Eventually it appears things got so bad that Rachael must have had enough of his drinking and other foolishness. Or maybe she was afraid for herself and the boy but whatever it was it all reached the boiling point one night in March 1964. The Mounties later said it was a real mess. Actually, I still can't believe what happened. I find it hard to accept that Ben would do anything like they claim he did but I never tried to make excuses for him. I had seen him in action and I knew of his quick temper. After their investigation, police told a horrific story that people are still talking about today. It seemed too sensational to be true but sadly, it was. It was one of Liverpool's darkest moments. Even today it's too horrible to forget and too painful to remember.

Police were called to the house by a neighbour who heard a gunshot. Based on what they found at the scene, police said it looked as if Ben and Rachael had a fight that night. They said there was broken glass throughout the house and furniture strewn everywhere ... and blood. There was lots of blood. We later learned that Martha told the police Rachael had been planning to leave Ben. He had been beating her and in the end had been hitting the boy. Martha claimed Rachael had told her Ben was drinking more heavily and she couldn't stand it anymore. She was afraid Ben would hurt her or, worse yet, that he would hurt Billy. Ben would seem fine one minute and then, out of the blue, he would snap and lose control of himself. He became someone else ... someone she didn't know. He became someone she feared. When that happened, Martha told police, Rachael believed Ben was capable of doing just about anything. She felt her only protection was to get away from him but back then it wasn't normal or even practical for women to leave their men. How would she survive? Where would she go? If she went back to her parents' house, he would surely go there looking for her. Besides, people actually believed the man was the lord and master of the house and that women should be seen and not heard. A little slap or kick in the butt every now and then was just what a woman needed to keep her in line and that was acceptable, or at least that's what some people thought in those days.

In the eyes of those who lived then in this backwater town it would have been an awful thing for Rachael to have left her husband. Naturally, everyone would have felt bad for Ben. They would have blamed Rachael for the failed relationship and would have found a few select labels for her. There's no doubt that she would have been ostracized and ridiculed in a cruel, mean way. That night, though, police figured it finally came to a head and that Rachael most likely had told Ben she was leaving. What happened next is really just speculation. Police said based on their investigation of the crime scene they were able to reconstruct the violent events as they had taken place. They said the detonation point obviously came in the kitchen. They believed that's where Rachael must have confronted Ben with her decision to leave. Police figured Ben exploded in a fit of rage and lost all control of his senses. I figure he was so pissed he blew his freaking top like I'd seen him do many times in the past. I think Ben went crazy that night and struck out at the first thing he could get his hands on. Apparently that was Rachael. He had to be insane for him to do something so horrible.

From their investigation, police said it was clear that a terrible fight had taken place that night and in the process Ben was somehow stabbed by a kitchen knife. They said it was only a small steak knife but they found a wound in the left side of Ben's chest and there was a knife on the kitchen floor with traces of blood. Tests later confirmed it was Ben's. They said it didn't look as if Rachael was attempting to kill her husband but maybe trying to protect herself. Anyway, they said Ben must have snapped and chased Rachael through the house as she ran for her life. They found Rachael's body in the living room covered in blood. She had been stabbed twenty-seven times and her throat had been slit almost from ear to ear, nearly taking her head off. Police painted a gruesome picture. Lying beside her body police found Ben's favourite hunting knife. It was the same knife I had seen him use the few times we had gone deer hunting when we were younger. His grandfather had taught him how to cut a deer's throat so he could "bleed" the animal. When his grandfather died, he left Ben the knife and I know he treasured it. He carried it with him all the time on his belt. It was sad to think that he would use the weapon in such a violent way.

I can't picture any man doing anything so terrible to a woman, or anybody, no matter how mad he was. She was the mother of his son. How could he do that? It was so brutal and cold-blooded that I found it difficult to comprehend how even an insane person could inflict that much damage on someone else. It left the entire community in shock. We were all numb. It wasn't a planned murder, police said. More like Ben had kept stabbing Rachael over and over and over like you would do in a mad rage. But that wasn't the worst of it.

No one knows why he did it. Everyone who knew Ben said he loved his son more than his own life. They said that love was evident when the father and son were together. Ben truly cherished his child but there wasn't any love in Ben that night. There couldn't have been. Police found the boy's body in his bed where he must have been hiding as the fight raged outside his bedroom door. We can only imagine how scared the boy must have been hearing that racket and the screaming. It must have been god-awful for the little guy cowering there under his covers as his mother was stabbed to death. They found him with the sheets pulled up to his chin or what was left of it. He had died instantly from a single gunshot wound to the face. There was no explanation then, and there is none now to justify why a father would do that to his own child. We'll never know what Ben was thinking when he fired the shot that ended young Billy's life that night. That was the saddest part of the tragedy. The kid was only six and still had his whole life to live.

No one can explain what possessed Ben that night. It defies all logic. But some forensic psychologist later put forward two theories in hopes of helping the community heal. Without knowing the family dynamics, the doctor explained it is impossible to say for sure why a parent kills his or her child. In Ben's case, he said, it would seem logical that the father killed his son for one of two reasons - either that he could not stand the thought of someone else raising his son in the absence of the biological parents, or that he was so confused and delusional that he believed the best way to protect Billy from the same tormented life that he had led was to put him out of his misery. It's very likely Ben knew what he was doing when he pulled the trigger but felt he was doing what was best for the child. It's hard to imagine a parent doing such a terrible thing but who am I to question the theories of such a qualified professional?

As for Ben, police found his body slumped over in a pool of blood on the cold basement floor. He had shot himself. Apparently, after he had killed Rachael and the boy, he must have figured his life was worthless and that he had nothing to live for. Police said it was the same gun he had used to kill Billy. After the carnage that unfolded in the main level of the house, Ben went down in the basement where he sat on the damp cement floor with his back propped up against the washing machine. It's not clear how long he sat there and no one knows what was going through his head at that point but finally, in one last act of desperation, Ben put the barrel of the rifle into his mouth, pulled the trigger and blew his brains out. The blast was so powerful that it damned near blew his head completely off. The poor bastard never knew what hit him. He probably never felt a thing once the gun fired. It's a good thing he killed himself that night. If he wouldn't have, I'm sure someone else would have done it for him. A deep river of hate ran through Liverpool after word of the murders got around.

Ben obviously felt remorse of some sort. He left a note. Police found it in his shirt pocket, covered with blood. It simply read: "I hope you're happy, Ruby." The note had been hastily scrawled in pencil. You can bet there was a great deal of speculation around this town about what that note actually meant. Many of the people in town at that time didn't even know who Ruby was. But I knew. And I understood Ben's message. He had been dancing with the dead for too many years and he finally snapped. "There, but for the Grace of God go I," I remember thinking.

I felt like a piece of me had died when I finally heard news of the tragedy. I was working at the mill by this time and had been on the late shift that night. I was just finishing up when one of the replacement workers arrived fifteen minutes before his six o'clock shift. He asked if I had heard about the commotion over at Ben's. Naturally I hadn't since I had worked through the night but I made a bee-line over there just as soon as I finished work. Instead of going straight home, I seemed to be pulled to Ben's place where five RCMP cruisers, a coroner's van and dozens of onlookers had gathered. It was raining hard that morning - pouring cats and dogs as my mama was fond of saying. Once I arrived, it was all I could do to keep myself together. I felt as if I wanted to jump out of my skin and run and hide in the nearest, deepest manhole. I hurt so bad on the inside that I wanted to throw up as my stomach flip-flopped from side to side. And my head felt like it was in a vice, squeezing my life away.

The flashing red lights on top of the police cars were hypnotic as they reflected in the wet, morning air. The lights were a beacon for all the pain and sorrow that existed in our world. My head was swimming. I felt as if I could pass out. I couldn't believe what had just happened. Disbelief. Shock. Disgust. Sadness. Remorse. Anger. Confusion. ... Responsibility. I felt all of these emotions, and more, as I stood for hours outside the once cosy, brown bungalow and watched as police officers in their blue plastic-like protective gear came and went. Finally, they performed the grisly task of removing the bodies from the blood-stained house. First they brought out Rachael, then little Billy. There was a united gasp of disbelief and a chorus of sobs from the crowd as a lone officer carried the remains of young Billy in a small black body bag. My knees went weak and my legs all but buckled under me. It was almost another hour before they brought out Ben's body, and when they did the crowd went silent.

The only sounds I could hear as they carried Ben's remains past the dazed crowd was the endless tap, tap, tap of the rain splashing down on the wet, black asphalt. My heart was beating fifty miles an hour, as if it was going to explode in my chest. My head was pounding like someone was hitting my brains with a hammer. I was in a state of shock. There he was, the last of my childhood friends. Gone. They were all gone now. I wondered why all my friends had died such tragic, horrible deaths.

As I watched the officers load Ben's body into the back of the black panel van, images of my long-lost friends flashed before me ... Ben, Hank, Bunny and Levi. How had our lives' journeys gotten us to this point? Even after the crowd started to thin out, I lagged behind for what seemed an eternity, fixated by the bungalow that had been the site of such terrible bloodshed ... and then, suddenly, there he was again.

Sure as I was standing there in front of the house of death, so was the mysterious man in black. Like a quiet sentinel he had come again, only this time I recognized his form immediately as he appeared, out of nowhere, on the front doorstep. He stood still for a minute, maybe two, his face unrecognizable in the shadows. It seemed as though he was staring directly through me. His eyes went right to my very soul. Then the tall dark figure in his now-familiar trademark long black overcoat and large-brimmed hat, slowly and deliberately, like he was floating on thin air, went inside through the open front door. It was only a matter of seconds but sure enough, he had been there. I'm sure I wasn't imagining things. Even in my emotional state, I knew what I saw.

The cold icy fingers that I had felt too many times before over the years, once again made their journey up my spine until I could feel the tiny hairs on the back of neck standing straight up. It's a sensation I don't like. I was stunned, unable to move a muscle. It was like I was frozen in time but eventually I regained my composure as my curiosity was aroused. Who was this mysterious man who seemed to follow me whenever I was in despair? What did he want from me? I just had to know.

The house was still cordoned off with a police line. Naturally I couldn't get in. Police officers also guarded the crime scene to keep out nosey people like me. Upon questioning two officers about who was still inside, I was told rather sternly that it was none of my business but then, out of some act of compassion, they informed me that the investigation had wrapped up for that morning. No one, they assured me, was in the house.

Wrong, I thought. Someone was, indeed, in the house, only I didn't know who, and I wasn't going to find out that morning.

It wasn't easy to feel sorry for Ben but I did. Naturally, everyone in town grieved for Rachael and the boy, as I did. I hated it that Ben could do something so evil but I couldn't help thinking about Ben and wondering what in the hell could push him to the boiling point that he would do something so violent as kill his only child. Loving parents don't do that no matter how desperate or stressed out they get. Ben and I had grown up together. I thought I knew him. Obviously, I didn't. How had his life gotten him to that terrible night? It didn't make sense to me back then and it still doesn't, even after all these years. Christ, me and Ben were together through a lot of things as kids and I never would have guessed he was capable of doing something so horrible.

Rachael's family buried her and little Billy side by side in the family plot out in the Anglican cemetery on Bog Road but they sure as hell weren't having anything to do with Ben. Couldn't blame them after what he had done. His sister, Beth, took care of all his arrangements. If Bunny's funeral was a sad affair, Ben's was beyond words. Beth was there. His mother had long since passed away. There was me along with a couple of other guys he worked with down at the shipyards, and that was it. Beth didn't have much money to spend on an expensive funeral for her brother and since he had killed himself, she couldn't collect any insurance money to help pay for it. So it wasn't a fancy affair. That wouldn't have been proper anyway considering what Ben had done. The coffin was appropriately a plain, black box. A single bunch of yellow daisies rested on top with a little white tag that said "Brother" on it. It's strange that I remember a minor detail like that but when something tragic happens, I think your mind focuses on the little things to keep you grounded.

Ben was buried about two years after Bunny but their funerals kind of blend together in my mind. From where I was standing that day for Ben's burial, I could see Bunny's grave and the fresh flowers left there just recently by his mother and sister. As the minister performed the committal and asked God to forgive Ben for the evils that his weak, human mind had allowed him to commit, my thoughts drifted back to Hank who had been buried years earlier some place over in England and of Levi up in Ontario somewhere, separated by time and space. We had all been kindred spirits, connected by our pasts and a friendship that had been stretched and pulled beyond natural limits. Now I stood alone.

After Ben died I was like a sole castaway lost here in Liverpool, adrift on a stormy sea of memories. Levi had never returned and Hank had died a long time ago and was buried some place far away. They had been gone so long that most people in Liverpool had forgotten they had even existed. Bunny had been killed and buried a few years back, and now Ben was gone. That was a rough time for me. Not only trying to put Ben's actions into perspective but also struggling to come to grips with being the last survivor of our group. The town was changing in many ways and now all my childhood companions were gone. We had drifted apart and that separation made me uneasy and sick to my stomach. It was like I was walking alone in some dark, scary place. It was creepy and depressing. I wasn't sure if I would be able to escape from that mysterious place where ghosts have taken up permanent residence.

Even though I was married and had my own family by that time, I still felt very lonely. But my life story is better left for another day. I'm tired now. I would like to rest but I hope you will come back so I can finish my story. There's lots more to tell.

Chapter 18

Where have you been? I've been awake since early this morning with no one to talk to. It's depressing when you're alone in this place.

Yesterday, you wanted to know what happened in my life after that hot summer when Ruby Todd went missing. If you still want to hear it, I could run through it quickly for you.

I've lived in Liverpool my entire life. In fact, I have never been past Halifax. I like this little town very much, even though sometimes it does get on my nerves. It's got a lot of character, and many secrets.

As the guys started to leave home, I decided that if I was going to stay here in Liverpool, then it was time for me to settle down. I had to put things in their proper perspective and get on with living. You could have a good life in a place like Liverpool if you didn't expect too much. It also helped if you caught a few lucky breaks and if you met the right people. I was fortunate enough to eventually meet the right person for me. In fact, she was the most important person I ever met in my entire life.

I was twenty-three when I really noticed Victoria Wright for the first time. The Wrights had lived in Liverpool for many years. I had seen the girl around town and thought she was pleasant, but I never paid her any attention until she started working at J.P.s. She was five years younger than me, and that's probably why I ignored her as she was growing up. I remember her as a flat-chested, skinny kid with knobby knees and reddish blond hair. She was kind of tomboyish as a child. As she matured though, she blossomed into a beautiful young woman and I finally realized what I had been overlooking. There, in front of my eyes all those years, had been the woman I was going to marry. From that first day when she walked up to the booth where I was sitting and took my order, I knew she was the one for me.

I remember our first conversation. Every word, just as if it was yesterday.

"And what would you like today?" Her voice was sweet but I can't say I had ever really paid her much attention. That morning wasn't much different until the games began.

"Just coffee." I was on my way to work and wasn't hungry. Sliding into my favourite booth, I quickly ordered and settled in to get caught up on the day's news as I did every morning. Listening to the gossip in the soda shoppe was more informative than any newspaper could ever hope to be. The place was like a beehive with everyone talking all at once.

"You'll have two sugars and milk in that, right?"

This girl was amazing. She had only been waiting on tables for a few days at J.P.s and had never taken my order before but she knew how I liked my coffee. It may seem like an over-reaction but I was impressed.

"How did you know that?" I asked. "Who's been telling you my secrets?" For some reason I instantly felt comfortable with her.

She continued to play games, shrugging off my question as if it wasn't important to her. "Don't really know," she answered with a sheepish grin. "Guess a little birdie told me."

I never learned how she knew the way I liked my coffee. Maybe one of the other girls told her. But her playful manner caught my attention. I thought it was a sweet gesture that she would have gone to so much trouble to find out something about me even before we met. When she brought the coffee, I couldn't resist asking her out for a date. It probably was forward in those days to think she would go out with me. But what the hell, I thought, going with the impulse.

"Why Jack Webster, I don't know if I can," she answered. "I don't know you all that well and you're so much older than me. What would people think if I went out on a date with a working man your age who has so much experience?"

"Experience?" I shot back with a self-assured smile. I was feeling pretty high on myself even though I knew she was exaggerating. In truth, I had only ever dated once before. That was Patty Fergusson. It was clear this girl in the coffee shop was having me on. "Who's been spreading stories about me?" I played along. "Don't believe everything you hear, young lady. As for age, well, that doesn't mean anything. And besides, you owe it to yourself."

"Excuse me?" she said. She pretended to be surprised but I knew she was hooked. "I owe it to myself? You are a cocky one. Maybe your reputation isn't so far off the mark after all."

"Not at all," I argued. "You owe it to yourself to get to know the man you're going to marry."

"Whatever are you talking about, Jack Webster?" It was obvious she enjoyed this verbal sparring very much and quickly rose to the challenge.

"I know I haven't paid you much attention in the past, Victoria Wright, but that's about to change. I'm noticing you now. I hope you don't mind me saying but I like what I see very much. At least give me a chance to show you what I'm really like."

"I'll have to think about it." With that, she turned and left to wait on customers at a nearby booth. Over the next half hour, as I nursed my coffee and observed her going about her duties, I could see her watching me from the corner of her eye. She tried pretending she wasn't interested but her actions told me otherwise.

Finally, she came back to my booth. "Will there be anything else this morning, Mr. Webster?"

"No, thanks," I replied, fully expecting to get her answer. Instead, she quickly turned and walked off. She played this game very well. I liked her style.

Five minutes later she returned and placed my bill face down on the table and then, before I had a chance to ask her if she had thought about my date proposal, she beat another hasty retreat to a nearby booth and some new customers who had just come in.

I was dumbfounded; disappointed by her lack of interest and put out that she hadn't had the decency to give me a straight answer. If she didn't want to go out with me, she could have just said so instead of leaving me hanging.

I sat there for maybe another ten or fifteen minutes thinking she would come back but she didn't. Finally, I had to leave. My shift was about to start and I always prided myself at being on time. I was frustrated, maybe even a little angry, at being shunned by a pretty young woman. But upon flipping over the bill I found myself smiling again. Written in red ink, the bill said "Paid in full. Pick me up at seven."

I chuckled and left J.P.s with a grin on my face that must have gone from ear to ear. I tucked that little piece of paper away for safe keeping. And you know what? I still have it stashed away in a corner of my wallet. Go on. Get my wallet. It's over there in the drawer. Go get it and take a look.

There. I told you I still had it after all these years. It's a little ratted around the edges but it's still there, just like my love for Victoria is safely stashed in a corner of my heart. She was a special woman. No one has ever touched me the way she did. I miss her very much.

I was still working at Tupper's when me and Vic started dating. That's what I called her sometimes. She didn't like it much. She said if her parents had wanted her to be called Vic or Vicky, that's what they would have named her. She hated nicknames. I used to do it just to bug her but she knew it was all in fun, another one of our little games.

I remember our first date. I was so shy and nervous that I could hardly get out of my own way. I desperately wanted to make a good impression on her. Vic was different from the other girls I knew. I felt deep down inside that I had to treat her special. She deserved it.

Like me, she was an only child and her parents were protective of her.

They wanted Victoria to be happy and they promised they wouldn't interfere with her life; that they would allow her to make her own decisions and her own mistakes, as long as she carefully thought things through. They were honest and friendly people who put their daughter's health and happiness ahead of everything else. I liked Vic's parents from the first time we met. They told Victoria that no matter what happened, she was always welcome in their home. It was clear to me they deeply loved Victoria and they had a good relationship.

The war had just ended so money was tight. In those days, we had to make a good time the old-fashioned way. There were no fancy theatres or bars. That wouldn't have been for us anyway. Vic was a simple girl. That's one of the things I liked about her. She didn't pretend to be something she wasn't. Our first date was memorable. It was a hot night in July and we went to a ball game down at the old field that used to be located near the swamp and the main road. There's a grocery store on the site now. Baseball was a big game around here at that time. Liverpool played teams from all over the South Shore and our local boys were actually quite good. There was one spell when they went all the way to the provincials and won the championship two times in a row. A few of the boys were even scouted by major league teams. They played some exciting ball and everybody got behind the team. We all went to the games to support the boys when they played at home.

I liked baseball a lot. It's always been my favourite sport, though I never played it myself. One of the highlights of my life was the day Babe Ruth came to town. The slugger himself; the Home Run King right here in this little backwater town. I heard about the Babe on the radio and read all about him in the newspapers. I knew the legend. He was playing with the Yankees at that time and he was in Nova Scotia on some kind of publicity tour. I was only young but I remember it was a big day when Babe Ruth came to Liverpool. Imagine that, the best baseball player of all time coming to this little place because he had heard so much about the good baseball we played here. I'm still impressed by that. He was something to see. A giant of a man, almost as big as his legend, and he was genuinely cordial to everyone he met. There has never been another one like Babe Ruth, and there never will be. I liked the way he played the game. He was honest about his approach, and he never took it too seriously. He went out on the field and played the game the way it was meant to be played. I sometimes wonder what he'd think about the game today if he was alive. He played for peanuts compared to what these guys are getting today, and none of them are worth it. You tell me if any single man is worth ten million dollars a year to play a game. I don't think so. Imagine what a real player like Babe Ruth would be worth by today's standards. It's staggering to think about.

The night of our first date I went by the Wrights' home just before seven o'clock to pick up Victoria, like the note had instructed. As she came down the front staircase in the entry-way, she looked radiant. Her hair was down, falling onto her shoulders. I was breathless and weak in the knees. My heart skipped a beat and my head felt as light as a balloon. The waitresses had to wear their hair up in ponytails under nets at J.P.s for health reasons. That was the first time I noticed how long hers really was. It was lovely. The Wrights' house was nestled under a tiny grove of chestnut trees down by the river but it's gone now like a lot of other things around here. The town council bought the house and tore it down fifteen or twenty years ago so they could put that sewage pumping station on the property. Shame, really. But I guess that's what you call progress.

Victoria was ready when I got there. After some quick introductions to her parents, we were off. She seemed happy, practically bubbling with excitement. In a lot of ways, she reminded me of a small child going to the candy store for the first time. As we walked to the ballfield, she confessed this was her first date with an older man. She had been out with boys her own age but this was the first time she had agreed to date someone of my "maturity level" as she jokingly put it. Her honesty and natural beauty won over my heart during the first five minutes of our date. It felt right being with Victoria. It was like we belonged together, as if fate had made it possible for us to find each other. I couldn't believe my good fortune.

We had a great time that night. I enjoyed Victoria's company very much and while I knew I had already fallen head over heels in love with her, we used the opportunity to get to know each other better. We laughed and talked about what we wanted to do someday. We shared our goals, our hopes and dreams, our likes and dislikes. There was an instant connection. Vic wasn't a big dreamer. She made it clear that she was perfectly content to stay in Liverpool where she hoped to get married, find a nice home and have children, if God was willing. That was fine by me, I told her. Victoria wasn't much for trying to chart a course for her future. She said a person's life should unfold as it's meant to happen; lives should evolve and develop. Having too many plans wasn't healthy, she believed. For some people, those dreams become obsessions and if they don't realize them, then they feel like failures. Victoria felt that too many people lose too much of their lives trying to plan their way instead of letting things happen as God intended them to. I don't think there's anything wrong with people setting goals for themselves but Vic had a point. She firmly believed in that old philosophy that what will be, will be. No amount of scheming could alter the plan that God has for each of us.

"You cannot avoid your fate or your future no matter how much you scheme and maneuvre," Victoria said matter-of-factly. I learned a great deal about Victoria that night. I knew I could be content making my life with her. You might call it love but it was something more than that. It was much deeper. The connection went well below the surface. My love for Victoria was true and honest. There was a bond that drew us together. She recognized it that night as well.

We were at the ball game a couple of hours and watched the hometown chalk up another victory. Afterward we went to J.P.s for a milkshake and then I took her home at ten o'clock, like her parents had asked.

"I had a great time this evening, Jack," she whispered as we said goodnight on the front step. "You know how to make a girl feel special."

"Yeah, me too. It was great." For the first time in my life, I was nearly speechless.

"I felt so comfortable with you tonight, Jack. Maybe, if you want, we can do it again sometime real soon."

"If I want? I'd like that a lot. When?"

"Easy, Jack. We don't have to rush. Drop by J.P.s tomorrow and we'll talk about it."

"Okay. Well, I guess I should let you go inside before your folks think I've kidnapped you or something."

"It's okay, Jack. They trust us."

"Maybe they shouldn't."

"Why do you say that, Jack?"

"No reason. But do you ever really know another person?"

"No, I guess not, especially at first. But why would you say something like that, Jack? Is everything alright? All of a sudden, you seem so far away."

"I'm fine. It's just that I was remembering something that happened a long time ago."

"What was it? Want to talk about it?"

"It was nothing really. It wasn't all that important. Just something from my past. Let's just forget about it."

"If you wish."

"I do. ... I'll see you tomorrow."

Quickly planting a light kiss on my lips, Victoria slipped inside. "I'll see you tomorrow at J.P.s," she whispered as the door snapped shut.

That first kiss was quick but it was special. From that night on, I knew Victoria and me would spend the rest of our lives together. We'd see each other two or three times a week, sometimes even more. It was like we had an instant connection. There seemed to be a special bond between us that I didn't understand, but I didn't question it. If we were meant to be together, that was fine by me. I could be myself and she accepted me for what I was. She made me feel special and I hope I made her feel the same way.

Within a few months we started talking about marriage. A year later, on

June 16, Victoria Wright became my wife.

She wanted a June wedding because her parents had been married that month. She wanted to make it a family tradition. Victoria took pleasure in explaining that it was customary for Romans to marry in June to honour Juno, the queen of the gods. Juno was also the goddess of women and the Romans believed that getting married in June would win her favour. In turn, that would make the marriage last and it would also make childbirth easier. Victoria thought the tradition was romantic and I agreed to go along with anything that would make her happy.

My wedding to Victoria was the happiest day of my life. She looked so beautiful coming down the aisle on her father's arm that I had to pinch myself to see if I was dreaming. I couldn't believe my good fortune in finding her. I often found myself shaking my head to see if the love we shared was a cruel joke, but it was very real.

It wasn't a fancy wedding. Even though Mr. Wright had a good job at the mill, money was still tight. After all, he had a house and things to look after. But while the wedding may have been simple, it was still wonderful; picture-perfect in most respects. Many people came, but mostly they were friends and relatives of the Wrights. I didn't have much family and most of my friends were gone. Bunny was my best man and Ben came for the reception. I would have been surprised if he had showed up at the church for the service. For as long back as I can remember, I don't think I ever saw Ben in church. But he came to the party afterward to be with me, and that was nice. I was glad he and Bunny were there. It proved to me that even though we had grown apart, we still had some kind of connection that would keep drawing us back into each other's lives. Little did I know that a few years later they would both be gone.

I was glad they were there on that special day. But I knew there would be trouble. Ben couldn't go anywhere without fighting. He had a knack for somehow getting into trouble. More to the truth, he was a shit disturber. He couldn't control his temper even on an important day like his friend's wedding. He thoroughly embarrassed himself that night. As usual, he was drinking heavily and he got into a fight with one of Vic's cousins over some girl I can't even remember. When Ben hooked onto a girl he demanded her full attention. Ben would get jealous if she danced with any other guy and the situation would always turn sour. He met up with this particular girl at my wedding almost from the instant he walked into the hall and they stuck together most of the time, dancing and going outside to drink. Vic's parents wouldn't allow alcohol in the church hall. They were religious people and felt it would be morally wrong to have drinking on God's property. Although I haven't been known as a heavy drinker, I didn't think a little alcohol would hurt anything but I kept my opinion to myself. I didn't want to spoil the day for Victoria. It was important to me that this day go off without a hitch. And it almost did, except for Ben.

Ben and that girl had been drinking quite heavily since the reception began. I could tell they were feeling their liquor by the way they were hanging all over each other and staggering around the hall. I should have seen it coming a mile away and asked them to leave before trouble started. It isn't hard to recognize when someone's getting drunk. Vic's cousin Frank tried to quiet things down by asking the girl to dance with him but it backfired. Before Frank knew what hit him, Ben was all over him like a dirty blanket ... fists flying, legs kicking and blood gushing. It wasn't pretty. I knew this was not going to sit well with Vic's parents. I had to stop it fast. It took some doing, but me, Bunny and a couple of other guys somehow managed to pull the two men apart and I asked Ben to leave. It's a hard thing to ask a good friend to leave your wedding reception, but I did and I'd do it again for the same reasons. I told Ben he had no right spoiling this special day for me and Victoria and suggested it would be better if he left before he caused any more trouble.

He didn't argue with me, although I'm sure he wanted to. He stood in the middle of the church hall staring at me through glassy eyes for a few minutes as blood trickled down his chin from a cracked lip. It was an intense moment. When our eyes met, I could see the anger. I really didn't know what to expect from Ben. I knew with his temper this confrontation could quickly get out of hand. I got the feeling he was pissed at me for finding happiness. It was more like envy than jealousy. Maybe he was glad the fight had happened because he wanted to ruin my day. I wouldn't like to think that a friend would do that, but you never know. I believe he was trying to tell me he didn't think it was fair I was happy while he was having such a shitty life. Then, as he picked up his torn jacket from the floor, the emotions finally boiled over and he angrily shot back at me with an intensity I hadn't seen in Ben for many years. His words were cutting and hurtful, clearly the product of years of pent-up anger.

"It's all right for you, Jack," he said. "You've found a way to be happy but some of us can't do that. Some of us haven't been able to put things out of our minds like you so conveniently seem to be able to do."

"No! You can't do that to me, Ben. I won't let you ruin this day for me. You can't blame me for your miserable life," I snapped back, feeling my own anger rushing to the surface. "It hasn't been easy for me, but you have to make yourself move on. I've had to push myself every day and I won't feel sorry for you. You have no one to blame for the way things have turned out in your life except for yourself. People always get what they deserve. You're responsible for your own actions and your own decisions. You've made your own life and regardless of how things have turned out, you've got to live it. If you don't like it, change it. If you're not happy with the way things are going for you, then do something about it. But don't come around screwing up someone else's chance at happiness. I wouldn't expect this from you today, Ben, not from a true friend."

"Friend? Huh! What in the hell do you know about being friends?" he fired back, pulling on his jacket and wiping the blood from his chin onto the sleeve. "You wouldn't know anything about true friendship or the way my life has turned out, so don't lecture me, Jack. You don't know anything about my life. Don't be so damned cocky. You got lucky, that's all," he said through clenched teeth. Then he stood quietly for another minute or two, glaring at me. It was as if he wanted to say more, but he didn't. He bit his cracked lip, then finally turned and left the hall. It was a strange and awkward encounter between two people who were supposed to be life-long friends.

I didn't see much of Ben after that night, but when we met we never once brought up the wedding reception fight. That was just as well. Sometimes it's better to leave things alone. There are other times, though, I'm not so sure that's the case.

Other than the fight with Ben, our wedding went off without a hitch. It was a beautiful day and Victoria was very happy. I had promised her a wonderful day and I delivered despite Ben.

Chapter 19

After we were married, Victoria and I rented a compact, two-room apartment downtown over the doctor's office. It wasn't much, but it was our own place to do with as we pleased. We were comfortable there. We had a bedroom and our kitchen and living room were combined. It was small, but Vic had that special way about her. She could take any room, regardless of its size or shape, and make it look like a million dollars.

In a few weeks she had our tiny apartment looking like a castle and it was real cozy. She was proud of what she had accomplished, and I was glad for her. Vic kept working at J.P.s for a while to help with the expenses and I was still at Tupper's, only now the work was cut back to less than part-time. The war was over and the contracts were drying up. They didn't need as many men, so they started cutting back from the bottom of the ladder. Unfortunately for me, that's where I was. They were tough days. I had wanted to give so much to Vic ... a bigger place to live and lots of nice things to wear, but we couldn't afford anything extra. With what we were pulling in from our two jobs we barely had enough to cover all the bills, but somehow we managed to get by. It wasn't easy but we made it work. And we were happy despite the struggle.

My mother had offered to allow us to move in with her but I didn't want that. The house I grew up in would have been too small for all of us. Vic's parents had offered to let us live with them until we could get on our feet, but neither of us wanted that either. Even though they were wonderful people, I wouldn't have been comfortable around her parents. I would have felt like I was scrounging off them. Besides, Vic believed newly-married couples should have their own space and privacy. I agreed. She was determined that we were going to do this on our own and I admired her spunk even if it sometimes seemed as if that's all we had going for us.

Vic's father worked as a planer at the sawmill. Eventually he pulled some strings and got me steady work over there. It was a good job in the woodyard where we'd help to unload the logs as they came down the river or, in later years, as they came in on the trucks.

When I first started at the mill, log drives down the river were very common. It was a spectacular sight to see those logs floating down the river. You won't see that today with all the trucks on the roads, but it was one of the most memorable things about working at the sawmill back then. It's a part of this town's long history but it's gone forever. Most people don't remember the log drives, but at times the logs were packed in so tight you could walk across them from one side of the river to the other without falling through.

After I took on the new job, things got better for Victoria and me. The night of our first anniversary was a big celebration for us. I suggested that Vic should quit her job at J.P.s and stay at home to take care of things. We had been talking about getting a bigger place and maybe even starting a family. But she was way ahead of me. That was the night Victoria told me we were going to have a baby. In the two years we had been together, I had never seen her looking any happier. She was meant to be a mother. She was absolutely glowing when she sat down beside me on the old plaid couch that used to belong to her parents and told me the news. She was so radiant and happy she could hardly control her excitement. She was like a small child on Christmas morning.

At first I didn't know what to say or how to react to the news. Naturally I had always thought that someday I'd be a father, but now that it was coming true, I couldn't believe it was happening.

"What's the matter?" Victoria asked, sensing my apprehension. "Aren't you happy about the baby?"

"Yeah," I said. "Of course I am. It's just that it's such a surprise. You caught me off guard. Why didn't you tell me sooner?"

"I wanted to be sure," she said. "I didn't want to get your hopes up in case something went wrong."

"So how is everything?"

"Perfect," she said. "The doctor says everything's just fine. You do want this, don't you?"

"Want it? You bet I do."

When the shock wore off I came to love the idea. Finally, I thought, I was going to have a child all my own to share things with and do things with. It was going to be wonderful.

Victoria had an easy pregnancy until the last month. Then things got scary. She started passing blood almost four weeks before her due date. The doctor ordered absolute bed rest for her. He wanted her off her feet until the baby arrived. These were the 1950s. They didn't have any fancy hospitals or machines or specialists like they got today so the doctor thought it best that we not take any chances. Vic was terrified. She said she could feel inside that something was wrong with the baby. But the doctor said there was no way of knowing. All we could do was wait to see what God had planned for the little one. He said sometimes expectant mothers jumped to conclusions when this sort of thing happened and there was a good chance the baby was just fine as it was so close to the delivery date. He said that meant the baby should be almost fully developed. Furthermore, he said, both the mother and baby appeared to be strong. He didn't think we had anything to worry about, especially since the baby had a strong heartbeat.

But Victoria wasn't convinced. She was an emotional wreck. She believed the doctor was wrong. She was convinced the baby was in trouble, and that stress added to her physical problems. Vic's mother stayed with her during the day while I was at the mill. I had to keep working even though I couldn't stop thinking about Victoria and our baby. Some nights Vic's mother stayed over in case we needed her. I couldn't relax. I was so worried that something was going to happen and I was going to lose Victoria. She meant the world to me and I don't know what I would have done if anything would have happened to her.

About two weeks after spots of blood appeared, Vic woke me up early one night crying, saying something was wrong. She had sharp pains and she was bleeding heavily. We both knew these weren't good signs. It was about nine-thirty. Her mother had stayed over because I had to work an early shift and would be leaving around four the next morning. She was asleep on the couch in the living room and I thanked God she was there.

I woke Mrs. Wright to stay with Victoria while I went for the doctor. By the time we got back to the apartment about half an hour later, Victoria was in a bad way. The contractions had started and the baby was on its way.

That was one of the longest nights of my life. Victoria was in pain and I couldn't stand to see her like that. Her screams were hard to take. I knew it meant she was hurting bad and I was still afraid something wasn't right. I felt helpless. I didn't know what to do or say to relieve some of her anxiety. I would have done anything to ease her suffering but all I could do was offer her my hand to squeeze. I kept thinking over and over and over that I was going to lose Victoria. I would have died that night too if anything would have happened to her, I just know it.

Seeing your baby born should be one of the most joyful events in your life, but it wasn't meant to be for me and Victoria that night. The doctor and Mrs. Wright worked on Victoria for more than five hours, and finally the baby arrived. It was a boy, but he was stillborn. The doctor tried everything he could to bring our little boy to life but he couldn't work miracles. He just wouldn't breathe.

Where was Nanny Vera when I needed her?

They say your life flashes before your eyes when you're facing a terrible tragedy, and they're right. That night, watching my dead son come into this hateful world, my mind quickly jumped back to those stories of Old Flossy and Nanny Vera and how they had struggled to rescue me from death's grip when I was born. I wanted the doctor or Mrs. Wright to perform the same miracle. I wanted someone to breathe life into my son, to pull him back from the threshold of darkness, but it didn't happen and I resented the fact that death had won this battle. I hated it that death had gotten its revenge.

The doctor couldn't explain what had happened. He couldn't tell us what had gone wrong with the pregnancy. There was no medical explanation for why my son was born dead. Only God, he said, could explain why things happen as they do, and although I knew he was right, his words made me angry. He knew he had made me angry and he stopped talking and backed away from the bed. That was probably a smart move on his part considering how I was feeling. I wanted to blame someone and if it had to be the doctor, then I didn't care.

I knew Victoria was a strong woman and in good health. I also knew everything should have been fine. Logically my mind said there was no explanation for what happened but my heart wanted to scream at someone. I needed to blame something for this tragedy. All the doctor could say was that he was really sorry and that sometimes these things happen because God has a plan. That's supposed to make you feel better at a time when your heart is breaking into a thousand pieces? It might have been better if the doctor hadn't said anything at all. While he said he understood that we were upset, he also added there was no reason to think that Victoria couldn't have more children. In the morning, after the shock had worn off, we'd see things differently. He tried hard to convince us that everything would be all right, but I wasn't buying any of it.

I trembled with sadness and anger as I stood beside the bloodied bed, watching Victoria hug our dead baby boy tightly to her heaving chest. My heart was broken. I wanted to scream to the top of the hills but what do you say at a time like that? It wasn't fair; it wasn't right that such an innocent life would be taken before it even had a chance. I hated everything about life at that moment and I hated the doctor for what he had said. I couldn't help but think such words from a doctor were insensitive. Certainly they were ill-timed. How could he have been so callous in front of my wife? My first instinct was to throw him out but then I thought of Victoria. She didn't need any more stress. So, as hard as it was for me to do, I kept my mouth shut.

It was painful to watch Victoria with the still, lifeless body of our little boy. She didn't react like I thought she would. She seemed calm and relaxed, even in the face of such a terrible tragedy. Her faith was awe-inspiring. She wasn't crying or behaving in any way like I imagined she would. Instead, she kept rocking the baby back and forth, and whispering to him. "I know you're in heaven, my precious little boy. I know you're safe in God's hands," she said.

It was the most amazing thing I ever saw. I knew Victoria was a strong and special woman, but I never thought she would take something like this so well. In fact, she took it better than me. The whole scene was too much for me. I had to leave the apartment. I don't handle being around death very well. I needed to catch my breath and come to grips with what I had just witnessed. I knew it was going to be hard but I had to find a way to accept my baby's death.

I had sent word to the mill that I wouldn't be in for my shift. Instead I walked the streets of Liverpool for what was left of that night. It must have been at least two hours. Up one side of the street, down another, not going any place special. It was dark and lonely but I wouldn't have welcomed any company. I needed to be alone. Finally I ended up on the front steps of Henderson's store.

It had been a familiar and comfortable place when I was a kid so I felt drawn to it. Sitting there on those steps I thought about a lot of things while trying to put the world into perspective, but you can never make sense out of some things. I thought about my father and Hank and how I missed them both so much. I thought about Victoria and wondered if she was going to be all right. And I thought about my dead baby boy. I wondered if this was some horrific prank or some type of revenge that God was playing on me, but in the end all I could think about was the son that I would never know. It made me sad to think about the things we wouldn't do together and I cried that night. It was one of the few times in my life that I cried, but I wept for my little boy and asked God to take good care of him. If possible, I suggested to God, that maybe he could arrange it so that Hank could take care of him until me and his mother got there, but then I realized I wasn't even sure if Hank would be welcome in that place where only righteous people go. For a brief minute, I laughed at my stupidity.

Try as you may, when faced with death, there are never enough answers to satisfy all your questions. I wanted someone to tell me why God would take an innocent baby, who had not wronged anyone, but yet allow some of the worst criminals to walk the earth. I don't understand how such an injustice can happen. My sadness ran deep that night. I didn't think I'd ever get over it. Eventually though, while sitting on Henderson's front steps, a weird sensation washed over my body. It lasted only seconds, but after it passed I felt more at ease, more content with the way things had turned out. I realized that although we expect perfection, we cannot fix everything that's broken, and I understood that Victoria had accepted that. Instead of allowing her emotions to tear her apart, my wife had found the courage to face the reality of life, or death, as it were. I understood that I had to do the same. If I didn't, I knew my grief would consume me.

It was near dawn when I returned home. As I entered our apartment I remember looking back at the early morning sun as it broke over the rooftops. In that instant I felt as if my burden had been lifted. As I had travelled along Liverpool's deserted narrow streets toward the apartment, it seemed as if I was walking with a friend. Then I recalled the words Mama used to speak whenever I seemed sad as a child. "You never walk alone in your hour of despair," she would often tell me. For a minute, at least, I'm sure I smiled.

By the time I arrived back at the apartment, the doctor had gone and Mrs. Wright had cleaned everything up and put fresh blankets on the bed. She had asked the doctor to stop by Cushing's Funeral Home and send someone for the baby. Since Victoria was sleeping, I remained in the living room where me and Mrs. Wright talked over a cup of tea. We both needed to reflect on what had happened. That morning, while we were trying to ease each other's pain, Mrs. Wright shared a secret with me. She told me that, in fact, she wasn't surprised that the baby had been born dead because the same thing had happened to her with her first baby. I hadn't known it before that night, but Victoria would have actually been the Wright's second daughter, just like I was the second child.

Here we were, the both of us being the second and only children. It was an odd coincidence. For some reason Mrs. Wright felt she had passed her own defective genes on to her precious daughter as if it had been some weird family curse. She understood the pain and suffering I was going through, but she also reminded me that if there was any comfort in her own experience, then she knew we could have more children. After all, she and Mr. Wright had another child. The revelation didn't make up for the loss of our baby, but eventually me and Victoria found the happiness we wanted.

Chapter 20

Time eases all sorrow and although it wasn't easy, I learned to accept my baby's death. Two years after the sad birth of our first child, we had moved to our own house to be closer to the mill. Miraculously, Victoria healed, both physically and mentally with no lasting scars. And finally we had our baby, a healthy eight-pound girl. We called her Katherine, after my mother and Vic's grandmother. Our baby girl was beautiful and everything we could have ever hoped for in a child. After the loss of our first baby, Katherine brought much joy and happiness into our lives. We felt truly blessed. It was as if our little girl was a gift sent from Heaven. She was our little angel.

Victoria was the best mother possible. Katherine was a smart little cookie. She walked when she was only nine months old and she started talking by the time she turned one. She loved being around people. That's the way she was throughout her life. She was a quick learner and very sociable, not afraid of anyone. On the other hand, her brother Thomas, who arrived almost two years later, was another story. He was a bad little Christer almost from the time he was born. The two were as different as sugar and salt. Where Katherine was kind and gentle, Thomas was like a bull dog. He'd rip and tear around the house running his poor mother off her feet. Thomas was an independent and curious child, qualities that led him to trouble when he was young. They are still leading him to trouble today.

After the children were born, life went along well for a few years without many bumps. That summer when Ruby Todd went missing was like a dream. It was like nothing had ever happened. Finally, I thought, my time had come. I had a good job. Me and Victoria were happy and the children were doing fine, but you can't depend on that kind of comfort to last forever. Fate never reveals what it has planned. All seems well, and then, in an instant, your life falls apart. Everything changes without warning.

It was a fall day and I had gone to work as I had done for years. I was working in the woodyard and everything seemed normal, until just before ten o'clock a strange sense of foreboding came over me. It was so intense that I stopped working. I found it hard to breathe and my head started to spin. I had to lean up against a guardrail to keep from falling over.

"Are you okay, Jack?" one of he other guys asked. "You're as white as snow. Maybe you should take a break."

The other men on the shift thought I was having a heart attack but I told them I would be all right after I caught my breath. I told them I had just gotten a little light-headed from the heat but it was more than that. I knew something was wrong.

I'm sure the other men would have thought I was completely nuts if I had told them what was going on in my head at that time. I hated it when those feelings came. It usually meant something terrible was about to happen. Such feelings came to me quite often, but they usually passed quickly and were sometimes followed by minor mishaps with no major consequences. This day, however, the sensation lasted for ten, maybe fifteen minutes, and it shook me to the bone, leaving me with a deep sense of loss. Call it intuition or whatever you want, but I knew something terrible was about to happen.

I later learned the accident occurred at about ten after ten that morning. Katherine was nine and Thomas was seven by this time. That day my son's curiosity led to tragedy, changing our lives forever. Thomas and Katherine had been playing in our bedroom when he found my rifle standing in our bedroom closet. I had been cleaning it a few nights earlier to get it ready when deer hunting season opened in October. I didn't know Thomas had earlier discovered where I hid the shells. I was stupid. I should never have had guns in the house with children around but in those days guns were no big deal. Hunting was a normal thing for men my age and guns were commonplace in most homes around here. Victoria was down in the kitchen getting ready to make lunch for the kids when she heard the gunshot. By the time she got up to our bedroom it was too late; she found Katherine lying motionless on the floor next to the bed, a puddle of blood quickly forming around her head. Thomas was standing over his sister, screaming and yelling but still holding the rifle in his trembling hands as smoke filtered from the end of the muzzle.

Victoria knew right away that it wasn't good; there was so much blood. Her first instinct was to get Katherine to help and the only place close by was the mill. She knew there was usually a nurse on duty there because of all the heavy equipment and the potential for accidents. She scooped up Katherine's limp body and carried her all the way to the mill, about a ten-minute walk from our house at a fast pace. I don't know how she managed to get there carrying our blood-covered daughter without breaking down but she made it with Thomas in tow.

When Victoria got to the mill, people there reacted quickly. The duty nurse immediately rushed Katherine into the examination room and sent someone to come fetch me from the woodyard. It was now close to ten-thirty and I knew right away that something was wrong when the messenger told me to go directly to the first aid room. They only do that when something tragic has happened. Instinctively, my first thought was of the kids or Victoria, but I had no idea what I'd find when I got to the clinic. It took me about five minutes to reach the first aid room from the woodyard. All the way there I could see their faces in front of me. Which one of them was hurt, I asked myself.

It was like I had rushed blindly into one of my worst nightmares. The first sight that greeted me was Victoria standing in the dimly-lit hallway in tears and her dress covered in blood. Naturally, I thought she had been injured because of the blood. Then, when I saw Thomas curled up on a bench, I knew it was Katherine.

The nurse didn't give me a chance to ask Victoria what had happened. "Mr. Webster, I think if you want to see your little girl before it's too late, you should come quickly," she said quietly, leading me into the small, sanitized room where she had placed Katherine on an examination table covered with white paper. The table and floor were now awash in blood. The white paper was almost completely red and a large pool of blood was forming beside the table as it dripped and splattered to the tiled floor. It wasn't good. I knew I was going to lose my precious little girl.

My first reaction was to close my eyes. Maybe this was all a bad dream and if I kept my eyes closed, it would all go away. I wasn't sure if I wanted to see my little girl like that. I was confused, too afraid to open my eyes and too afraid to keep them closed. The nurse told me she had sent for a doctor from town but she said, based on her examination, she feared there wasn't much they could do for her. The bullet had entered Katherine's skull just above the left ear and become lodged in her brain.

Although my little girl was still breathing on her own, the nurse told me and Victoria that she thought it would only be a matter of time. By the time the doctor arrived a few minutes later, Katherine was dead. I held her tightly for an hour that day before they finally pried her dead body from my aching arms. I loved that child with all my heart, with every ounce of my body. A large part of me died when Katherine died that day. I found it hard to understand why God would take away another one of the people that I held so dear. It was probably then that I concluded there was no just God, only a mean, vindictive entity who believed in making sinners pay for their deeds ... over and over and over, until they break. It wasn't fair that He took another of my babies, but it was obvious that it was all part of His plan. I accepted that I had to make amends for what I had done. But my children should not have had to pay. They had done nothing wrong.

The doctor told me and Victoria, based on the entry wound and the location of the bullet, there wouldn't have been anything he could have done for Katherine. "But," he said, "if there is any consolation, you can take comfort in knowing that she was not in any pain. Katherine didn't suffer." But that didn't make it any easier on me or Victoria or Thomas.

"No pain?" I blurted out as the doctor explained that, when the bullet entered her brain, she went unconscious immediately. In his opinion, he said, she never knew what hit her.

"How in the hell do you know she was in no pain?" I said as my grief took control of my entire body. "You doctors got so much book knowledge in your god-damned heads that now you can tell when someone feels pain or not? Tell me, doctor, just how do you think my little girl felt when she heard that gun go off? Did she know what was going to happen to her? Did she have time to panic? Did her short life flash before her eyes? Did she feel the bullet enter her head? You can't say if she felt anything or not, so you should just keep your well-educated opinions to yourself."

After saying my piece, I left the room. I should have stayed with Victoria and Thomas, but I needed to be alone. I had to get away from that place where the lifeless body of my once sweet and energetic little girl was laid out. I walked and I walked for a very long time until, finally, I reached the cemetery where my parents were buried. My mother had died by this time, and kneeling down beside her grave, I prayed to her to give me enough strength to survive this unholy tragedy. Here I was only thirty-six and I had already lost two children. This just wasn't right. Parents should not outlive their offspring. I felt God had forsaken me. Katherine was loving and thoughtful. She never hurt anyone or anything in her whole short life.

For some reason unknown to me, I had been drawn to the cemetery that day. Maybe I thought being close to the dead would make this nightmare go away, or perhaps I was trying to get back to the past, to a time before all this pain began. I talked to my mother that day and I felt her presence all around me as if she were trying to embrace me and ease my sadness. At one point, I could have sworn she ... or someone ... was standing directly beside me. It was a sensation I had experienced before ... on the night before my Old Man died and many times after. In fact, the feeling was so strong that day, that I looked around the cemetery to see who else was there. But there was no one, except for me and the wind. It was an eerie feeling. I shivered despite the warm sunshine that fell from the clear sky.

I remained at my mother's grave side for almost two hours, hoping to find the answers I was searching for, but there were none. Finally, I went home to find Victoria and Thomas huddled together on the living room couch. He had cried himself to sleep and she had hugged him, giving him the comfort he needed. In all the confusion surrounding Katherine's death, Thomas had gotten lost in the shuffle but I now understood we were dealing with the loss of more than one child that day.

After we buried Katherine, things were never the same again in our house. Victoria went into some kind of withdrawal. We hardly spoke. I understood how she felt. After all, she had buried two of her babies and that's not easy for any mother. She refused to enter our bedroom even though I had scrubbed the blood off the floor. That's one of the hardest things I've ever had to do in my life. Scrubbing away Katherine's blood was like washing away her very existence. But even with the stains gone, Victoria could not enter the room without seeing her baby girl lying on the floor in a pool of blood. I had to move all our things into a small room downstairs next to the kitchen.

As for our relationship, it went way off track after Katherine's death. She never said it, but I know Victoria blamed me for what happened to our daughter. I blamed myself. It was my gun and my bullets that killed her. Such personal stress can strain a relationship no matter how much in love two people are.

Thomas was never the same after that day. How could he be? Outwardly I never blamed him for getting the shells and loading the gun. He didn't know any better. He was a curious child. He didn't know the gun was a dangerous weapon that could kill. He probably thought it was a play rifle like his own. It was an accident, but unfortunately it left Thomas with deep scars that never healed. There's no doubt he blamed himself for his sister's death and that's a tremendous burden for a child to carry around. After that terrible day he withdrew into his own world, blocking out me and his mother in the process. We both tried talking to him and we even took him to see several doctors but we could never reach him. Over the years he drifted further and further away until, one day, he was gone as well. As Thomas went through school he became a loner. He wouldn't play with any other children and once he got to high school, he wouldn't make friends or date. Finally when he finished high school he left town without so much as an explanation as to where he was going. I hear from him every now and then but we don't have much contact. I get a Christmas card or a quick phone call every couple of years, but few words are spoken between us.

There's a wall there that neither of us can get through. Last I heard he was working for some movie company out in California.

It's hard knowing you have a son out there somewhere in the world that you don't have any contact with, especially at a time like this when you know your jig's just about up. I don't blame Thomas for the way things turned out. None of it was his fault. He blamed himself for his sister's death and, as a parent, I failed to find a way to help him understand that it was an accident. When the story's written, each character must play out his role in the plot, even when it's a tragedy. Sadly for Thomas, he was given a shitty part. When the gun went off that day, it destroyed the lives of my two children. The bullet shattered our lives and my family never healed.

The last time I saw Thomas was in 1982 at his mother's funeral. I wasn't sure if he'd come home to see his mother buried, but he surprised me. It had always been Victoria's wish to see the family reconciled before she died, but she never realized her dream. And after the funeral I knew it was never going to happen; not in my lifetime. I had always thought I could make it work between us if he ever decided to come home again so we could have another chance, but I was wrong. I don't think he was in the house for any more than an hour before we were arguing. He stayed two days and then left without so much as a goodbye. We buried Victoria in the afternoon and he left the same evening. At a time when the two of us should have put the past behind us, we dwelled on the pain, dredging up all the bad things that had happened in our lives. Instead of rejoicing in each other's company, we relived the suffering that had kept us apart. We took our frustrations and anger out on each other, just as we had always done.

We argued over insignificant things, picking up where we had left off years earlier. The tension was thick from the moment Thomas walked through the front door. Instead of greeting him with a warm hug and welcoming him back into our home, I said something stupid like, "So, you decided to come home for the funeral. You couldn't bother to come home to see your mother when she was alive. I'm surprised you could pull yourself away from your busy life with all your big-shot movie friends to come see her planted in the ground. Nice to see you, Thomas, after all these years. It's too bad you couldn't have come while your mother's eyes were open so she could see how you really turned out."

It was stupid, I know that now. I should have tried to make him feel more welcome, but I was hurt and I was angry.

His reaction was quick and predictable. "Look Dad, I'm not going to argue with you over Mom's funeral," he shot back. "I'm only here because of her. It's the right thing to do, but you wouldn't know anything about doing the right thing, would you? I'm not here to see you and we don't even have to talk to each other. I don't even have to stay here, if you don't want."

The kid was astute, I'll give him that much. He knew me very well, perhaps even better than I knew myself. It was a learned behaviour. It surely didn't come from talking to each other. That was something we had never done.

"No, you can stay here in your old room," I said. "Your mother would have wanted that and I intend to do whatever I can to honour her wishes." But I knew her ultimate wish, a reconciliation of the family, would never happen. Thomas was too much like his father, and two people who are so much alike just can't see eye to eye.

"Look," he demanded. He stared me directly in the eye when he spoke. "There wasn't any love lost between us when I lived here, so don't think there's any chance of having a reunion over Mom's death. If you wanted that, you could have asked for it a long time ago. As far as I'm concerned, it's way too late for any reconciliation. The only thing we share is the blood that runs through our veins."

Thomas knew how to get to the meat of things, but like the bulldog that I am, I couldn't drop the argument. I could never let things go. "Sonny boy, you ain't got any idea how many times over the years your mother pleaded with me to call you. But I figure you were the one who left this house. It was your decision to run away from this town ... from your home ... from your family. I've seen other people do that and they lived to regret it just like you will. Don't expect me to lay the welcome mat down for you as if nothing has happened. You know you can always come back here anytime you want, but if you're waiting for me to ask you, you'll have one helluva long wait." I could be pig-headed when I wanted to be. But I should have made an effort to reach out to Thomas. It was stupid, a missed opportunity. It's something I dearly regret and something I'd change if I had it to do all over again. There are many things I'd change if I could.

"Yeah! So what else is new, Dad? I learned long ago not to wait for you or count on you for anything. I've always had to do things your way, and look where that's gotten us. You won't have to hold your breath. I won't ask you do anything for me. I don't have any intention of staying any longer than Mom's funeral."

"Fine. You do whatever you want."

He stayed for the funeral. Then he left. I haven't seen him since, but I have missed him. I miss them all very much.

Chapter 21

When Victoria died, my life may as well have ended too. We never did get to be as close again as we were before Katherine's accident but we still cared deeply for each other and looked out for one another over the years. Eventually we came to terms with the tragedy and somehow found our way back into each other's hearts. After time I think we both forgave me in our own personal ways for the accident, but regardless of how hard we tried, it seemed there was some kind of barrier between us. None of that mattered. I still loved Victoria with all my heart.

It was a sad day when she died. It was the last time I cried and the last time that I felt alive. When I lost Victoria, I lost everything in this world that mattered to me. I know life has to end, but I always figured I'd be the first to go. I wasn't ready to live my life without her and, like I always knew that it would be, it has been a miserable existence.

On days of tragedy everything starts out normal as it did on the day Victoria died. I remember that morning very well. It was the day that life as I knew it came to an end. I had gotten up about fifteen minutes earlier than Vic, like I did every morning since we had been married. That routine started in the winter, first to get the house warmed up for her, and then for the kids when they started going to school. It was six o'clock that day. I had to be at the mill by seven for the shift change. And just like Vic had done every morning, she got up at quarter past six and went to the bathroom before getting dressed. As usual, we talked while she washed and brushed her teeth. I heard her turn the bathroom tap on and then the water kept running and running and running.

After a few minutes, I knew something wasn't right. I couldn't hear her but I could still hear that damned water running. I called to her several times, but I couldn't get an answer. When she didn't respond, I immediately knew there was trouble. I found her sprawled on the bathroom floor with her toothbrush still clutched in her hand, the unopened tube of toothpaste lying next to her and that damned water tap running. She wasn't moving and she was turning blue. I knew right away it was bad and quickly called for the ambulance to come.

I sat there on the bathroom floor, holding her still body close to me until help arrived. It seemed like it took forever for the ambulance attendants to come but they later told me it took less than five minutes from the time they got the call. The doctor told me it wouldn't have mattered how quickly they had gotten there. Victoria was dead before her body hit the floor.

I agreed to let them do the autopsy. Like the doctor said, we had to know what really happened. Vic had been a healthy woman her entire life except when she lost the first baby and a few times when she got the flu. Other than that she had always been in good health.

The autopsy revealed she died of a brain aneurysm. There may have been a few small warnings in the months leading up to her death, such as tremors in her fingers, blurred vision or headaches. But if there had been, Victoria hadn't complained of anything. Naturally, she wouldn't complain. Basically, the doctor said, there wouldn't have been any way of knowing what was happening in her head. Chances were, he said, the blood vessel had been weak for many years, and over time the pressure built up until that June morning when it finally burst. Even if they had known sooner, the doctor said, they couldn't have done anything for it. The clot had formed in a part of the brain they couldn't reach without too many risks. There was no way to prevent what happened to Victoria, but the doctor said I should take comfort in the fact that she didn't suffer.

It's amazing how many doctors over the years have told me I should take comfort in someone's death just because they didn't suffer. Well, that don't make it any easier to deal with. It don't make the pain go away or fill the emptiness those people leave behind. I don't know why doctors feel they have to say anything like that. Just let people grieve for the loss of their loved one. That's the kindest thing they can do.

Victoria didn't know what hit her that morning. One minute she was getting ready to brush her teeth and the next minute she was gone. It happened in the blink of an eye. You never know how or when it's going to happen. You better make sure you're living the right kind of life. You may not have the chance to go back and make amends. As my Old Man always said, you never know when you may have to answer for what you've done. You better be sure you're doing the right thing.

It has been a miserable life since Vic died. It's hard spending so many years with someone and then just when you're getting ready to retire and planning to spend the last twenty or thirty years together, all of a sudden you find yourself alone. I never did get used to living in that big old empty house all by myself and now that I'm stuck in here they'll finally be able to sell it off to a large family who can really use that much space. It was a nice house but it was built to accommodate more people. It's gone to waste for nearly twenty years with only one senile old man rambling through it. A house like that can be a lonely prison for a man living by himself with only his memories and ghosts to keep him company.

If Thomas would have been any kind of a son, he would have come back more often to spend some time with his old man. But why would he do that? I certainly hadn't made him feel welcome the last time he came home. Maybe that was too much for me to expect. I shouldn't blame him for not coming to see me. I should blame myself for not making him feel more like my child and for not helping to ease his pain. If I have but one more regret before I die, it's that I can't set things straight with Thomas. The doctor told me they've sent word to him that if he wants to see me alive one last time he should come quickly. But I don't expect for him to come. Any bond between us was severed years ago. I'm not sure what it was that drove us apart. I understand that Thomas took his sister's death personally, because he pulled the trigger, but I think he believes I blamed him for the accident. I didn't. I should have made sure he understood that. Instead I allowed us to drift apart. The ghost of his sister's accident kept pushing at us like two magnets. I know now that it was a mistake not to make sure he understood that I didn't blame him, but I was caught up in my own self-blame and kicking myself in the ass for putting that gun where the kids could find it. I should have told him that I loved him and that his sister's death was an accident plain and simple. I could never bring myself to tell him anything like that, but now I know I should have been more helpful and loving. Now it's too late to mend those fences and the last person left on this earth that really means anything to me is thousands of miles away when I could use him the most. All because this cranky old man was too proud and stupid to say the right things.

Victoria constantly told me it wasn't healthy for me to keep things bottled up inside. She knew when things weren't right or if something was bothering me and she'd try to get me to talk. She said she could see it in my eyes when something was wrong. And when I became quiet, she'd often get mad at me for not sharing my problems with her so that she could help. But there are some things you can't help with. Some things are better left alone, or so I thought. I no longer believe that, and that's why I'm glad you're here now.

The time has come for me to get something off my chest. It's something that's been bothering me since the summer of 1940.

Chapter 22

    This is not going to be easy. You must promise to listen carefully. It's going to hurt me to do this, but it has to be done. It's something that should have been done a very long time ago. This is the day I finally get this tremendous burden off my chest once and for all.

    We'll only get one shot at this. I know, deep down in this tired old heart, that I won't have the guts to tell you this but once, so be sure to take it all in.

    I have to warn you, though, it's not for the faint of heart. But if you're sure you are ready, I will take you back to that dark period in my life ... a time when my whole existence changed forever; a time when this entire town entered an empty void, changing in ways I could never have imagined. My life has been a virtual blackhole ever since.

    It's 1940. The war is raging. The people of Liverpool are struggling to survive in tough economic times. Five young men on the eve of their lives make a dreadful mistake.

    Everything is rushing back at me and there's no stopping the flood. Life is funny but it's no laughing matter. When you're young, you wish you were older so that you could benefit from the wisdom and knowledge that maturity brings. When you're older you wish you were young so you could enjoy your life all over again while avoiding the mistakes you made the first time. In the process, your life passes you by. In the blink of an eye, it's gone. In a heartbeat your life has slipped through your fingers while you stood by and allowed it to pass. The challenge, of course, is to take advantage of every opportunity, no matter how big or small. Mama used to say that she was too soon old and too late smart. The Old Man said youth is wasted on the young. They were both very wise. I wish I had listened more carefully to their words. My life might have ended differently.

    It has been my destiny to arrive here in this hellish place. The question is, what is my legacy? There's so much that has to be said and so little time left. Thinking about this reminds me of something I heard a long time ago ... you best be aware of your past indiscretions because they'll catch up with you someday. I know all too well exactly what that means.

    That's another piece of advice my mother used to give me when I was a kid. I thought I knew everything, but Mama couldn't understand why I was in such a hurry to grow up. She knew all too well that life passes by soon enough and she didn't want me to piss mine away. She tried to share her wisdom but I was too stubborn to pay attention. The Bible teaches us to ask God to forgive us our past indiscretions but there are some trespasses that even He cannot forgive. My mother knew what she was talking about when she spoke those words.

I was a cocky brat, a real asshole with a tendency to get into trouble. Let's be honest about that. But Mama never got angry or preached at me when I did something stupid. She was crafty that way. She never gave up on me. Instead of scolding me like most parents, she'd take a more subtle approach, finding some tactful way of pointing out my mistakes without being judgmental.

My mother endured many hardships in her lifetime but I don't remember her as an angry or resentful person. She learned things the hard way - by experience. Most importantly, she learned not to question one's lot in life. That's a valuable lesson she acquired from the school of hard knocks. Her life experiences taught her well, and she tried to pass that knowledge on to me. But it didn't work. She didn't fail as a teacher. I failed as a student. Mama knew how to survive no matter what curves life threw at her. I would have done well to heed her words. I know that I should have paid better attention when she spoke. But not me. I was a know-it-all smart-ass with shit for brains who refused to listen to what any grown-up had to say, particularly my parents. I was one of those kids who thought I knew everything, but, truth be told, I knew very little about life. Common sense, my mother would tell me, can't be borrowed or bought, it has to be earned.

I know Mama didn't say these things to be mean. I'm sure she hoped she could smarten me up with a dose of reality. It took awhile to get through this thick skull of mine, but eventually I listened to Mama's words. And I learned a great deal from her even though I didn't recognize it back then. I heard her message and I realized soon enough that Mama knew what she was talking about. I just wish I had listened to her a whole lot sooner.

She told me if I didn't mend my ways, my life would go nowhere. Basically, she was telling me that if I wanted my life to end up in the shitter, then I was on the right road. She told me to be steadfast and wise as I went through life. She urged me to make my decisions using my brains, and to chose my friends carefully. She was afraid I'd throw my life away. "It is the wise man who knows with whom he is sleeping," she told me. And always be honest, she said. I had to live with my decisions and the actions that came from them. I had better make careful choices or be prepared to face the fallout. You only get to go through life once and everything in your future depends on your actions today. You can't undo the past, so you better make sure it's done right while it's still your present.

I didn't know it sixty years ago, but I now understand. Mama was right. I wish I could tell her that I appreciate what she meant to me, but it's too late. Why is it that by the time you recognize your mistakes, you can't do anything to correct them? The real irony in all of this is that your future is so connected with your past, that the two become one. I'm not sure that it matters when the revelation comes, all I know is that the moment when you understand you've made a mistake, you should correct it. No one expects us to be perfect. We all make errors in judgement. The challenge is to recognize where you took the wrong turn, then go back and get on the right road.

Excuse me for getting off on a tangent.

Come in and sit for awhile. It's nice to see you this morning. You're a welcome sight for these tired old eyes. I'm not feeling very well today. They gave me an extra shot earlier because the pain was worse. The nurses say the doctor told them to increase the dosage but I can't have any more for at least two hours. Apparently it's dangerous to get it in large doses too close together. They said it could affect my heart or my breathing or something like that and it could kill me. I said, big deal. That's all the more reason to give it to me, but they weren't amused. I don't know what all the fuss is about. If they give me an extra large shot and kill me, what the hell? Who cares? I'm going to die soon anyway. But they have their orders. They have no choice but to follow them. But you're a nurse. You know what that's like. They can't give me the drugs because that little shit of a doctor says not to. So here I am stretched out here like a pin cushion, suffering real bad, and praying for the pain to stop, hoping to die.

This is stupid; so unfair. What gives anyone the right to keep me alive in pain like this? I didn't ask them to keep me breathing. It isn't right ... it just isn't right.

No. This is a good time to talk.

Please sit down.

I really don't want you to go. I'll be fine. I'll behave and stick to the story if you'll stay awhile.

There's no need to leave.

I'm feeling well enough to talk. That's all I have going for me. If you leave now, I'll go stark raving mad. Between the pain, the stink in this God-forsaken place and staring at the ceiling, it's enough to drive anyone over the edge.

Company is the only thing I have to look forward to. Besides, we haven't finished what we started. I can't die until you know everything there is to know about me. There's a lot more to this decaying old man than meets the eye. You wouldn't want me to leave with my story only half-told, would you? You don't know the ending yet.

By the way. Did you hear the news?

One of those cleaning men with the shiny white suits was in here this morning. He told me that someone has finally moved into the old Hadden House. Imagine that! That's the place where the Todds lived when they moved to Liverpool in 1940. It's strange that after all these years someone would move in there now. Don't suppose it's much of a house any more. Whoever bought that place has got their work cut out for them if they intend to live there. That house will need a lot of repairs to bring it back. I can only imagine how rotted everything is after all these years. It's a damned shame. It used to be a spectacular house, but it's too late for that place now. It should have been torn down years ago. It's another reminder of what happened way back then. Why do you suppose somebody has decided to move in there now?

Liverpool has its share of mysteries, not only the one of Ruby Todd's disappearance. For one thing, people around here say the bay out near the Head is haunted. They say that every July 28th, a ghost ship comes into the bay. Under full sail. Then catches fire and burns for a few minutes before it's gone.

It's the kind of story those Hollywood types would love to get their hands on. They'd screw it up like everything else they touch. Anyway, it's one of our most popular mysteries. People around here say the ship actually belonged to pirates a couple of hundred years ago. The story goes that it was chased into the cove by the King's navy where it was burned and the crew killed. Most of them, anyway. Some people say that somewhere, either on the bottom of the bay or maybe on the shore where some of them pirates might have hid it, a pirate's treasure waits to be found. But they also warn there's a curse connected with the treasure and whoever finds it will have to battle a dozen pirates before claiming the prize. Legend says they've been guarding it ever since it was hidden hundreds of years ago and they won't give it up without a fight.

Imagine what you could do with a treasure worth millions of dollars. Money. It's a curse in it's own right. Many people have tried to solve the mystery and find the buried treasure. They've dug around the shore and searched for years, but I don't suppose they ever will know the truth. I'm sure over time that story has been stretched so much it's probably so far from what really happened by now it's all lies. I don't believe the stories of buried treasure, anyway, but it's a fun legend. These types of lies are harmless, they don't hurt anyone. Some lies do, though.

Lies are a terrible thing. They're like a cancer, gnawing at your insides until you're weak and hurting. It was a lie that led Mr. Copper to kill himself a number of years ago, or that's what people said. Truth is, I've always thought he was murdered.

Garth Copper was a bookkeeper at Tupper's Shipyards. He started working there a few years after Mr. Todd left Liverpool. He worked there for almost thirty years before the truth finally came out. Some accountant discovered Garth Copper had been skimming a percentage off the company's books all those years. And when he realized the truth was finally out, people said Mr. Copper shot himself to keep from going to jail. But I didn't buy that. Everything was too cut and dried. It didn't make sense to me how one man could get away with doing something like that for so many years without being caught. Someone else higher up in the company was in on it with Mr. Copper. There had to be someone helping him keep the secret. But if there was, it has remained a mystery all these years.

Police said, on that October night in 1968 Garth Copper must have figured investigators were getting too close. He went to his office where he placed one bullet in the side of his head. They found him next morning, sprawled over his desk in a pool of blood. He had a gun in one hand and a suicide note in the other. In the note he apologized for what he'd done and explained how he'd pulled things off for all those years. Miraculously in his open safe they also found a duplicate set of books exposing how much money he had taken over the years. Stories around town said the amount ranged from less than $20,000 to more than $100,000. But I didn't buy any of it. All of a sudden, when the police are starting an investigation, these books show up and the only man who supposedly knew the truth turns up dead. No way. It was too neat and tidy, if you ask me. I think someone made it look like suicide. Someone got away with murder and a lot of money to boot. The cash was never recovered. But like me, not everyone in town bought the suicide story. Over the years rumours have come out about the Coppers and the company. For instance, why was it that the family of one man who also worked in the shipyard offices seemed to be better off than the rest of the office workers? And why was another guy fired just a few weeks after Mr. Copper was found dead? Such coincidences make for a lot of talk and speculation in a town like this, and it makes for a good mystery. There were too many things that didn't add up.

It was a sad thing, but young Missy Goodwin gave Liverpool another good mystery when she disappeared in the early 1970s. Missy worked as a cashier at the grocery store down on Main Street. She was a nice young girl but kind of on the slow side. She was friendly to a fault and liked to gossip. Problem was, she talked too much. She asked too many questions about things that didn't concern her. Missy was the type who had to know everyone's business, and she didn't hesitate asking. She should have been taking care of her own business.

Missy was born and raised in Liverpool, and I figured she'd meet some nice young man, settle down and have a bunch of kids. But like everything else in this backwater town, you can't count on anyone to do what they're supposed to do. Somehow Missy became involved with the wrong crowd and got into trouble. She was raised in a by-the-book Christian family and that's where the problems began. Her parents were very protective and strict. They didn't want Missy having boyfriends. The Goodwins were an extremely private family but I don't think they felt she was capable of handling a relationship. They especially didn't like her seeing boys who consumed alcohol. Well, you know what people are like. If you keep them under your thumb for too long, they're going to rebel. That's just what Missy did. Like a bitch in heat, that young girl ran directly to the nearest young stud she could find, and when she got there, she cut loose.

I remember Victoria thinking it was such a terrible and shameful thing for a nice young girl to behave in such a way, but I think Missy did it to spite her parents.

She was in her late teens when she started seeing that young fellow, Steve. The story goes that he was into drugs and other criminal activity ... a real little shit, in other words. Missy's parents had a fit over their relationship, and from what I heard, you couldn't blame them. People were shocked by her actions, as if they needed anything else to talk about. But I never got caught up in all that gossip and it didn't seem to bother that little girl that her actions were hurting her parents. She was constantly fighting with her parents, and finally the Goodwins kicked Missy out of the house. They just couldn't stand to watch what was happening to their daughter and she didn't care about what she was doing to them. Missy moved in with another young girl here in town, but kept right on seeing that young stud.

Then one morning in November, 1971, a few weeks after Missy left her parents' house to live with her friend, they found her car parked down by the water not too far from the bridge. It was empty. Her purse was on the front seat with her money, bank book and all her important papers. There was a man's jacket balled up on the back seat, but nothing else of Missy's was found. There was also a half-full package of cigarettes laying on the floor of the passenger side but people said Missy didn't smoke so they couldn't be hers. It turned out they were the same brand her boyfriend smoked but that didn't prove too much ... or so the police said. He could have left the cigarettes there any time. They had a point. Besides that, there was also an empty coffee cup and a full bottle of Coke on the front seat of the car. And in the trunk there was a bag of groceries that Missy apparently bought three nights earlier before she left the store. The police said there were no signs of a struggle and they didn't find anything else suspicious in the vehicle, but they didn't find Missy either.

When Missy didn't show up for work that first morning, the store manager called to see if she was sick. Her roommate said she never came home the night before. Upon receiving a concerned call from the roommate, Missy's parents notified the police that their daughter was missing. Naturally the police figured Missy ran off somewhere with that young fellow, but when he showed up at the service station where he worked as a mechanic, they ruled out that possibility. But they didn't rule out suicide or something worse. They talked to that young fellow, Steve, many times over the course of the investigation. Even though those cigarettes were the same brand he smoked, the police never could place him in the vicinity of Missy's car in the days that she was missing. The cigarettes could have been there from sometime earlier, since he and Missy spent a lot of time together, or maybe they belonged to someone else. The police said the cigarettes didn't prove anything. As for the man's jacket, the boy denied it was his and no one could ever prove that it was.

Were the cigarettes and jacket clues to Missy's disappearance? Who the hell knows? Nothing is ever what it seems.

Eventually the police admitted they couldn't solve the case and closed the file. It remains unsolved to this very day. Not surprisingly, just like in Ruby's case, there was a great deal of talk around town about what happened down on the waterfront. People in Liverpool love to sink their teeth into a juicy mystery. Naturally there would be lots of theories. Isn't gossip a wonderful thing? I don't know what some of the people in this town would do without it.

A scandal was just what this town needed. Some people figured Missy killed herself because Steve wanted to call it quits. Others figured he killed her after he found her cheating on him, or maybe she was pregnant and he didn't want to have to take care of a baby. Police carried out an extensive search of the river and the banks around the harbour but they never found her. If she went into that water, no one knows for sure. Maybe she's still alive and laughing at everyone from some place far away from Liverpool. Wouldn't that be a funny thing.

Mysteries are a funny thing. They all start from some nugget of truth. Then, over the years, as people spread the story and add their own version of the facts to what they think they've heard, everything gets changed and twisted. Eventually the truth gets all blown out of proportion until you have a story that sounds nothing like the real thing. But the fact is, someone always knows. That's the one absolute truth about mysteries. Someone always holds the key to unlock the door to the truth. That's the way it has been with the mystery of Ruby Todd.

The speculation and rumours surrounding Ruby's disappearance never died. If anything, they intensified. The truth got so blown out of proportion it's impossible to tell where the facts end and the fiction begins. Even today people still talk about the mystery of Ruby Todd's disappearance.

The more people talked about it, the more it took on a strange, twisted life of its own. Now it's unrecognizable. It's more like a piece of fiction instead of the tragic true story of a missing girl. Today the mystery of Ruby Todd's disappearance has become an integral part of Liverpool folklore. There are many different versions of the story, most of them far from the truth. Sadly people today don't understand that Ruby Todd was a real person. They don't appreciate that the disappearance of that young girl over a half century ago caused a great deal of pain and suffering for many people ... for her family ... for all of us. That's right. The mystery surrounding Ruby's disappearance caused a lot of grief for Hank, Levi, Ben, Bunny and me. No one knows how much her disappearance affected us, but I'm going to tell you. I'm the key that can unlock the mystery. I'm the last living person who knows what really happened to Ruby Todd. It isn't a pretty picture, but then again, the truth is seldom pretty. However, the truth is even uglier when it's kept secret, hidden away, buried beneath a bed of lies.

Chapter 23

The day was muggy; almost suffocating.

It's difficult to imagine Liverpool in 1940. It seems so far away. Not in distance, but in time. The years have slipped by so fast. I never appreciated my life. Now time is my enemy.

I met Ruby Todd a lifetime ago and many things have happened since then. I've seen many changes in this small town, some for the good and some not. People have come and gone from Liverpool; many of the old buildings have fallen to the wrecker's crew and many new ones have been built up. Friends and family have died, but still the memories of that sickly hot August day come back to me as if it was only this morning. Truth is, I still get cold chills when I think back to that time. It's a feeling I've experienced many, many times over the past sixty years, but I never get used to it.

As usual the highlight of that day was going to be hanging out with the guys. This was our last summer together and we wanted to make the most of it ... lifelong friends spending their last few months together before going our individual ways into a future that would separate us forever. That's how some childhood friendships end. We knew that. That's why we planned to spend as much time together as we could before the company dissolved. Although we didn't know what was going to happen to any of us in the fall, we knew our lives would change forever.

That August day we met at J.P.s. Bunny had to work at the store and Levi had to do something with his family. If we didn't get work at the shipyard, me, Hank and Ben were to hang around town until after lunch, then we would go out to the Grove for the afternoon. The others would meet us there later in the day.

When I got to J. P.s that morning, Hank and Ben were already there. They were sitting in a booth talking to Ruby Todd and Patty Fergusson. The girls had something planned for the day and they left almost as soon as I arrived. I remember thinking that Ben was upset at something, although I'm not sure if I ever found out exactly what had him so riled up so early in the day. Ben seemed more restless than usual. He didn't say anything when I sat down or when the girls left a few minutes later. He didn't even acknowledge when they said goodbye. But that wasn't so unusual for Ben. He was a moody son-of-a-bitch who often withdrew into his own little world. Sometimes it bothered me that Ben could sit with us for hours and not even let on that he knew we were there, but I learned to accept that characteristic.

When I joined the others in the booth, I decided not to press Ben about his mood. Whatever had crawled up his ass could stay there. I knew if I questioned him it would piss him off even more and maybe ruin our plans for the day. Later, when Ben wasn't around, Hank told me Ben and Ruby had been arguing over something, although he wasn't sure what. Ben didn't seem particularly happy about the way things ended. That wasn't anything new, though. Ben was never happy with the way things turned out as far as Ruby was concerned.

Ben sulked for a few minutes. Then, just like that, he was fine, almost like he had been in some kind of a trance. He joked and made plans for the afternoon's trip to the Grove. Whatever had made him so angry at Ruby disappeared after the girls left.

He wanted to talk about anything else other than Ruby. He bragged to me and Hank that he had taken a bottle of whiskey from old Ralph Burchell's kitchen the day before when he had been there helping out. "I'm gonna bring it with us this afternoon when we go to the Grove," he announced. "We can thank ol' Ralph for the hangover we're gonna have in the mornin'." He seemed pleased with himself that he'd stolen the whiskey from an old man.

Me and Hank weren't impressed but we didn't say anything to Ben. We knew he'd call us wimps and tell us to lighten up. He'd say that Ralph had plenty of whiskey laying around and wouldn't miss one measly bottle.

Ben and old Ralph had developed an odd relationship. Ben was the last guy I would have thought would find compassion for the old man but that's what happened. He'd go over every day to help out that cranky old man and not expect to get paid for the work he done.

Ben said he liked helping out. It gave him something to do. Ben wasn't afraid of work. And I'm sure old Ralph Burchell appreciated the help. After all, he wasn't a young man any more, and taking care of his cattle had become quite a chore for him. I still can't explain why Ben and that old man became so close. I sometimes wondered if Ben was trying to make up for the five of us burning down his barn back when we were kids. I never asked him though. I figured whatever deal he had made with old Ralph was his business, but it was clear that Ben thought a great deal of him. When the old man died, Ben took it hard. Actually, Ben found him that morning when he went out to the farm to help fix some fences. Ralph Burchell had taken a heart attack and died in the barn that he had built after the fire. It seemed only fitting he would die there next to his cattle. He thought a lot of them animals. He lived alone and didn't have anyone else.

It was obvious to all of us the old man's death bothered Ben a great deal but all that came a few years after this particular August morning when I ran into Ruby Todd and the others down at J.P.s. That day Ben seemed proud of himself for taking a bottle of the old man's liquor. It wasn't an expensive whiskey. It was some cheap shit that tasted like smelly perfume. It was ugly but it had a mean kick. A bottle of that stuff could set you back on your ass. You wouldn't exactly call me an alcoholic, but I wasn't against a drink every now and then.

Me and Hank weren't sure that Ben should have taken the whiskey since we knew the old man had to work for every cent he got. But Ben didn't seem to think much of it. That wasn't so unusual, though. Ben never stopped to think about the consequences of his actions. He never thought about how hard old Ralph Burchell worked to get enough money to buy that bottle of whiskey. All he thought about was the good time he could have with the liquor. And for Ben, that's all that was important. He always came first.

Just like every other morning, we were disappointed by the response down at the shipyard that day but we did leave with some hope. The war was picking up and that meant more jobs. They told us to come back the next morning as they were expecting several new boats in for refit over the next few days and they'd need more men. So while we didn't work right away, at least our prospects were looking better and we thought for sure we'd soon get hired. That put us in a good mood. We were up for a party, especially since we knew Ben had that bottle of whiskey stashed away. We knew it was stolen alcohol but we wanted to celebrate, so Hank and I overlooked that minor detail.

For the next few hours, we hung out around town, at my house and at J.P.s, hoping Levi or Bunny might soon be able to join us. But we were getting restless. It was hot in town and we wanted to get away. At about one-thirty Hank finally suggested we might as well head out to the Grove. Bunny and Levi knew where to find us when they were ready, he pointed out, and it didn't take much convincing to get me and Ben to agree. Like Hank, we were anxious to get out of town to escape the suffocating heat. Actually, it seemed like the town was shutting down early anyway. We knew it wouldn't be long before Bunny would be able to join us.

This sweltering part of August was known as the Dog Days of Summer because the intense heat made you pant like a parched pooch. We didn't have air conditioning back then and those little stores could get mighty hot and stuffy. Nobody shopped in such heat. Most people were staying at home or getting out of town to find some place cool. The heat had become so intense, I remember it was unbearable. There was no way to get comfortable or escape the temperature. There wasn't much to do in Liverpool on a day when the mercury was climbing through the roof. It was so humid that just thinking made you sweat. For the five of us, suffering it out meant going to the Grove to lie in the shade of the thick pines or taking a refreshing swim in Brier Lake. Liverpool wasn't a place you'd want to be on a hot August day and we wanted to get away early.

It was nice at the Grove, just like we'd expected it to be. The shade was a welcome change from the humidity and dust of the gravelled roads in downtown Liverpool. We no sooner got there before Ben cracked open the whiskey he had taken from old Ralph Burchill and passed it around. If we felt guilty about drinking liquor stolen from a sick old man, the guilt didn't last long. It sure as hell tasted good that day. It hit the spot after losing so much body fluid to the humidity. Whiskey was about the absolute worst kind of alcohol as far as I was concerned, but I drank it anyway. A few drinks of that crap and I'd be done for, especially with the shit we were drinking that day. The whiskey today is nothing like it was back then.

By the time Bunny arrived at about four o'clock, me, Hank and Ben were pretty loaded. We were feeling no pain and having one helluva good time when Bunny showed up. His old man had allowed him to leave early that day. Business was slow and he knew Bunny wanted to be with us since it was to be our last summer together. That's how Sam Henderson was. He always put his kids ahead of everything else. He understood how important it was for the young people to earn their own way in the world but he also knew being young was a time to have fun and enjoy friendships. He wanted Bunny to learn how to run the store but that could wait. He also wanted his son to have a good time while he was still young and not tied down with responsibilities, so he gave him the rest of the day off to be with us and celebrate what was left of the quickly dying summer. I had great respect for how that old man treated his kids.

We enjoyed having Bunny with us. He could be a hoot when he got away from his mother's watchful eye and the four of us had a great afternoon together. We drank and swam most of the time and by early evening, as the euphoria-like effects of the whiskey wore off, we were pretty much wiped out. But even though we were exhausted, we weren't ready to go home. Years later though, I regretted that we didn't call it a night after we sobered up. But we didn't. Instead, we made a fire and waited at the Grove for Levi to show up. After all, we had promised we'd wait for him. We felt we should at least be there when he showed up. Besides, we had nothing better to do back in town. We knew the heat would still be hanging in there like a shroud, so we flaked out in the cooler evening air and talked about the better days ahead, conveniently pushing the war out of our minds. We were still young and optimistic that the future held promise for each of us. We didn't know that same future could also hold many dark times.

Naturally, me, Ben and Hank all hoped we would go to the shipyard in the morning and land jobs right away. That'd be great. We were still living at home but we could all use the cash. But finding jobs wasn't the only thing on our minds that night. We talked about the girls in Liverpool and about who we'd like to go to bed with. It was the stuff guys talk about when they're together. It's the kind of bullshit we say in a group hoping to impress the others, but it was all talk. We were all mouth and no action.

In those days people didn't talk openly about sex, but we were five healthy and virile young men. Growing up in that old-age period was hard. We had to sneak around and whisper about these things. We talked about it every time we were together. You didn't dare mention it any place out in the open. Sex was a no-no. It was taboo, something everyone did but no one admitted to. Sex was like something evil and dirty. It was not to be enjoyed and it sure as hell was not to be mentioned in public, so we did all our talking when we were together, just like that night. Everything we learned about sex, we had to learn through our own experience or from our friends. So we talked and bullshitted, hoping to pick up some tips from each other. It didn't matter that most of the stories were made up.

Ben was the best bullshitter of all. He could tell a good tale and always came across as very convincing. He said he'd been with many girls since he was young but none of us really believed all his talk, although you never knew for sure with Ben. That was one of his quirky characteristics. He could be telling the truth or lying through his teeth and you couldn't tell the difference. He seemed very knowledgable, even though we didn't want to accept that he actually might have had some real experience. It's just possible he did know a thing or two. But it was hard for the rest of us to admit that he might have had more experience than ourselves. We would've been terribly jealous if we'd thought for sure that one of us had been with a girl and we hadn't. Of course you never said anything about this to the other guys. You wanted them to think that you had already done it. As a way to keep up the charade, you lied through your own teeth, just like the rest of them. If you wanted to be a real man, you never admitted the truth. What a mistake that was.

Ben's favourite stories were the ones about his sexual exploits with the next-door neighbour, Mrs. Bates, who liked to have sex when her husband was at work. Ben described Mrs. Bates as a slut who enjoyed sex anywhere and any way she could get it. She liked younger men and, Ben added with some embarrassment, younger women, as well. I can't say if I believed Ben about that part, but he swore on everything he held dear that he could see into his neighbour's bedroom from the attic window of the house he lived in following the fire. He insisted that he saw her on more than one occasion making out with other women right there in her bed. We weren't sure if we should believe him or not, but I couldn't argue with him. I knew parts of his story were true. I didn't know for sure if he was lying about the other-woman thing or not. But I can say that Ben was telling us the truth about being able to see into the bedroom from his attic, because I saw that for myself. He showed me one day, just to prove his point. Sure enough, there she was in all her natural-born beautiful glory strutting around her bedroom like it was nobody's business. And it wasn't. After all, she was in the privacy of her own house.

Ben said that's how he got to be with her. He could tell it much better than me, but he said that one day as he was watching Mrs. Bates from the attic window, she caught him spying on her. He was afraid she would be angry he had seen her naked and report him as a Peeping Tom. But instead of closing the bedroom curtains like you might think a woman would do when she was caught by a young boy lusting over her body, she stood in the window and touched herself in intimate ways for a few minutes. Then she waved for him to come over.

Ben was just about going crazy by that time. He took her up on the offer without hesitation and why wouldn't he? He was fourteen at the time. She was in her mid-thirties. Like I said, Ben could tell the story better. You're getting it second-hand from me. When Ben told the story, he included all the intimate details but I'll tell you what I remember.

After being caught spying on his beautiful, naked neighbour, Ben said he was excited about her offer but also very nervous at the same time. However, it was a chance most young boys long for and Ben wasn't stupid. He recognized the opportunity that he was being given and seized it. Flying down the stairs, out of his house and across the grassy yard to the neighbour's house faster than a dog chasing its tail, Ben said his mind was a blur. What if Mr. Bates came home early from work and caught them? Surely he'd be pissed to find a kid in bed with his gorgeous wife. Maybe he'd kill them both in a fit of rage. And what about his lack of experience? When he got to the house, would he know what to do? Would she like him? All of that uncertainty, however, was erased once he reached the neighbour's house.

Mrs. Bates was a good-looker and Ben knew many men around Liverpool would die to be with her. He threw caution to the wind. He wasn't about to blow this chance. None of the danger mattered and, in a naughty way, added to the excitement. Any risk was worth taking to see this woman up close and personal.

Ben knocked on the back door and waited for Mrs. Bates to answer, but she didn't. For a minute he felt the blood freeze in his veins. Had she changed her mind in the short time it had taken him to get over to her house? Ben waited a while longer, then went in. After all, he had been invited over, hadn't he? He knew Mrs. Bates was waiting for him. Once inside, he paused to catch his breath. His heart did palpitations as if he was running a marathon. His mind raced with nervous anticipation and confusion. Could he do this? Yes! He told himself. The burning in his groin told him he could.

Climbing the hardwood steps one at a time, Ben cautiously made his way to the bedroom where he had seen the beautiful and naked young woman only minutes earlier. The door was closed as if protecting a hidden treasure on the other side. He knocked and waited.

"Come in, Ben," a sultry voice said from the other side of the closed door. "You don't have to knock. I've been waiting for you."

Gingerly pushing open the door, Ben entered the room. She was perched on the edge of the bed smoking a cigarette like some silent movie seductress. Her beauty caught Ben's breath. She was wearing a flimsy nightgown but her wares were not a secret. Ben had already seen the treasures the flimsy material was covering, but only from a distance. Now he was close and he could barely contain his excitement.

"Actually, Ben, the truth is I've been waiting for you for a long time," she said. "I've been thinking about this day for months. Do you want to come in? Don't be shy. I know you do. I've seen you watching me from your attic window. I think you've liked what you've seen, haven't you, Ben?"

Ben's mouth went as dry as the hottest desert. "Yes," was the only word he could manage.

"Good," she said. "Come on in here then. I've been wanting to see what you have to offer me. Since you've been spying on me all these years, you know what I can give you, but now it's your turn for a little show and tell."

"Come over here and let's have a look," she whispered, taking him by the shoulders and positioning him in front of a floor-length mirror. "Why Ben, you're trembling. Don't be afraid. I'm not going to hurt you. Now, take off your shirt," she instructed. "But please do it slowly ... there's no need to rush."

Ben did as he was told. He undid the buttons one at a time and slipped his shirt off his broad shoulders, and dropped it to the floor.

"My, you do have a nice body," she said. "I like my men to have huge shoulders. Now, remove your pants."

Ben quickly slid down his pants to expose his short, muscular legs. Mrs. Bates slowly nodded her head as if giving her approval for what she saw.

"Very good, Ben. You're turning out to be every bit of the man that I imagined you to be. But that underwear is really blocking the view," she whispered in his ear. Her warm, sweet-smelling breath tickled his neck.

Ben reached down and removed his shorts.

"Now let me see the complete package," she said moving behind him, pressing her warm body against his. "I am impressed. You are a mature fourteen-year-old, aren't you. Now look at yourself in this mirror, Ben." She moved her hands over his shoulders and around to his chest. "Do you see it, Ben?" she asked. "Do you understand what it is about a man's body that excites a woman like me?"

Ben hesitated, searching for the right words. He didn't want to say the wrong thing and spoil the moment. "Yes, ma'am. I think I understand," he said.

"Do you really?" she toyed, moving closer. "Let's see if I can make the picture even clearer for you." She began to kiss and caress his body. First his neck, his shoulders, then the small of his back and then around front to his chest, lingering on his nipples. "Is this what you want, Ben?"

He couldn't move, let alone say anything. Instead, he stood perfectly still with his eyes clenched tight. She moved behind him again.

"Open your eyes, Ben. Look into the mirror and see for yourself," she said as she moved her hands down his shoulders, across the small of his back and ass, and then around front to his penis. Ben gasped. He thought he would faint as her hands wrapped around his penis. It was the first time another set of hands had touched him there. "This, young Ben, is what drives women like me crazy," she said. "Don't be shy, Ben. Don't turn your head away or close your eyes. Look at it, Ben. Be proud of it. This can do a lot of things for you if you learn how to use it."

Ben remained speechless, his mind swimming with wild excitement and ecstasy. "Now, Ben, it's your turn. You must see up close what you've only been able to glimpse from a distance." Moving around to face him, Mrs. Bates slid the nightgown down off her shoulders and dropped it to the floor. Her beauty was exquisite. It was even more breathtaking up close than it had been from across the yard. It was as if a master artist had chiselled her from the finest piece of marble in the earth, Ben told us.

"Do you like it? This, my young Ben, is what drives men like you crazy. Men and women are a strange bunch. People around this town are prudes. We tease each other with our bodies, yet we think they're an instrument of evil and we keep them covered up. But I don't think that way, Ben, and I hope you don't either. Don't ever let anyone tell you that our bodies are dirty or evil. I think our bodies should be enjoyed and cherished. Touch me, Ben, if you want to."

Want to? If only she knew how badly Ben wanted to touch her. Slowly and nervously he reached out and scooped her breasts into his hands.

"Relax, Ben. There's no need to be nervous," she said, placing her hands over his. Her touch was gentle, relaxing. "I understand this is your first time, but don't be scared ... enjoy it. That's what our bodies are for. Don't ever let any of the hypocrites in this town ruin that for you. Don't listen to their talk. It will scar you forever, and that would be a dreadful shame for someone so young with such a wonderful body."

She smiled and looked him square in the eyes. "I know what you need, my young Ben. You need something to help you relax." Instead of going to fetch them a drink, as Ben had been expecting, she pulled him close and kissed him hard on the lips. Her tongue pushed into his inexperienced but eager mouth.

"Relax, Ben," she whispered into his ear as she began to kiss his neck ... his chest ... his stomach ... and then, without warning, she slipped his rock-hard penis into her mouth. Ben all but passed out. His knees went weak. It only lasted a minute or two, and then it was over. Ben was not mature enough to hold back.

Rising from her knees, Mrs. Bates whispered, "That was wonderful, Ben. You really are good at this. Can you make it work for me again?"

It didn't take much coaxing to get him back into form. Taking him by the hand, she led him across the room and pushed him down onto the bed. She paused a minute to eye him from head to toe, then she climbed onto him. It was the moment most young men dream of and it was everything he had ever imagined it would be. She knew exactly what to do and Ben just lay there wallowing in the pleasure she was creating with their bodies.

When it was over, she rolled off him and left the room. She said he should leave as it was getting late, but she suggested with a wink, he could come back again whenever he felt the urge.

That was Ben's version of his first experience with a woman. Although he may have embellished some of the details, I would never call Ben a liar. Much of it probably happened like he said it did. Many stories about Mrs. Bates had been going around town. If they were any indication, then she really was a slut. She had a bad reputation, so it's very probable that Ben did lose his innocence at a very young age to the woman next door. And if it wasn't true, then it was still a good story, especially to a bunch of tipsy young men hung up on their own virility. The truth was, a good story is all we cared about that night.

Ben was proud of his accomplishment. His stories always left the rest of us jealous and longing for our own experiences with the opposite sex. He bragged that making it for the first time with a woman more than twice his age was the best way to be broken in. She was experienced and knew exactly what to do. He claimed he spent many afternoons at the neighbour's house and he always came home smiling. It could have all been lies. Who can say for certain? But it sure as hell made for some fun talk for a bunch of horny young men. We always allowed Ben to spin his stories and every now and then, one of us might jump in with our own version of our sexual experiences, but there was no doubt that Ben had the talent for getting our interest.

Chapter 24

It was almost eight o'clock that August night when Levi finally showed up at the Grove, but to our surprise he wasn't alone. He had Ruby Todd in tow. I could tell from the first minute the pair walked into the fire-lit clearing that Ben was upset. He didn't want her there. Ruby and Ben couldn't get along. As soon as they were within five feet of each other, you could feel the bad vibes. It was like fingernails on a chalkboard. That night, the heavy tension immediately descended over the gang, snuffing out our mood like a bucket of water quenches a campfire.

Ben was jealous over Ruby. We all knew how he felt about her. Levi knew how Ben would react. I'm convinced Levi brought Ruby that night just to tick Ben off.

I don't think Ruby and Levi were in any way romantic, but I'm sure Ben didn't see it like that. When he got mad, there was no reasoning with him. It wouldn't have mattered what we said. Instead, we let Ben stew in his own way, hoping that it would quickly blow over without any trouble, and we would get back to having a good time. After all, that's why we had gathered.

Levi explained he had been on his way out of town earlier when he met Ruby walking home. She had spent the afternoon with Patty and a few friends helping out down at the church's weekly picnic. Throughout the summer, the local church held a picnic in the town park every Wednesday afternoon for the young kids. The minister liked to get the girls to help out. Some people in Liverpool said Rev. Henshaw had an eye for the young girls, but no one ever knew for sure. As far as I know, the rumours were never verified.

That evening, Levi said, Ruby looked hot and sweaty when they stopped in front of J.P.s to talk, so he generously invited her to come along. He thought she might enjoy a swim in the lake, he explained. How thoughtful. Naturally we were all worried about what Ruby's father would say if he ever learned that she was out in the woods with us. But Ruby promised he would never know. If her father asked where she had been, Ruby would tell him she had gone to Patty's house after the picnic. If he ever asked Patty about it, Ruby said her friend would back her up.

I still wasn't comfortable about Ruby being there. I knew the kind of fuss her father would raise if he ever discovered the truth. But even though I understood there could be trouble, I kept my mouth shut. I figured if the young girl wanted to get herself into trouble with her old man, that was totally up to her. She'd have to suffer the consequences. I kept quiet, especially after Levi produced a full bottle of whiskey he had confiscated from his father's private stash. Levi knew his father would be pissed when he found the bottle missing but figured what the hell. He wanted to have a good time with his buddies so it was worth getting his father a little hot under the collar. He'd scream and yell for a couple of minutes then lecture Levi on the evils of stealing. It was the kind of talking to that Levi had heard many times before. He'd learned years earlier how to block out his old man.

Once the whiskey started flowing, most of us forgot about Ruby being there. While the five of us started drinking right away, Ruby was reluctant to join in. She told us she never had whiskey before. She didn't know if she'd like it or not. In time, though, she warmed up to the idea and, after a little coaxing from us, had a few sips. With the whiskey quickly disappearing, it wasn't long before we were all feeling pretty damned good again and slipping back into a partying mood.

By around nine o'clock we were all drunk as skunks at a roadside barbecue. That's when Hank suggested we should go for a swim. I thought it was a good idea until Levi dared everyone to go skinny dipping. We'd never done that sort of thing before. It was clear what was on Levi's mind and I didn't like it. It was obvious that Bunny and Hank were against the idea too but Ben, well, he was all for it. In fact, he was the first to get undressed. In just a few minutes flat he had dropped his clothes and was prancing around the fire buck naked. Ben was proud of his body. It didn't seem to phase him one bit that there was a girl present.

Ben began taunting. He called us chicken, especially Levi since it had been his idea in the first place to go skinny dipping. "C'mon, don't be sissies," he teased. "You afraid to show off your little weiners?"

It took a few minutes but Ben finally embarrassed Levi into joining him. Before we knew it, like little sheep being led to the slaughter, me and Bunny had joined in as well, but not Hank. To this day, I can't explain my actions. I don't know why I followed Ben and Levi but Hank wouldn't have any part of it. He was not impressed with our actions. He could see where this was heading and that trouble wouldn't be far away. Hank said he hadn't come up to the Grove for this bullshit and he wasn't about to stand by and watch. He said he was going home and he left us there naked by the fire.

"You guys are headin' for trouble. I ain't havin' any part of it," he said as he left.

Hank seemed embarrassed that the four of us had stripped off in front of Ruby. Maybe he was uncomfortable that we had stripped off in front of him. I don't know which it was, but I know he didn't like it. Hank seemed more uneasy than Ruby, even though she hadn't yet taken her clothes off. After me, Bunny, Ben and Levi all ran into the water, Ruby began to ease up. I guess the mood and the whiskey got to be too much for her. It was only a matter of minutes before she stripped down to her underwear and joined us in the lake. She never did strip completely nude, but I figured she did take a big step by at least getting down to her bra and panties.

I don't know how long we played in the water. We were all having a good time. It was fun for awhile until Ben started messing with Ruby. That's when everything turned sour.

"C'mon, Ruby. Let's have some real fun," Ben said. At the same time, he started pulling at her, like he was trying to force her to do things she didn't want to do. "Let's find some place where we can be alone."

"No, Ben, I don't want to," she insisted. "Let's just stay here with the guys." Ruby didn't like Ben's rude and forceful advances, not one bit. "I don't like it when you behave like this, Ben. Please leave me alone before you ruin everything."

"They don't care what we do. Let's leave these guys here," he shot back. "You and me can go off some place else on our own. We can find some place private." Ben had his own ideas of the kind of fun he wanted and there was no stopping him.

But we should have. We could see he was getting rough.

"No, Ben. I just want to stay here," Ruby pleaded. "Let's go back by the fire. I'm starting to get cold."

"I can warm you up," he said. Ben had been diving under the water and pulling at Ruby's panties, trying to get them off. "I know a real fun way to warm you up."

"Stop it, Ben. Don't do that. I don't like it."

But he wouldn't.

"What's the matter, Ruby? You afraid to show us everything you got?" Ben taunted. "If the rest of us can go naked, then you can damned well go naked too. Or do you think you're too good for us?"

"Stop it, Ben. Right now." Ruby wasn't having any of Ben's foolishness. "No, I won't do that, Ben. I'm getting my clothes and I'm going home."

The mood changed quickly.

"No, you don't want to go home yet, Ruby. We're just startin' to have fun," Ben insisted, grabbing her by the shoulders again and forcing her under water.

"Stop it, Ben. You're hurting me," Ruby screamed, pushing back at Ben's rough horseplay.

She started for shore, half running and half swimming. Ben got angry. He became forceful. The more Ruby protested, the more insistent Ben became.

"Damn it, girl," he yelled. "I told you to stay here with us. We ain't done yet." He became violent and grabbed her by the shoulders one more time. She spun around, lost her balance and slipped into the water.

The rest of us were in shock. We couldn't believe what was happening. Ben forced Ruby's head under water and, grabbing handfulls of hair, began pulling her towards the shore. He slapped her on the back of the head a few times, trying to force her into submission.

"Stop it, Ben," Ruby cried. "You're hurting me." She begged him to stop. But he wouldn't. The more Ruby struggled and resisted, the harder Ben pulled on her. With clenched fists he grabbed more hair. His attack was brutal. He punched and slapped her as she screamed out in pain.

"Shut up, bitch," he screamed back. "It's no use fighting. I got you now. You won't get away from me this time. You and me got some catchin' up to do. You owe me and I'm gonna collect."

"What are you going to do, Ben?" Ruby wailed. "Please don't hurt me. Can't we just talk this through?"

"There's no more time for talkin'," Ben snapped.

As the rest of us stood back and watched, Ben finally got Ruby to shore. It was wrong ... it was very wrong. I know that.

Once on shore, Ben became brutal. That's where the real attack began. "I told you to shut up and stop fighting," he ordered, planting several blows across Ruby's face with the back of his hand. He then pinned the helpless, screaming girl to the gravely sand like a little rag doll.

"Let's get a better look at what's under here," he snarled, throwing his weight on top of her to keep her trapped there as he tore off her bra.

"Ben, please don't do this," she pleaded. "You're hurting me. Please get off."

But Ben had lost control. It was like he was someone else.

I don't know exactly what I was feeling at that moment as Ben ripped off Ruby's bra, her bare breasts coming into view under the glow of the full moon. Maybe it was the sight of her creamy white skin or the booze or the sex talk from earlier in the night, but I didn't do anything to stop what was happening right in front of me.

I kind of went numb and blocked out the screams as Ben's hands moved down her thrashing body and ripped off her underpants. She was trapped, like the prey of a beast, and her attacker was relentless. But I did nothing.

"Get off of me," she screamed, punching at Ben, trying to get him to loosen his grip. Clawing at him with her fingernails, the only weapon she had. She fought back with every ounce of energy she could muster, but he was too strong. "Don't do this to me, Ben," she cried.

I felt dizzy. It was like the world was spinning out of control. It all happened so fast. I didn't know what to do or how to react. It felt like I was in a dream. My mind told me I should stop Ben but I felt completely powerless.

I could do nothing, but from somewhere on the shore, Hank quickly ran to the water's edge to intervene. We had all thought Hank had gone home earlier, but he hadn't.

By the time he got to where Ben had forced Ruby to the ground, it was too late. Ben was on top of her. As he forcibly penetrated her, Ruby screamed, pleading with him to stop.

"Get off of me. Ben, please stop. You're hurting me," She cried over and over and over. "It hurts real bad. Please don't do this. Someone stop him ... help me."

But there was no stopping Ben. He was a madman on a mission.

"Shut up," he shot back. "Stop pretendin' you don't like it. You know you want this. You're all the same. You tease and pretend you don't want it but I know you really do. I'm gonna show you what you've been missin' all these weeks."

For some reason, Ben had come to believe Ruby had been leading him on since she arrived in Liverpool, but I didn't see it that way. However, there was no stopping him.

"Please help me," Ruby begged of us. "Don't let him do this. Why won't any of you help me?"

For as long as I live, I don't think I will hear anything as pitiful as that girl's screams of pain and agony as she begged him to stop. It had only taken seconds for Ben to force the girl's legs open. He planted his mouth over hers in a vain effort to drown out her screams.

"Shut up," he said, delivering two solid slaps to her face. "Stop fighting. If you just go with it, it won't hurt as much."

Hank sprung into action. "Get off her," he screamed rushing to the shore. "Stop this Ben. You're going too far. You're hurting her."

Reaching the edge of the water where Ben had pinned Ruby down, Hank bent over, picked up a heavy tree branch from the ground and struck Ben on the side of the head with it. The impact of wood connecting with Ben's skull bone was sickening and loud. I could hear it way out in the lake where me and Bunny were still standing. That must have been a few hundred feet away. The force was so powerful that it knocked Ben off the girl, sending him sprawling to the wet rocky shore.

"Get off her, I said. You're hurting her," Hank screamed at Ben.

"Christ, Hank. What the hell you doin'," Ben cursed. "Stay outta this. It ain't none of your business." Bleeding from the resulting gash over his left eye, Ben now turned his anger on Hank. "If you don't want any part of the girl, stay the hell outta the way. I ain't done with her yet. Ruby likes it. Can't you see that? If she didn't want it, she shouldn't have come around teasin' like some dirty two-bit whore," he said. "Now she's gettin' what she deserves and if you get in the way, then you'll get yours too."

Hank was a big guy. He wasn't easily intimidated by Ben. "I don't think so, Ben," he said, planting himself directly between the sobbing girl and her assailant. By this time Ben had gotten up to his knees and could see Ruby struggling to get up.

"If you want to get back at Ruby," Hank said, "you'll have to go through me." That wouldn't be easy. Hank was built tough. He wouldn't easily be pushed around.

"Look, Hank," Ben yelled. His anger was intense. "This ain't between us. You and me have been friends for a long time and I don't think you want this little bitch comin' between us. She's had this comin' to her since the first day she showed up here in town. I ain't never been good enough for her. Don't try to stop me, Hank, 'cause I ain't gonna be responsible for what's gonna happen if you do, friends or no friends."

I looked at Bunny. He looked at me. We were stunned. It was impossible to believe what was happening. I didn't know what to do or what to say to make Ben stop. He was raging like a bull in heat and he wasn't about to be stopped. That much was obvious. But while me and Bunny stared on in disbelief, it was Levi who surprised me the most.

While Hank was bent over trying to help Ruby to her feet while still keeping an eye on Ben, Levi came up from behind, and grabbed Hank around the neck and waist. He locked his arms around Hank's neck and forced him down to the ground, face first into the sand. Hank had been so preoccupied with Ben and Ruby, that he hadn't noticed the sneak attack from behind. He was trapped.

"There Ben," Levi barked while holding Hank down. "Finish what you started. This little shit ain't gonna get in your way."

Recognizing the opportunity with Hank out of commission, Ben quickly sprang to his feet. Ruby had been clawing her way through the wet sand, trying to regain her footing, when he caught her. Flinging the helpless girl to the ground yet again, he jumped on Ruby one more time.

"No, Ben. Don't do this," Ruby screamed. "Listen to Hank."

But Ben wasn't listening. Again, through tears and screams of protest, Ben forced her to submit, pushing himself into her battered body.

Me and Bunny had made our way back to the shore by this time but instead of stopping Ben and Levi, like we should have, we ran back to the fire and hurried into our clothes. I don't know what we were thinking.

"Jack. Bunny. Do something. Don't you see what they're doing? You've got to stop them before it's too late," Hank called out, begging us to stop Ben and Levi, but we didn't do anything. By the time me and Bunny got dressed, Ben had spent his load and was sprawled out on the wet gravel as Ruby lay, sobbing, curled up in a ball next to him. She was trying to protect her savagely violated body.

The girl was injured, we could see that. Ben's attack had been brutal. She was in pain, her battered and bruised body trembled in the cooling night air.

"Why, Ben? Why?" She sobbed. "Why did you do this to me? ... Why did you hurt me so bad? I thought we were friends." Ruby seemed to find some force deep within and recoiled like a trapped cobra. "I hope you're satisfied with yourself. You should be proud of what you've done, Ben. You're a real big man now."

Trickles of blood ran down from the corners of her mouth as she cried while painfully pulling herself up to her hands and knees. I knew she was preparing to make a run for it.

But Ben was no longer a threat. He remained silent. He didn't respond and he didn't raise another hand against her. He totally ignored Ruby.

But Hank didn't. He tried to coax her to get back up on her feet and run away. "Get outta here now while you still can," he urged her as Levi began to loosen the grip that he had maintained during Ben's assault. "C'mon. Get goin'. You've got to go now. ... Run Ruby, run, before it's too late," he begged her. "Run for your life as fast as you can."

Ben may have finished his dirty deed, but Hank knew the assault wasn't over. Now Levi wanted his turn.

"I can't," she said. "I can hardly move. It hurts too much. Ben hurt me really bad." Slowly, Ruby struggled back to her feet, stumbling as she went and holding onto her right side as if her ribs might have been broken during Ben's assault. From where I stood by the fire, I could see that her body had been battered pretty badly. I knew she had to be in a great deal of pain.

Pushing herself with some inner strength she managed to muster, Ruby slowly picked her way over the slippery rocks along the lake shore in a feeble attempt to get away from her assailants. But her efforts were to no avail.

Levi pounced. "Where do think you're going? You're not going anywhere!"

He grabbed Ruby by the shoulders and threw her to the wet gravel. The back of her head struck the rocks.

"No, Levi, please, don't," she protested. "No more, please. I thought we were friends."

"Just shut up, Ruby. Don't fight me on this," he demanded.

Ruby's will to survive was strong, though. She wasn't giving up. She reached out in one last desperate attempt to save herself and found two large rocks in the gravel. Somehow she managed to find the weapons she needed. Scooping up a large rock in each hand she found her target on each side of Levi's skull. The impact of rock on bone was loud.

"Jesus Christ. Are you trying to kill me?" he screamed. The counter-attack did slow Levi down for a few seconds but Ruby obviously didn't have enough strength left to make it count. Shaking off any pain Ruby's defensive maneuvre may have caused him, Levi quickly recoiled like a tiger. "You'll pay for that." Grabbing her by the hair with both of his hands, in one swift motion he pushed Ruby over on her stomach and forced himself into the girl from behind.

Again, Hank tried to stop the assault, but this time, Ben held him back. "No Hank. You got to watch this," Ben said. "She's only pretendin' not to like it. That's part of the game. She likes it rough, can't you see that?"

"All's I see is two punks terrorizin' an innocent, helpless young girl," Hank said. "Can't you see he's hurtin' her? Let me go so I can help her while there's still time. ... It's not too late to stop him, Ben. If we let this continue, somethin' bad's gonna happen. ... I just know it."

It didn't matter what Hank said to Ben, he couldn't get through to him. All Hank could do was watch as the assault progressed and Ruby called out to him.

"Help me! Somebody, help me! It hurts real bad, please stop." She cried over and over but Hank was helpless under Ben's grip. He couldn't do anything and me and Bunny were too stunned to interfere.

Ruby did the best she could to fight off the attack. She struggled with every ounce of energy she had left in her broken body, her arms and legs flailing around, trying to push off her assailant. But it was impossible from the position she was in and, besides, Levi was too strong and forceful. She was like a rag doll under his weight.

Then, in an instant, her body went limp ... there was no movement ... and the crying stopped.

The Grove grew silent for a few minutes. Even the crickets and loons which only minutes earlier had been singing their summer serenades, became silent. Then hysteria set in.

Chapter 25

"Jesus, she's not movin'," Levi cried. "I don't think she's breathin'. Somebody do somethin'."

He pulled back from Ruby's still form. "Com'on, Ruby," he pleaded. "Stop messin' around. Listen, guys, somethin's wrong over here."

Something was wrong, all right. Something was very wrong.

We knew immediately what had happened. Levi had killed Ruby. When he rolled her over onto her stomach, he forced her face into the water and she drowned.

"What have we done?" Levi was beginning to panic. "What have we done?"

I'm not sure how his attack on Ruby became "we" but suddenly, in Levi's eyes, we were all responsible.

I can't begin to tell you how I felt. "Jesus, Levi," I cried. "You idiot. You've really done it this time."

And Bunny was so worked up, he threw up beside the fire.

"There, you stupid assholes," Hank snapped at Levi and Ben. "You done it now. Ain't you proud of yourselves? You've gone and killed her. Now what are we gonna do? I got half a mind to walk outta here right now and find Chief Frasier. I'm sure he'd like to hear all about what you've done."

"Com'on, Hank," Ben snapped. "Take it easy. Attacking us ain't gonna solve anything. It ain't gonna fix things."

"Take it easy? Don't tell me to take it easy!" Hank screamed. "How the hell can I take it easy after what just happened? Don't you realize what you've done? What do think the Chief will do to you when he sees Ruby like this? I told you somethin' bad was gonna happen, but you guys wouldn't listen. You never listen to anything I say."

"Shut up," Levi snapped. "I gotta think."

"Think? That'd be different," Hank fired back. "If you'd been thinkin' with your head instead of your dick, none of this would have happened. We better go to the Chief before things get any worse. ... We messed up real bad this time."

"You ain't gonna do nothin' except keep your mouth shut," Levi demanded. "If you go to the chief, me and Ben will tell him that you were in on it too. We'll tell him that you wanted the girl just as much as we did ... and you guys, too," he said, motioning toward me and Bunny.

"Yeah. She wanted this and she got it," Ben piped up. "She deserved what she got, the little whore."

"And you shut up too, Ben," Levi demanded again. "If you wouldn't have started this, we wouldn't be in this shit right now. We got to figure out what we're gonna do. We can't let anyone know what happened or my ol' man will kill me. We gotta take care of this and no one can ever find out what we did."

"Deserved this?" Hank screamed. "How in the hell can you say that an innocent young girl deserved to be tortured and killed like this? What the Christ you got up there? Shit for brains? Don't you realize what you've done?"

"If Ben hadn't started screwin' around, none of this would have happened," Levi huffed. "It's all his fault."

"There he is," Hank said.

"Who?" Ben asked.

"Good ol' Levi. The same Levi we've known all these years," Hank answered. "I wondered when the real Levi would show up. He killed Ruby and now he's turning the blame on the rest of us. That's how he does things."

"I'm telling you to shut up, Hank," Levi insisted. "I'm warning you to back off."

"And of course he'd be more concerned about what his ol' man would think than the fact that a young girl had died only minutes earlier by his own hands," Hank continued.

"I said to back off, Hank," Levi yelled. "It's all Ben's fault. If he hadn't started it, none of this would have happened."

"My fault? Now just wait a god-damned minute," Ben argued. "I'm not takin' all the blame. I didn't kill her and I ain't takin' the heat for it ... at least not by myself. You had his dick in her when she died, not me."

"It don't matter who was doin' what when she died," Hank interrupted. "I can't believe I'm sayin' this, but Levi's right. Me and Jack and Bunny didn't do anythin' wrong, but we didn't do anythin' right either. We should have stopped this. We were here and they'd blame us just as much as they'd blame you two. We're all in this together."

"Hey! Now hold on," Bunny jumped in. "What the hell's all this *we* shit? I didn't do nothin'. Me and Jack weren't close enough to do anythin' to the girl and we sure as hell weren't close enough to stop it."

"It won't matter," Hank reasoned. "They won't listen to none of that, even if it is the truth. We should have stopped them. Maybe we didn't try hard enough. If anyone finds out about this, they'd take one look at the five of us out here drinkin' with a good lookin' girl. They'd figure we were all in on it together right from the start. They'd conclude that we planned this all along, that we lured her out here for one purpose. It won't matter to them who actually did what. They'd just figure we all had our way with her and then killed her to keep her mouth shut."

"But that's not what happened," I piped up. "Ben and Levi did it, not us. And Ruby's death really was an accident. Levi didn't mean to kill her. Maybe they'll go easy on all of us if we just tell them the truth."

"The truth? Do you really think any of that will matter?" Hank asked. "Ask yourself what you'd think if you were the police. They'll come up with their own conclusions. You're forgettin' Bert Frasier. He don't like none of us. He'd jump at a chance to catch us in some trouble like this. We won't stand a chance if he gets wind of this. Ain't no court gonna believe that we didn't mean to kill Ruby. They'd say we brought her out here with this plan in mind, and I'm not so sure that's not what Levi did."

"You back off, Hank Thompson," Levi argued. "I never meant for any of this to happen. But I can tell you all, I ain't goin' to jail over the death of some little whore. You better understand that. You all may as well know right up front that if I do go down, you all go down with me. I don't care who did what."

"Well ain't that great," Bunny shot back. "I ain't goin' to jail for somethin' I didn't do just to save Levi and Ben's asses. I don't care if we're supposed to be friends or not, I'll tell them what happened. Maybe they'll go easier on Hank and Jack and me. Anyway, Hank tried to help Ruby. That should count for somethin'. He tried to stop you two assholes so they'll really take it easier on him."

"Give me a break," Ben started again. "Listen Bunny, you little shit. They ain't gonna believe you, any more than they're gonna believe me or Jack or any of us. Hank's right. You three may as well accept that you're in this right up to your balls whether you like it or not. The question is, what the hell are we gonna do about it so none of us gets into trouble?"

The air in the Grove grew silent. Even the crickets and loons became still once again. It was almost as if the entire universe had come to a halt. It seemed like an eternity as we, five conspirators on our covert operation, stood vigil around the dead girl's naked body trying to devise a plot that would ultimately save our own skins. It was a morbid picture, one I'd love to be able to put out of my mind after all of these years but the sight of Ruby's bloodied and bruised lifeless body glowing under the bright moonlight has stuck with me. It's a lasting impression that has become a vivid image burned into the far recess of my mind. I carry the pictures around with me every day.

Then finally, Hank spoke, assuming the lead. "Okay, then. It's settled. We're all in this together. Now what are we gonna do about this mess?"

Someone had to take charge. The time had come to unite; to put our differences aside like we had done so many other times over the years. It didn't matter that only minutes earlier we had been on opposite sides of the fence, that some of us were rapists and murderers while others were innocent, if not partially responsible because of our inaction. We now understood we had to pull together. It was a matter of survival and we were all in it together whether we wanted to be there or not.

Chapter 26

Experience had taught us that when Hank took charge, it was time to fall in behind our leader like obedient troops. The jockeying for position was over. We knew that when Hank stood up to lay out a plan, we should listen. Simply put, he always seemed to make sense. It came naturally that way.

Over the years, Hank had shown his leadership abilities many times. We never questioned him. Besides, no one else could ever come up with any ideas that were better than his. That's the way it was with Hank. He was like our unofficial general. It was time to stop the argument that had been pulling us apart. We had to become one. We had to think of a way to get ourselves out of the mess we were in and the only way to do that effectively was to have everyone on the same side. We knew that we stood a better chance of getting out of this if we stayed united. But finding that togetherness was not easy.

Hank made the first suggestion and most of the guys followed right along, like little sheep. Did you know the herd will follow the lead sheep right off a steep cliff to their sure death without any consideration for themselves? That's just what we were. Little sheep, only we were looking for a way to save our asses, and Hank seemed to have an idea that just might work.

"Now we gotta think of somethin' that can't fail or we're all in deep shit," Hank began, placing his hands on his hips as if to project an image of authority. "It's time to stop arguin' and get down to business or our asses are gonna fry. We got to do this as a team or it won't work. If anyone wants to back out, now is the time to speak up. But keep in mind, that none of us wanted this to happen. And none of us wants to spend the rest of his life in jail so whatever we do, we all got to go along with it no matter if it turns your guts or not ... and we all got to agree that we will never tell anyone about what has happened out here tonight. We got to swear it on everything that is dear to us. Silence will be our best ally in the weeks ahead, do you all understand? We have no choice but to do this if we don't want to get caught. If one of us goes down, then we all go. From this point on, we're all in this equal. If this unity cracks even a little, then we are each on our own. But remember, if that happens, you won't be able to trust anyone. God knows what will happen 'cause the truth will be so screwed up that no one will believe anythin' we say. We got to decide if we're all in or if we're out. What's it gonna be?"

Hank paused. He looked around at the four of us, waiting for our answers. It was clear to me he didn't like what he was proposing, but for some reason I still don't understand he felt obligated to help the others out of the mess they had gotten us into.

Levi and Ben were quick to acknowledge their agreement to any plan that would save their asses. They'd do that naturally. They had nothing to lose.

But I was amazed that Hank would lay his own self on the line to protect the two young men who only minutes earlier had been his adversaries. Hank had been the most sensible through the whole ordeal. He had actually tried to stop the rape, but for some reason he felt compelled to be a part of the plan ... or part of the group. ... Maybe it was out of friendship or some twisted sense of loyalty, but I could never figure it out.

Bunny hummed and hawed for a few minutes. "I don't want to be a part of any plan that's gonna make matters worse," he said. But eventually, when he understood the type of intense scrutiny we'd be under if the truth ever got out, he came around and reluctantly joined with the others. "I'll do this, but I don't really want to. I don't think it's right, but I don't see how we got any other choice."

I wasn't so quick to jump in even though these guys were my friends. I loved these guys like brothers but I wasn't so sure I wanted to destroy myself to protect them. "Why should I risk everything after what they've done?" I said. "I'm not convinced that if we go to the police we'd all be in so much trouble."

I knew Levi and Ben were in deep shit right up to their armpits but I didn't think they'd be so hard on Bunny, Hank and me once they knew the entire truth. So I hesitated, which only made the rest of them pressure me all the more.

"I don't know if I want to do this, guys. It's only makin' matters worse for all of us," I said. I thought a different perspective on the situation might cause them to stop and think for a minute. "It seems to me like we're all settin' ourselves up to take the fall for somethin' that Levi and Ben have done. I'm their friend too and I don't want to see them get into trouble either, but they should have thought of that before they attacked poor Ruby here. They should have been thinkin' with their heads instead of with their dicks. Now we got to go out on a limb to cover up for them. This is not gonna be so easy to hide. We've got a dead girl on our hands and there's gonna be hell to pay when they find her. You guys ain't stupid. She's gonna be missed. ... Hell, she's probably bein' missed right now. Are we all prepared for the kind of heat this town is gonna be under when they realize Ruby didn't come home tonight? I think we're takin' a pretty big risk if we don't come clean."

"Com'on, Jack," Ben said. "We all got to agree or this won't work."

"I don't think I can, Ben," I said. "What about Ruby? She didn't deserve this. She was nice to all of us and she died like an animal. ... That makes me sick. Actually, Levi and Ben, you make me sick for what you've done to Ruby and for what you're forcin' us to do. If we take care of ourselves, who's gonna take care of her? ... What about Ruby? What's gonna happen to her? Shouldn't we think about her for a minute? Like I said, Ben and Levi are my friends, but I'm not sure that buryin' ourselves along with them is doin' them any favours."

The four of them applied pressure but it was Hank who did most of the talking. "Listen Jack, we're in a whole lot of trouble here. I think you're wrong. I think they'll go tough on all of us if they find Ruby's body. Believe me, I'm pissed at Levi and Ben too, but I don't think we got any choice. We all feel bad about what happened to Ruby. Hell, it makes me sick to my guts but what's done is done. We can't undo it. All we can do now is take care of ourselves, but to do that we got to stick together. If one of us don't join in, then we're all messed up. If you don't help us then you let us all down and that means our friendships don't mean nothin' to you."

They continued applying heat until, finally, but reluctantly, I agreed to be a partner in their hideous crime. They were all relieved that I was in, but I've never forgiven myself for giving in to the pressure and going along with their plan. I should have said no and walked away that night. I should have let things work out on their own. Life would have been a whole lot better for all of us if that had happened.

Chapter 27

The wheels were already in motion and I was sucked into their wake. We knew we had one thing going for us and that was the isolation of the Grove. The location would afford us the secrecy to hatch our morbid plot and the time we needed to execute it. We were a long ways out from town and not many people ever came out to this spot, especially at that hour of the night. The chances of us being seen by anyone else were pretty slim. We knew that whatever we decided to do, we could carry out our plan without fear of being discovered and the truth would stay with the five of us.

Despite my earlier reservations, once I said I was in, I was in for the long haul. The secrets we were making were the kind that we'd take to the grave with us.

"The key," Hank explained, "is not to panic. If any of us panic, we'll blow the whole plan and it will be game over for all of us."

As disgusting as it was, I will give Hank credit for coming up with a plan that was obviously foolproof. Over the years, no one ever learned whatever happened to Ruby Todd.

The plan was a simple one. I think that's what made it so effective.

"Jack, you and Bunny go back into town to Henderson's and get some kerosene oil," Hank said. "Come straight back and make sure no one in town sees you coming or going. We have to remain unseen if this is gonna work."

As we made our way to Henderson's along the same beaten path that we had travelled many times before, everything seemed different, kind of foreign to me, most likely because of the confusion and fright in my mind. I was scared shitless. It was a dangerous game we were playing, one that could be lost any second.

On our way back into town, me and Bunny didn't talk much. I didn't know what to say and I'm sure Bunny was feeling the same way. Words didn't seem appropriate after what we had just witnessed. And considering what we were about to do, anything we would have said might have only contributed to our guilt. After all, Bunny and I didn't actually participate in the crime, yet here we were participating in a plan designed to protect those responsible, our friends. Naturally, that made us just as guilty as Ben and Levi, if not even more so on a moral plane.

As we neared the outskirts of town, Bunny finally broke the silence. "Just what the hell are we doin', Jack?" he asked, stopping to gather his thoughts.

I was caught off guard by the question but quickly picked up the query. "Well, I guess we're about to make the biggest mistake of our lives. We're gonna make matters worse by goin' along with this hair-brained scheme. I think we're about to piss our whole lives away, if you really want to know what I think."

"Then why are we doin' this?"

"Are you really sure you want to do this, Bunny? I'm damned sure I don't but I don't see that I have any choice. If we get the oil and take it back there, we'll be just as guilty as the others. I hope we all know what the hell we're doin' 'cause our whole god-damned futures are restin' on this. It better work or we're all screwed."

"Exactly," Bunny said. "So let's get outta here while we still have time. Let's not do it. ... Let's not be talked into doin' somethin' that we know is so awfully wrong. The others can worry about themselves. Maybe we should go see Chief Frasier right now and tell him everythin'. Maybe it's not too late to come clean. We've got the chance to tell our side of what happened. We've got the chance to tell the truth before Levi and Ben can tell their version. I think that's what we should do, Jack. We should take our chances with the truth. They always say the truth is your best defence. We should go talk to the Chief."

"I don't know, Bunny. That'd be takin' an awful chance," I said. "What if Chief Frasier don't believe us? Remember, he don't like us much. He probably won't listen to anythin' we have to say, even if it is the truth. And, besides, it doesn't matter what we say now. Once he talks to Levi and Ben and they tell their version of what took place, they'll make it sound good. In the end, it will still be our word against theirs and no one will know who to believe. No, Bunny, I don't think goin' to the police is an option for us. Besides, you should have spoken up earlier. That was the time to tell them what you think. Now it's too late to back out."

"So what then? What are we gonna do? Just go along with the others without lookin' at other options? I don't know about you, Jack, but I don't want to go to jail for somethin' I didn't do and I'm sure you don't want to either. Maybe we didn't try to help poor Ruby but we didn't lay a finger on her. That's got to count for somethin' in the eyes of the law. We've got to think things through before we end up screwin' ourselves. I'm really leanin' toward just walkin' away and sayin' to hell with you all. Let the others take the heat for what they've done."

"I hear what you're sayin', Bunny, but I'm not sure what other options we have. To me, it looks like we have two choices. We either go along with the others and hope no one ever finds out what we've done, or we go to the police and take our chances. That will mean goin' to jail and I can't do that. You have to do whatever you think is right for you, Bunny, but I have to go back to the Grove and fulfil my end of the plan. If we don't go back, we're not only screwin' Ben and Levi; we'll be lettin' Hank down as well. I can't do that to him. He's like a brother to me. I can't leave him out there in a lurch like that, even if he is the one pushin' along this whole sick plan. If it was just Ben and Levi, I'd say to hell with them after what they've done. But I can't do that to Hank. He's countin' on me ... on us. I know he would never let us down and I can't just turn my back on him. I'm afraid we've got to do this, whether we like it or not."

"Christ, Jack! This is so wrong. This ain't the way this night was s'pposed to go." Bunny was nearly hysterical. I understood his emotions perfectly well. "Why the hell did Levi have to bring Ruby out there with him in the first place?"

"Yeah!" I said. "It sure as hell ain't the kinda night that fond memories are made of, but sometimes, Bunny, you just gotta roll with the punches. We've been sucked into somethin' bigger than us, and now we gotta fight for our own lives. That's how I look at it. I feel pretty sick about what happened to Ruby. It's eatin' me up inside that two of my best friends could be responsible for somethin' so wicked, but now we've got to help ourselves. I don't look at it as if I'm helpin' them. ... I'm doin' this for me."

"I guess you're right, Jack. ... But this is so terribly wrong. How can we do this even if we are lookin' out for ourselves? That's such a selfish thing to do. How are we ever gonna put this behind us? How are we ever gonna look at ourselves in a mirror again?"

"I can't answer that, Bunny. All I know is that we've been pulled into this dark hole and we're bein' swallowed up by it. We're into this up to our asses, regardless if we like it or not. We might as well get what we came for and get it over with so we can all go home. Maybe things will look better in the mornin'."

At that, Bunny stopped talking again, keeping his thoughts to himself. I can't help but think that I somehow failed Bunny as a friend that night. He was looking for reassurances that things would be all right. But I couldn't give him any. We both knew things would not look better in the morning ... they wouldn't ever look better again.

Me and Bunny went to the store and got the kerosene. It was late. We knew no one would be around. At least our secrets would be well guarded. That was a small comfort. On the way back to the Grove, neither of us spoke a word ... but I thought a lot.

Chapter 28

It took us almost an hour and a half to go to the store, pick up the oil and get back to the Grove again. By the time we returned to the clearing, Hank, Ben and Levi had moved Ruby's body onto the little raft that we had built a few years earlier. We used to push it out to the deep water to dive from. That crudely-constructed craft gave us many hours of happiness. Now it was Ruby's final resting place.

The trio of conspirators who I called my friends had fashioned a bed of brush and placed her terribly beaten body on top of it. They had also picked up all her clothes and her shoes and piled them onto the raft with the body. And then they had positioned some brush over top of everything. It was a morbid sight. It was a vision I've seen many times over the past sixty years in my mind's eye. The pale, white skin of Ruby's once vital body gleamed from under the shadows as light from the full moon penetrated the brush cover. Her strawberry blond hair was now matted and knotted by the sticks and branches that had become her burial bed. But of all the vivid pictures I have of that tragic night, it is her eyes that I remember most.

Ruby had died with her eyes open. Now her once bright blue eyes were dark and hollow. They stared out from under the brush pleading, "Help me! Help me!" just as the girl had pleaded only minutes before her death.

I couldn't stand the thought of someone dying with their eyes open. It just didn't seem right. It's as if people who die with their eyes open are defying death. That's what Ruby was doing. Mama used to say people who died with their eyes open had unfinished business to attend to. I shuddered at the morbid thought. Instinctively, I reached under the brush and closed her eyelids. It was something I've regretted doing for the rest of my life.

Her skin was cold to the touch but it was then that I connected with the dead girl in some sort of lifelong bond that has been haunting me ever since.

For a brief moment that night, I danced with the dead. I've been doing the dance ever since, waltzing with Ruby's ghost in the far recesses of my mind and in all the corners of my heart. That touch was like the cold of ice and the heat of fire all at the same time ... like cold chills running up your spine while sweat pours from your brow and goose bumps skip up your arms making the little hairs stand on end. I shivered at the touch. When we connected, I went weak. It was as if someone had backed me up against a wall and kneed me in the guts. It was the most extraordinary sensation I had ever felt or would ever feel again in my life.

My heart pounded like a drum as Hank took the oil from me and Bunny. "Good job, guys," he said. "Anyone see you?"

"Nope," I stuttered. "Wasn't a single person around town. We don't have to worry about that."

"Good," he said. "We can't be too careful."

I watched, speechless and almost breathless, as our friend dumped the kerosene over the body, the brush and the raft. Me and Bunny remained on shore as Hank, Ben and Levi carefully guided the raft out to the deep water where they set it on fire, and then returned to shore to stand vigil.

It was a quiet ceremony, except for a few words Bunny whispered. "Ashes to ashes," he said under his breath, as if giving Ruby her last rites.

The rest of us remained silent.

We stood motionless on the shore and watched the flames shoot into the night sky, the fire lighting up the darkness over the water with an eerie orange glow. And then it hit us. Like a brick hurled by some superhuman entity stationed out in the middle of the lake. The smell of burning human flesh, combined with the kerosene and brush, blew in from the smoldering raft, filling our nostrils with a sickly odour that remains, to this day, the worst thing I have ever smelled. It was yet another reminder of the night's crimes.

It took a good half hour for the raft to burn and then sink. We knew the water was deep enough out there near the centre that any large pieces of wood or bone which hadn't completely burned would sink out of sight, and we also knew that the current would carry away the ashes. We also hoped the water would wash away any other evidence of what we had done. It was a risky plan. We didn't know if the fire would have been hot enough to completely destroy the body. We didn't know if all evidence of the crime would be washed away by the lake water. But we had no other choice. We took our chances that the fire and water would remove any trace of Ruby Todd.

In only a few hours we had gone from five young men having a good time and enjoying each other's friendship to being murdering rapists. Not only that, but we had also conspired to wipe another human being completely off the face of the earth. It was as if Ruby had never existed, like she had been something out of our imaginations. But she had been real and we knew all too well what we had done. The plan was devious and disgusting, hatched out of desperation to save our asses. But that was no excuse. I knew it. We all knew it. That reality would eat at us like a cancer gnawing away at our insides for our whole lifetimes. In the end we deserved everything we got. Such actions are defenceless.

That night faded into history, leaving a legacy of mystery and heartache for many people but the memories lived on for the five of us.

After the last flames flickered out, we sat on the rocks for hours. Going home didn't seem right. Ruby would never go home again. None of us spoke a single word. What could we say? Sorry certainly didn't fit. Oh, we were sorry all right, but not for the death we had caused but for the fact that we had gotten ourselves into such a mess. No. Words would not heal the pain and guilt we were feeling. It was as though we were in a vacuum where we couldn't speak or even breathe. And we couldn't reach out to each other even though we were only a few feet apart. We would never reach out to each other ever again like friends should, like we had done over the years before this hellish nightmare began. Many things died that night out there at Brier Lake, things other than a beautiful young girl.

Finally Hank broke the silence with a stark dose of reality. "You guys know that if we get caught we're never gonna get out of this shit we're in. This is heavy duty stuff and we're all gonna pay dearly if they ever find out what happened up here. We all gotta swear that no matter what happens in the next couple'a days, we gotta stick with the plan. There's gonna be a lot of heat over Ruby's disappearance and a lot of questions. There's gonna be a lot of pressure to find that girl. It's gonna get pretty tough around here for awhile. They're gonna be lookin' at everyone, but especially the boys. You know we'll all be under suspicion of doin' somethin' to Ruby. We all gotta hang tough until the heat's off. ... If anyone caves in, you let us all down."

"I don't know if I can carry through with this," Bunny confessed as tears began to well in his eyes. "We've dug ourselves even deeper into this hole. This was all so wrong and they're gonna catch us ... I know they will. We should have gone to the police when we had the chance. Now it's too late."

I could relate with what Bunny was feeling as he continued to spill his guts. "I'm not sure that I'll be able to hide everythin' if they come around askin' questions." Bunny was getting near hysterical and I could tell the others, especially Ben and Levi, were losing their patience with him.

Ben snapped back. "They won't find out unless you tell them, Bunny. You got no choice but to keep your mouth shut. Just remember that it's not only you that'll be in trouble if the truth comes out ... and you can't let your friends down. You got to be tough for your sake and for ours."

"Tough! Is that what you call it, Ben? You ain't no friend of mine. Real friends wouldn't ask friends to do what we've done for you. You're the bastard that started all of this in the first place ... you and Levi." Bunny's emotions turned to anger, his eyes becoming narrow slits. I had only seen Bunny lose his temper once or twice, but I could tell he was nearing his breaking point. "If you'd kept your dick in your pants and left Ruby alone in the first place, none of this would have happened."

Hank tried to mediate, as only he could. "Come on, guys. We can't come apart now. We've got to stick together or we'll all be done for. Now's not the time to go losin' your head. The worst part's over." Getting between the two friends, Hank tried to reason with them but it was a futile attempt.

"Is it really, Hank?" Bunny picked up the challenge. "Are you really sure that the worst is over? Even if no one ever finds out about what we've done up here, does that mean that it's okay? I don't think it is. ... I don't think we've seen the worst yet. Maybe gettin' away with this is the worst thing that can happen to us."

"Who the hell cares what you think?" Ben continued in that irritating manner he had honed to a skill since he was a young boy. "It's a little too late to get all high 'n' mighty now, Bunny. You guys could have stepped in earlier, but you didn't. I think you were just waitin' your chance when me and Levi were done. I think you liked watchin' us 'cause you ain't never been with a girl before. You were watchin' us so you could see how it's done. Ain't that right, Bunny? If she wouldn't have died, ain't no tellin' what would have happened, or who would have done what. So you can drop the preachin' act and put this behind us. This is no place for a cry baby."

That was the final straw. Shoving Hank aside, Bunny flew into Ben like a rabid dog. First it was fists flying, then it was blood as he connected with Ben's jaw. The impact snapped Ben's head back with such velocity that it spun him around, knocking him off his feet. "Who's the baby now, Ben? I just want you all to know that this ain't over ... not by a long shot."

With that, Bunny left Ben sprawled on his belly. Things were never the same after that between Bunny and the rest of us. Or for that matter, they were never the same between any of the five of us. How could they be?

Silence settled over the clearing for a few more minutes as tempers cooled. Finally it was Bunny who interrupted the stillness once again. "I'll do the best I can, that's all I can promise. But how do I know I can count on the rest of you guys to keep your end of the bargain? How do I know one of you won't go to the police and tell what happened just to protect your own asses? Maybe we should all swear an oath or somethin'," he suggested. "You know, some sort of blood oath just to prove that we won't rat on each other."

"That's a pretty stupid idea," Levi piped up.

Ben remained silent, obviously smarting from his cracked lip, if not his bruised ego.

"No, I think it's a great idea," Hank said, defending Bunny's suggestion. "We must have a show of support so that we all know we can trust each other. It must be somethin' that will symbolize our unity. That way, if you don't take the oath, then we'll know who to blame if the truth ever comes out."

It's hard for me to admit but I devised the evening's next sinister twist. I suggested that the pact must have some lasting symbol to remind us of the oath we were making. I suggested a ritual I had read about that had been performed by some ancient civilizations in South America. In order to prove their loyalty to the tribe and that they could trust each other, the male members of these societies would form "faith circles" and, one by one, they would cut each other. They believed that if the wound wasn't fatal, then their comrade could be trusted.

At first, the others weren't impressed with the idea and, actually, I couldn't believe that I had told them about it once the words came out of my mouth. Deep down inside, I was hoping no one would take me seriously, but they did.

Bunny, of all people, got behind the idea and pushed the others to go along with the ritual. Reluctantly the others finally agreed it was a good idea. Systematically we formed a semi-circle and, one by one, we each cut the other. We had agreed the cuts would be on the left shoulder. That way the wound would be out of sight and the injury wouldn't interfere with our daily activities. We would use the hunting knife that Ben always carried after his grandfather gave it to him. I remember the order perfectly well. Ben went first, cutting Levi. Then, taking the knife, Levi cut Bunny. In turn, Bunny cut me. I then cut Hank. And the circle was completed with Hank cutting Ben. They weren't large cuts, but they hurt like a bastard. I guess that was only fitting in light of what we had done ... more spilled blood solidified our pact. We all deserved a bit of pain. It was small penance for the crimes we had perpetrated. We were branded for life.

If you look real closely you can see the scar on my left shoulder where I was cut. Victoria often asked me how I got the scar but I never told her. I made up some lie about being hurt while coasting one winter when I was a kid. It seemed like a reasonable explanation, but below that lie were layers and layers of deception and mistrust, the things that can ruin a person's life.

It was a morbid partnership, a sinister covenant made between five panicked young men. It was, in many respects, an agreement made in Hell. But we all took the oath, just the same. We swore on everything that was near and dear to us, that we'd never breathe a single word of what really happened that night out at the Grove. I can't speak for the rest of the guys but I never told a single soul until now. You're the first person I've told in all these years and it feels good to finally get it off my chest.

Chapter 29

Until that August night in 1940, summer was my favourite time of year. I loved everything about the season, the brightly coloured flowers, the buzzing insects, the birds and even the humidity as it clung to me. I liked the carefree attitude that came with summer and going to Brier Lake to swim. It was a good time; a good life with few worries. It was as youth should be.

Afterward, each year as August approached, I looked at the calendar with fear and loathing. One by one, as the days slipped by, the memories of that night became more vivid, more intense until, finally, on August 17, they became as real ... as real today as they were sixty years ago.

What we did all those years ago was unforgivable.

There is no excuse. I'm a monster. I may not have laid a hand on Ruby Todd that night but I'm just as responsible for her death as the others. My fingerprints are all over the corpse. My hands are covered in her blood.

There have been nights when I'd lay awake thinking about what we did. Whenever I'd close my eyes, she'd be there, crying and pleading for Levi and Ben to stop; reaching out to me for help, but getting none. I've seen her naked, bruised and battered body many times in my mind's eye, lying there on the slippery, wet rocks of the lake shore, her limp and beaten corpse glistening in bright moonlight. I've come awake at night with the feel of her rubbery touch on my face, as if she had once again connected with me like we did that night when I closed her eyes just before we burned her body. And can you smell that? Kerosene and burning flesh. I've had that disgusting smell on my hands and in my nose for the past sixty years. It's been burning a hole in my soul ever since that night, reminding me of what we did at Brier Lake. There have been days when I've heard her screams for mercy while I've been wide awake, her cries of despair ringing in my ears.

We danced the dance that night and now we've come to the last waltz.

I like to think that if I had it to do over again, I'd do things differently. But I don't know that I would. I've often heard people say if they could, they'd change things. But even with everything I know today, I'm not so sure I'd choose a different path if I was given a second chance. That's what makes this hard to live with. People think that, as you get older and you're waiting to die, you'd correct your mistakes the second time around. But I don't know if you would.

Shit!

What the hell is this?

What is going on here?

Where in the Christ am I?

Ben? Ruby?

What in the Christ am I doing here?

Bunny? Hank? Levi? You're here too?

Where in the hell did all you guys come from? How did we all get back here after all of these years? What are we doing back here again?

I may be a sick, old man, about to draw his last breath, but I know this place. It's the Grove. How can that be?

They're all here. But how?

It's that point in time, isn't it? That juncture in my life where I have to make the right decision.

Can I do things differently this time around?

I have to try. I owe it to myself ... I owe it to everyone.

"Stop it, Ben. Please stop it. I said to let go of me."

"Shut up, Ruby."

"Get your hands off me, Ben. You're hurting me. Let go."

"Let go? I haven't even started yet."

"You want me to beg? Is that it, Ben? Okay, I'll beg. Please let me go. Please stop."

"Keep quiet, Ruby."

"I won't give in to you, Ben. I thought we were friends."

"I like you, Ruby. I like you a lot."

"Then why do you want to hurt me?"

"You made me do this, Ruby. It's all your fault."

"My fault? How, Ben? How?"

"It just is."

"You're hurting me, Ben. Listen to me. You'll be sorry."

"If I don' do this, I'll be sorry."

"Let me go. I won't tell anyone about this. You can trust me."

"Shut up. The more you fight, the more it's gonna hurt. I'm just givin' you what you want."

"What are you talking about, Ben?"

"We both know this is what you've wanted ever since we met. No more talk. No more games."

"What are you going to do, Ben?"

"We're gonna take care of a little business."

"What do you mean?"

"You'll see."

"Don't hurt me, Ben."

"It will only hurt if you fight me. You're gonna find out how a real man plays."

"Is this what a real man does, Ben?"

"What do you know about it?"

"I know a real man doesn't force himself on a girl and I'm not going to make it easy for you."

"Whore. That's all you are. A whore who likes to tease."

"You're wrong, Ben. I haven't done anything like that."

"You don't even know when you do it, Ruby. You've always thought you were better than me ... better than all the people around here."

"You've got it all wrong, Ben. I'm not like that. You only see what you want to see. It's you who has the problem."

"Me? You think you're somethin' special lookin' down your nose at us. Well, you ain't no better than any of us. And now it's time you learned that."

"That's not right, Ben. I've tried to fit in."

"Fit in! Is that what you call it? Truth is, you've been leadin' all the guys on, teasin' us and drivin' us crazy. None of us like it. It ain't right, Ruby."

"So this will make you feel better, Ben? Will it finally make you the man you want to be?"

"Move it, I said. Go on or I'll give you another good one. If you want somethin' to cry over, I'll give it to you. Stop fightin' me."

"I'll never stop fighting you."

"You may as well learn to enjoy it. You're finally gonna find out what you've been missin' all this time. You're gonna like it, Ruby."

"You're wrong, Ben."

"All your kind like it rough. You always put up a fight at first. But you'll come around."

"No, you're wrong, Ben. Please don't hurt me any more."

"It's too late for talk, Ruby."

"Come on, Ben. I've always tried to be nice to you. If I hurt you or made you feel bad, I didn't mean to. If you think I've led you on I'm sorry for that too."

"I don't want to hear it, Ruby."

"Don't do this, Ben. You're making a mistake. Let me go before you do something you're going to regret."

"Shut up. I mean it, Ruby. Keep your mouth shut or I'll shut it for you. The only thing I'm gonna regret is that I didn't do this a long time ago."

"You're messed up, Ben. You aren't thinking."

"I'm thinkin' clearer now than I have in a long time. That sweet little girl act of yours might have worked for awhile but now it's time to become a real woman. You've led me on for the last time and now I'm gonna give you what you should have had right after you waltzed into town all fixed up in them fancy, frilly dresses."

"You're an idiot, Ben. This won't change anything between us."

"Yeah, it will. You'll remember for a long time what I've got in store for you the next time you prance your pretty little ass around town."

"Jack. Bunny. Please. Somebody help me. Don't you see what he's doing? Why don't you do something? You have to stop him. Please. He's hurting me!"

Chapter 30

Jesus!

What the hell's this?

This can't be real.

I can't do this again.

What was that about a second chance?

Is it too late for me?

Can we ever correct our destiny if we make a wrong turn? Do we get a second chance to get it right?

I had the power to save Ruby Todd's life once. But I took the wrong road.

Is that what this is all about? Is this my second chance?

"Jack! Jack! Come on man. What's wrong? You look like you just seen a ghost. What in the Christ are we gonna do about Ben?"

"Hang on a minute, Bunny. This ain't right. We ain't supposed to be here like this after all this time. It's been sixty years. You're all dead; you died a long time ago. None of this can be real. I must be havin' a nightmare. I know, it's those god-damned drugs again. That's it. What else could it be?"

"I don't know what the hell you're talkin' about, Jack. We're all gonna die someday. I don't know where in the Christ you think we're supposed to be, but I sure as hell wish I was some place else right now."

"I don't only mean some other place, Bunny. I really mean some other time."

"Ease up, Jack. You're really spookin' me with all this crazy talk. We ain't dead. We're right here at the Grove where we've been all night. Now, come on. Get your god-damned head outta your ass and help me out here. Ben's gonna do somethin' stupid. When he gets in one of them rages, there's no stoppin' him."

"I know, but we gotta think this through."

"He's gonna hurt her. What are we gonna do? What about it, Jack?"

"Take it easy, Bunny. It's now all makin' perfect sense to me. Of course you're right. When Ben starts thinkin' with his dick instead of his head, we're in for a whole lot of trouble. I know we just can't stand here and do nothin'. That's the mistake we made the last time. It's clear to me now. For some reason, we've all been given a second chance and we better do the right thing this time."

"The last time? A second chance at what? Now what are you babblin' about, Jack? I gotta say you're scarin' the hell outta me."

"Sorry, Bunny. I know it sounds crazy, but I ain't got time to explain. You gotta trust me with this. Just go with whatever I say and I'll fill you in later. Right now we gotta stop Ben before he does somethin' stupid that we're all gonna regret."

"I don't know, Jack. This all sounds kind'a far-fetched to me."

"Listen, Bunny. We don't have time for long explanations right now. He's almost got Ruby in to shore. Let's get in there before it's too late. We have to stop Ben."

"How in the hell are we gonna do that, Jack? You and me both know there ain't no stoppin' Ben when he gets all fired up like he is right now."

"I know, Bunny, but we have to do somethin'. This is our last chance, our only hope. Hey, Ben! Why don't you leave Ruby alone? She ain't ever done anything to hurt you. Just leave her alone and let's get outta here."

"I don't want to get outta here, Jack. I ain't done yet."

"Listen, Ben. You don't know it, but if you do this we're all gonna pay for your mistake."

"What are you talkin' about? Stay out of this."

"I know it sounds crazy, Ben, but you must listen to what I'm sayin' before it's too late for all of us. You have no idea how this will end. But it's bad."

"Stay the hell outta this, Jack. It ain't none of your business. ... It don't concern you."

"Listen to him, Ben. He makes sense."

"Shut up, Ruby. Listen, Jack, you know that she's got this comin' to her. Keep your nose outta my business."

"No, Ben. This does concern me. It concerns all of us. We can't stand by and watch you do this. Use your head, Ben."

"I don't want to think anymore."

"That's the problem, Ben. You haven't been thinkin'. But you have to understand. Ruby thought we were her friends. Looks like she misjudged us. What you do out here tonight affects us all so I'm makin' it my concern. I have no choice. For all our sakes, I've got to stop you."

"I'm warnin' you to stay outta this, Jack."

"You're like a brother to me, Ben. I can't stand by and let you do this. Someday you'll thank me."

"Listen to him, Ben. You're hurting me."

"Keep quiet, Ruby. What do you know about it, Jack? I'm tired of bein' treated like second-hand trash. I'm gonna show her once and for all what she's been missin'. If any of you get in the way, then the hell with you too."

"This ain't right, Ben. You know it ain't right."

"What do you know about what's right or not, Jack?"

"I don't want to argue with you, Ben. But don't hurt her. She doesn't deserve this. This ain't like you, Ben."

"What do you know I'm like, Jack?"

"I know if you do this, Ben, you're gonna screw us all in more ways than you know."

"Why, Jack? Why should I listen to you?"

"Because I wouldn't bullshit a friend ... a brother. You know that. There's a bigger picture here. Let Ruby go before it's too late. Walk away before you do somethin' we'll all be sorry for."

"Cut the shit, Jack. You back off and leave me alone."

"I can't do that, Ben. I'm askin' you to trust me. Listen to what I'm sayin'. Let her go before it's too late. I can't explain right now, but believe me, you don't want to do this."

"Yeah! I do. And you stay outta my way."

"Okay, Ben. If you're gonna make us do this the hard way, then that's the way we'll do it. We don't want to fight you, Ben, but we will if you make us."

"Us! Who the hell is us, Jack? You and Bunny? You gonna make me stop? Come on. I dare you. You know I can take you. It ain't gonna matter to me that we're friends. I'm warnin' you to mind your own business."

"You're wrong, Ben. I ain't alone. Hank is here. He feels the same way we do. Hank, I know you're out there somewhere. Come on, it's time to show yourself."

"Hank? What the hell is he gonna do? That little sissy went home an hour ago. He couldn't stand the sight of a naked girl ... or was it a naked man? Hank likes guys better than girls. He couldn't stand bein' around us naked men. He didn't think he could control himself. That's why he had to leave. You've been blind to that all these years, but it's the truth. He ain't gonna be here to help you."

"There you go thinkin' with your balls again, instead of with that little pea brain you got in that empty space between your ears. How did you know I didn't go home, Jack?"

"Just had a feeling, I guess."

"I knew there was gonna be trouble so I hung around back there by the thicket. I knew you'd cause trouble, Ben. That's just what I'd expect from you."

"Thank God, Hank. Maybe you can get Ben to let me go."

"I don't know, Ruby. He's pretty riled up."

"But he's hurting me."

"I know Ruby. C'mon, Ben. Let her go. I knew you couldn't leave her alone. But we won't let you do this to Ruby, so back off and leave her alone. We don't want to fight you, but we will."

"I'm shakin' in my shoes. It's Hank to the rescue. Is that supposed to scare me or somethin'? You listen here, Hank. I'll tell you the same thing I told Jack. Back off. Or else. I mean it. This ain't none of your concern."

"Let me go, Ben. You're hurting my neck. Help me, Hank."

"Shut up, Ruby. He can't help you. This is man business."

"You don't know nothin' about bein' a man."

"I know I'm more man than you are. I ain't afraid of you or Jack. If you want to take me on, come and get me. I'm ready for the both of you."

"Two to one odds, Ben? That don't hardly seem fair to me."

"Levi? You're sidin' with me over Hank and Jack?"

"Yeah, I'm with you, Ben. That little bitch had this comin' for a long time. I've watched how she's treated you. She deserves what she gets. I'd like to give 'er a go myself when you're done. But first it looks like we gotta take care of these two shits."

"Bunny's a wimp. We won't have to worry about him. It's just you and me against Hank and Jack."

"You boys sure you want to do this, Jack?"

"I'm surprised at you, Levi. I thought you had more sense than to rape a defenceless girl. Where's the challenge in that?"

"Stop it. Just stop it, all of you. I'm not a piece of beef to fight over. Just let me go, Ben, so I can go home."

"Not a chance, Ruby. We ain't done with you yet."

"Listen to her, Ben. She's right. If you're sure you want to do this you got to know that me and Hank can't just stand here and watch. It won't matter that we've been real good friends all these years. None of that will count for anything. Think about what you're doin'. You gotta know that Ruby didn't come here tonight to tease any of us. She thought she was comin' here to have a good time with some friends. And this is how you treat her?"

"Jack's right. C'mon, Levi. You and Ben can have any other girl back in town. What are you gonna do when you're done? Did you think of that? How are you gonna face her every day in town? How are you gonna live with yourselves? You're gonna have to hurt us to get to her. Are you prepared to go one on one with your best friends? Is this more important than friendship? Is it, Levi?"

"Listen, Hank, and you too, Jack. The time for thinkin' and talkin' is over. Why do you think I brought her out here tonight in the first place? What about you, Ben? You still in or not? Ben, what do you say?"

"I don't know, Levi."

"Don't tell me all this talkin's got you scared. These two shits ain't gonna be able to stop us if we stick together. C'mon, Ben, this is what you've wanted for a long time. Don't go soft on me now. Remember how she's always made you feel!"

"Don't listen to him, Ben. Do the right thing. Let me go."

"Shut up, Ruby. All of you shut up."

"C'mon, Ben. You really don't want to do this."

"Listen, Jack. You have no idea what it's been like. She made me feel like a piece of dirt."

"I did not, Ben. It's all in your head."

"Ruby, don't push him any further."

"Okay, Jack. Just get him to let me go."

"Ben, this isn't what you wanted. It's what Levi planned. He's using you."

"Christ, listen to what you're sayin', Jack. You think I've got that much power over Ben?"

"I think you do if you use Ruby. You know how he feels about her and you're using him to get to her."

"You're givin' me too much credit, Jack. C'mon, Ben. Let's stop all the talking. Are you still with me?"

"Shit, Levi. I don't know. Jack and Hank kind of make sense and, anyway, I sort of ain't in the mood any more. You might have planned this all along, but I didn't mean for things to blow up so bad like this. I just lost control. My feelin's just kind of took over when I saw her around the guys, and I lost it."

"Now what the hell are you talkin' about, Ben? You're the one who started this and now you're gonna let this bitch go? This is your chance. Don't blow it. You ain't thinkin' straight."

"I'm not sure anymore, Levi."

"You're better than that, Ben. I always thought deep down inside that you had the balls to do anythin' you wanted if you got out from under their thumbs, but I guess I was wrong. You've always let Hank and Jack run your life. When are you gonna become a real man, Ben?"

"Listen, Levi, just let Ben go if that's what he wants. Don't ask how I know. But I can tell you if you go ahead and do this, we're all gonna be sorry for it. It may be fun for you now. But if you do this you're gonna be sorry in an hour's time ... in a year's time ... sixty years from now. Someone told me some good advice, and I want you to hear it. You only get to go through this life once. You make decisions along the way. Every decision has an outcome. Every action creates a reaction. In everyone's life there are times that determine our destiny. We're at one of those times now. Our actions will change our destinies forever. This is our moment."

"What a pile of shit, Jack."

"Is it, Levi? Well, if you believe that rapin' this girl won't change the rest of your life, then go ahead and do it. I can't speak for Hank, but I'll tell you right up front that I won't fight you if you really think this is what you should do. Levi and Ben, this is your decision. Will you do the right thing? Or will you be selfish and cruel? What about it, Ben? How will you decide?"

"I don't know what you're talkin' about, Jack. I don't believe in that fate and destiny crap. It all sounds like a bunch of bullshit to me, but ... what the hell! All right. I'm done here. Levi's on his own."

"Thank you, Ben."

"Don't thank me, Ruby. I can't tell Levi what to do."

"That's a smart move, Ben. Now what about you, Levi? Are you gonna jeopardize your entire life and the lives of all of us here? Maybe you don't care about her or your friends, but are you willin' to compromise your own future for this? If that's your choice, then go ahead and get it over with. Just remember, though, you not only hold your own fate in your hands but you also hold the fate of all of us in those same hands."

"That's a real impressive speech, Jack, for someone who usually has a hard time puttin' two sentences together. I've never heard you talk so much bullshit in all the years I've known you. What I want to know, Jack, is who died and made you the keeper of our conscience? Fate has nothin' to do with it. As for the rest of you, I'm not sure I really care what happens to any of you. So what about it, Jack? I suppose you think the hand of God is gonna reach down and strike me dead right now. Is that what you're sayin', Jack?"

"No, Levi, but I know you will never be able to look at yourself in the mirror again. You will never again have a full night's rest. You will never again have a clear thought in your head. You will never again know true happiness. Trust me, Levi. I have seen what can happen when you make the wrong turn. But this is your call. Do what you will. Go ahead. Get it over with."

"No, Jack. What are you saying?"

"Easy, Ruby. I think Levi will do what's right."

"You don't know me as well as you think you do, Jack. Now it's me and Ruby."

"No, Levi. Don't do this. Don't hurt me. Listen to Jack. He makes sense. Why would you want to hurt me like this? Jack! Hank! Please don't let him do this. Please stop him."

"We can't do that Ruby. Me and Hank and the others might want to stop him, but this has to be Levi's decision."

"He won't stop, Jack. Can't you see what he's like?"

"I know that, Ruby. But he's got to do this on his own. Look at her, Levi. Look her straight in the eyes. Every night when you go to bed and try to sleep, you're gonna see those eyes. And listen real close, Levi. You're gonna hear those pleas for mercy ringin' in your ears for the rest of your life. Is that what you want, Levi? Is it?"

"Shut your mouth, Jack. I mean it or I'll shut it for you. She's only puttin' on an act. She likes this. You may have spooked Ben with your scare tactics, but it won't work on me."

"C'mon, Levi. Look at her. Does she really look like she's enjoyin' this?"

"Enough. No more talk, I said."

"No, Levi. Let me go. You're hurting me."

"Okay, Levi. If you want to play it tough, then you leave us no other choice. I said we wouldn't fight you, but maybe there's no other way. Quick, Hank, grab him."

"Back off, you two. Or I'll hurt her even more."

"He means it, Jack."

"I know, Hank. What can we do, Levi, to convince you to stop this before it's too late?"

"Nothing."

"C'mon, Levi. I don't care much for your ol' man, but he didn't raise you to be a rapist. What would he think about this?"

"He'd be pissed. But who cares what he thinks?"

"No one, I guess. But I bet your mother would care. Do you really want to disgrace her? Think about how she'll feel when word of this gets out. Believe me, Levi, she'll never be able to hold her head up again. Do you want to do that to her?"

"Shut up, Jack."

"I think it's workin', Jack. I think he's startin' to let her go."

"Maybe, Hank. But it ain't over yet. That's right, Levi. Pause and make a mental picture of this moment in time. It could be the most defining point in your life."

"Shut up, Jack. Your gettin' on my nerves."

"I'm just tryin' to help you see the mistake you're about to make."

"The only mistake I made tonight was bringing Ruby here with you guys. I should have taken her some place else so I could have been alone with her. Now all your talkin's spoilin' the mood. This is what I want. This is what I've been dreamin' of for a long time."

"But what price are you willin' to pay, Levi?"

"I ain't fallin' for any of that bullshit, Jack."

"Call it what you want, but you'll be sorry if you do this."

"Please, Levi. Listen to Jack. Please let me go home."

"Listen to her, Levi. Can't you hear the pain she's in?"

"Jesus, you guys are hard on the nerves. ... Oh, for Christ's sake, go on Ruby. Get outta here before I change my mind."

"There Levi, you've done the right thing. You may never know how close you've come to screwin' up all our lives. But believe me. It was real close. Luckily for us, you did the right thing. We all did the right thing."

Chapter 31

Sorry for drifting, but for a minute there your voice sounded familiar to me. I can't put my finger on it but you remind me of someone. For the life of me, though, I can't place it. These drugs have me so doped up and confused I can't even hear straight. And I find my eyes don't work too well either. Must be these lights. You look kind of fuzzy to me.

Just wait a god-damned minute. I know that voice. I've heard it many times before. There's something in the way you say my name that sounds familiar.

Please do me a favour. Go over to the window and tell me what the weather's like. My mother always told me that on the day I was born it was snowing hard. I'd like to know what it's doing outside, because this is the day I'm gonna die.

Well, Jack, when I came into the hospital three hours ago, it was a nice, early spring day. Actually quite mild. There's no way that it could be snowing.

Just humour a dying old man. Do this one little thing for me. Please have a look.

Well, would you look at that. It is snowing. And it's coming down pretty damned hard. The ground's white already. Isn't that strange?

I'm not sure it's so strange. I'm really not sure what's strange any more. Believe me, I've seen a lot of weird things in the past few days, but I know things are not always as they seem. Remember what Old Ralph Burchill used to say about snow so late into March?

He used it say it was the poor man's fertilizer.

Is that what this snow means for us? Do you believe in second chances?

Wait a second. I do know you. I have seen you somewhere before. But that's not important now. I just want to die. I want this pain to stop.

I've been down this road before, haven't I?

I thought you were someone I knew from a long time ago. You remind me of a bird that tries to fly through a window. He sees his reflection and flies right into the glass. Are you the real bird or are you the reflection in the window? Just who are you?

Does it really matter who I am? I am what you want me to be. I was meant to be here, Mr. Webster. That's all you need to know. It's what fate ordered.

I'm tired of being trapped in this dying body. I'm ready to die.

Let the dance begin.